THE LOST JOURNALS

ROBERT MASSETTI

Published by FEAR FILM Publishing
Orlando, Florida
www.fearfilm.com

ISBN: 979-8-9991587-0-3

First Edition

Cover design by Robert Massetti
Printed in the United States of America

This is for my father
who believed and supported
me in all my creative endeavors.
I miss you.

JOHN MASSETTI
1941-2017

And for my sister Gina,
for being the best sister EVER!
Thank you for always being there!

Contents

"Angels and Demons are real"

-Lucian Kane

THE LOST JOURNALS

Chapter 1

ANGELS AND DEMONS

Late at night, Aleister's father, Lucian Kane, sat in his study illuminated only by the warm glow of dancing firelight. He was a strong figure, his eyes dark and thoughtful as he sipped from a glass of brandy, lost in contemplation. Young Aleister burst into the room, his small frame trembling, his wide eyes reflecting terror. Lucian glanced up, his expression softening as he set his glass aside. He motioned to Aleister, patting his knee, inviting him to sit on his lap. Aleister hesitated before hurrying over, climbing into the protective circle of his father's arms.

"Father..." Aleister whispered, clutching at his father's sleeve. "There's... there's something under my bed. It says it's coming for me."

Lucian gave a reassuring smile, though a flicker of concern crossed his face. He rested a comforting hand on Aleister's back, his voice calm and low.

"Aleister, there's nothing under your bed that can harm you." He paused, as though considering his next words carefully.

"But yes... Angels, and even Demons, are real."

Aleister's eyes grew wide. "They are?"

Lucian nodded. His gaze distant for a moment. "Yes. I know several Angels I call friends, and I've done battle with the deepest, darkest Demons from the depths of Hell."

Aleister stared up at him, awe and fear mingling in his young eyes. Lucian seemed to sense this and reached for a silver ring on his finger. He slid it off and placed it in Aleister's small hand. The metal felt solid and warm, almost alive with its own energy.

"This is the Ring of Solomon," Lucian said. "It will protect you from anything that means you harm. Nothing will come for you while you wear it. Remember that."

Aleister tried to slip the ring onto his finger, but it was far too large, sliding off before he could secure it. He looked up, trying to hand it back.

"It doesn't fit, Father..."

Lucian interrupted him gently, placing his hand over Aleister's. "Wait. You must be patient and promise to do good with it."

Aleister glanced down at the ring, then closed his eyes tightly. "I promise to be good."

A slight chuckle escaped Lucian, and he gave Aleister a gentle squeeze on the shoulder. "Look at the ring now."

Aleister opened his eyes, glancing down to find the ring snugly fitting his finger, the metal cool and comfortable against his skin. His eyes widened, filled with wonder.

Magic.

Lucian's smile was warm, but his voice was serious. "Now, off to bed with you."

Aleister nodded, clutching the ring tightly as he slid off his father's lap and turned toward the door. But before he could leave the room, a chill swept through the air, and the warm firelight dimmed. Shadows lengthened across the walls, and an acrid scent, sharp and sulfurous, filled the study. Lucian's face darkened, his jaw clenched as he took a protective step between Aleister and the source of the stench. Then, a low, menacing growl echoed from the corner of the room, and Aleister's breath caught as a monstrous figure materialized from the shadows. Its twisted form loomed, eyes burning like hot coals, and Aleister felt the weight of an evil presence that made his blood run cold.

Lucian's voice was steady but fierce. "Aleister, leave. Now!"

Aleister shook his head, his voice quivering. "You need the ring!"

Lucian knelt and looked into his son's eyes; his face filled with an intense, final certainty.

"Remember what I told you about the ring," he said. "Nothing can harm you... I love you, son."

These were the last words Aleister heard before the room went dark, and the sound of ripping flesh filled the air. He stood frozen, unable to look away as the darkness swallowed his father.

"No!!!"

Aleister jolted awake, his heart pounding as he stared into the fire before him. The dream—no, the memory—still clung to him, its vividness refusing to fade. He exhaled slowly, his hand instinctively reaching for the silver ring on his finger. It was warm to the touch, as if still alive with the power his father had promised all those years ago.

"Nothing can harm you." His father's words echoed in his mind, a promise and a curse all at once. He stood, needing to shake the weight of the memory. The firelight flickered, casting restless shadows that danced across the room's many shelves and cases. The study was his sanctuary, a place that felt both safe and deeply haunted. Aleister moved to one of the display cases, his eyes scanning the objects within. Each one had a story, a purpose. He reached out and gently touched a dagger with an ornately carved handle, its blade etched with ancient symbols. This had once belonged to a man who claimed it could cut through the veil between worlds. Aleister hadn't believed him—until he'd seen it used to banish a shadow demon from a child in Ireland. Nearby, an obsidian amulet rested on a black velvet cloth, its surface smooth and cold as death. It was said to protect against possession, a gift from a reclusive witch he'd saved from a mob in Romania.

He sighed, his gaze drifting to the wall where a large map of the world hung, marked with pins and strings connecting countless locations. Each point represented a journey, a fight, a near-death encounter with the supernatural. Angels and demons were real, and Aleister had devoted his life to standing between their war and humanity.

"The war", he thought, his mind drifting. It had raged since the dawn of time, long before humans ever existed. The demons, hungry for power and freedom, had sought to break free of their infernal prison by crossing into the mortal realm. Possessing humans was their way in, a means to escape Hell and wreak havoc on Earth. The angels, divine protectors, had come to humanity's aid, their sole purpose to stop the demons from corrupting and enslaving mankind. But the war

had never ended. It continued in the shadows, fought in forgotten places by beings of immense power—and by mortals like him.

Aleister's gaze fell to a weathered book sitting on his desk, its pages yellowed with age. It was one of his most prized possessions, a grimoire he'd found buried beneath the ruins of a cathedral in Spain. The knowledge within had saved his life more than once, but it was a constant reminder of the cost of his obsession.

Revenge.

The word hung heavy in his mind, a forbidden whisper he never spoke aloud. It was the truth, though. It wasn't heroism or righteousness that had driven him to collect these artifacts, to plunge himself into the shadowy depths of the occult. It was his need to avenge Lucian Kane. His father's death wasn't just a memory—it was a scar that bled every time he closed his eyes.

Aleister moved to his desk, running his fingers over the leather-bound journal sitting there. *How many nights had I poured over texts like this? How many years have I spent searching for power—not to save the world, but to destroy the thing that destroyed my family?*

He closed his eyes, exhaling deeply. The truth was his obsession hadn't just consumed him—it had cost him everything.

His marriage. His home...

Mary.

The one person who had loved him enough to fight for the man beneath the mission was gone, locked out by the impenetrable walls of his obsession. Mary had begged him to stop. To live. To leave the demons to someone else. But Aleister couldn't—not when he was so close. The relics he'd collected over the years hinted at answers just beyond his reach, and one relic above all could put an end to it:

The *Staff of Infinite Light.*

The staff wasn't just a weapon—it was a beacon of hope, the ultimate tool to rid the world of the vile demons that plagued it. To banish the kind of darkness that had taken his father. Aleister's gaze fell on the shelves surrounding him, lined with artifacts, ancient books, and talismans—each one a testament to his relentless search. Yet for all his efforts, the staff remained elusive, a legend always just out of reach.

It wasn't just about the demons. It was the war itself. The eternal battle between Heaven and Hell, where mortals like him were nothing more than pawns in a divine game. He couldn't accept that. He couldn't let Lucian's death—his father's screams still haunted him—be just another casualty in an endless war. No, it had to mean something. He had to make it mean something.

For all his knowledge, all his careful preparations, there was one truth Aleister couldn't deny. He wasn't doing this for Heaven. He wasn't even doing it for humanity. He was doing it for Lucian Kane. He was doing it to avenge the man who had taught him that angels and demons were more than stories and that the world was far darker than most dared to believe.

The study fell silent, save for the crackle of the fire and the faint patter of rain against the window. The glow of the fire cast long shadows on the relics around him, each one a reminder of how far he'd come—and how much farther he had to go.

A sharp knock at the door broke the stillness of the night. Aleister froze, the room suddenly felt colder, darker. He glanced at the clock on the mantel—well past midnight. No one should be at his door at this hour.

The knock came again, louder this time. He stood cautiously, his heart quickening. Moving to the side window, he peered out into the rain-soaked night. Aleister reached for the Ring of Solomon on his finger, twisting it as if to draw strength from its presence.

Slowly, he unlatched the door and pulled it open. The storm greeted him with a gust of cold wind and the faint scent of ozone. Rain splattered the wooden floor beneath his feet. Aleister squinted into the darkness, but the porch was empty. He stepped outside, scanning the area. The storm had lessened to a drizzle, and the moonlight broke faintly through the clouds, casting eerie shadows across the lawn. He looked to the left and then to the right.

No one.

Frowning, Aleister stepped back inside, closing the door with a firm click. He turned the lock, his unease growing as he moved back toward the study. The firelight flickered as Aleister entered the room. He froze.

A soft blue glow emanated from the corner of the study, faint at first but growing stronger, its light filling the room with a warmth that chased away the chill. Aleister's breath caught in his throat as a figure stepped forward, emerging from the glow. Clad in radiant armor, his features sharp and commanding, the being was both otherworldly and familiar. The blue light surrounded him like an aura, pulsing with a power that Aleister could feel in his very bones.

"Michael," Aleister whispered, his voice trembling.

The Archangel's gaze settled on him, calm and steady. "Aleister Kane," Michael said, his voice deep and resonant, carrying a weight of authority that filled the room.

Aleister straightened, his heart pounding. "Why are you here?"

Michael stepped closer, the glow around him dimming slightly as he spoke. "The time has come for you to fulfill your purpose. The Staff of Infinite Light must be found. Without it, this realm will fall to darkness."

"And you think I'm the one to find it? I'm not a priest or even a soldier. I'm just a man—a man who's already lost too much to this war."

Michael's expression softened. "You are more than you believe, Aleister. You have been chosen not because of what you are, but because of who you are. The staff will not come to just anyone. It requires a pure heart, a worthy soul. You are both."

Before Aleister could respond, the temperature in the room plummeted. The fire behind him dimmed, and the scent of sulfur filled the air. Michael spun around, his hand instinctively grasping the hilt of a sword that had suddenly appeared.

Aleister followed Michael's gaze. The shadows in the far corner of the study twisted and darkened, coalescing into a form. Red eyes glowed from within the void, staring directly at him. A guttural growl echoed through the room, sending shivers down Aleister's spine. The figure stepped forward, its form humanoid but distorted, its claws dragging against the wooden floor.

Michael stepped protectively in front of Aleister, his sword blazing with blue fire.

"You dare step into this house?" the Archangel demanded.

The demon laughed, its voice low and menacing. "This house may be protected, but your mortal is not. He is weak. He will fail."

Michael's light flared, driving the demon back slightly, but the creature held its ground, its red eyes fixed on Aleister.

"You cannot stop us," it hissed. "The staff will be ours, and your little human will burn before it ever reaches him."

Aleister felt the weight of the Ring of Solomon on his finger, its metal growing warm. He raised his hand instinctively, and the demon recoiled, its laughter fading into a snarl.

"You're wrong demon." Aleister said, his voice steady despite the fear gripping him.

"See you in Hell!" the demon belched.

Michael stepped forward; his sword raised. The demon hesitated, its red eyes narrowing before it sank back into the shadows, its form dissipating like smoke. The stench of sulfur lingered in the air, a reminder of its presence. The blue light surrounding Michael dimmed.

"The road ahead will not be easy," he said. "But you are not alone. I will guide you, and the light will protect you. You must find the staff, Aleister. Time is running out."

"Then tell me where to start."

With a sweep of his hand, a faint glow appeared on Aleister's desk, growing brighter until it solidified into an object.

Aleister moved closer, he recognized what had materialized—a piece of parchment, aged and brittle, its edges curling with time. The markings on it were intricate and strange, a combination of symbols and a map that seemed to shimmer faintly with an otherworldly light.

"This will guide you," Michael said. "Your first step lies at Saint Mary's Church."

"Saint Mary's? That place has been abandoned for decades. There's nothing there but ruins.".

"The past is often buried beneath what we see. What you seek is hidden, waiting to be uncovered. Follow the map."

Aleister's fingers traced the lines and symbols.

"What am I supposed to find there?"

"The next step in your journey," Michael replied simply. His tone carried no urgency, no hint of the dangers that might await. "It's the path you must take."

Aleister glanced up, his eyes searching Michael's face for answers that weren't there.

"Why me?" he asked, his voice edged with frustration. "Why not someone stronger? Someone who—"

Michael cut him off gently. "Aleister Kane, you were chosen for a reason. This is your path, and yours alone. Trust in the light, and trust in yourself."

The simplicity of Michael's words did nothing to ease the storm brewing in his mind. He wasn't sure if it was anger, fear, or something in between.

Michael stepped back, his form beginning to fade, the blue light around him dimming.

"You must go. Time is not your ally, Aleister. Begin the journey, and all will become clear."

Before Aleister could respond, Michael disappeared, leaving behind only the faint warmth of his presence. The room felt colder, emptier without him. Aleister stared at the map, his mind racing. *Saint Mary's Church?* He had passed the ruins a hundred times, never once thinking they could hold anything of importance. Now, the idea of stepping into those shadows sent a chill down his spine.

As Aleister studied the map in the flickering firelight, his eyes locked on the name inked in faded strokes: St. Mary's Church.

He knew that name. Not from any journal—he hadn't found those yet—but from whispered tales and fragmented texts scattered across forgotten grimoires. It was the kind of name that came with no context, only a feeling. A warning.

St. Mary's wasn't just a church. It was a scar. Built in 1612 by early missionaries—or so the official story claimed—it had always been surrounded by unease. Local legends said the land had once belonged to a forgotten people who spoke in stars and shadows, and that the church had been constructed atop the remnants of a demonic gateway. A place where the veil between realms thinned to near-nothing. He remembered finding one brief reference to it, buried in the margins of a book on religious exorcisms:

"They buried the truth beneath the altar. God help the one who digs it up."

But what struck Aleister now, more than anything, was a vague recollection—something he'd once heard from a surviving monk of the Order of Light. An offhanded, wine-soaked muttering in the ruins of an abbey in Prague: "That's where Crowe made his choice...That's where the staff was nearly lost."

Aleister's grip on the map tightened. He had no idea what truly happened at St. Mary's Church. Only that it had been sealed for generations. Hidden from the world. Protected by magic so old, even demons couldn't whisper its name without burning their tongues. And now... it was where his journey would begin.

He took a deep breath, tucking the map into his coat pocket. The fire in the hearth flickered, its light growing dim as he extinguished it. Grabbing a lantern from the shelf, Aleister cast one last look around the study. The first step. That's all this was. He could do this. He had to. With the storm outside fading into quiet, Aleister stepped into the night, the faint glow of the moon guiding his way toward the unknown.

Chapter 2

SAINT MARY'S CHURCH

The ruins of Saint Mary's Church loomed in the distance, a silhouette against the pale light of the moon. The journey there had been uneventful, but Aleister couldn't shake the feeling that something was watching him from the shadows of the forest he had crossed.

He stepped off the main road and onto the overgrown path leading to the church grounds. The faint crunch of gravel beneath his boots was the only sound, the night eerily silent. No frogs, no crickets, nothing but the whisper of the wind.

Aleister paused, glancing around. The silence was wrong. It pressed against him, heavy and unnatural, like a warning. He tightened his grip on the lantern he carried, the faint light casting flickering shadows ahead of him. The closer he got, the more the church seemed to radiate an aura of decay and neglect. Its once-proud steeple had collapsed, leaving jagged edges of stone reaching toward the sky like broken teeth. Vines and moss crept over the crumbling walls, nature reclaiming what humanity had abandoned.

As he reached the rusted iron gate that marked the church grounds, Aleister hesitated. The gate hung ajar, its hinges squealing softly as the wind nudged it back and forth. He pushed it open fully, the sound echoing like a groan through the still night. Beyond the gate, gravestones jutted from the ground at odd angles, their inscriptions worn and illegible. A faint mist clung to the ground, curling around his boots as he walked. The air was colder here, biting at his skin despite the layers of his coat.

The church itself stood in the center of the grounds, its doors long gone, leaving only a dark, gaping entrance. Aleister stopped a few yards from it, staring into the blackness. His instincts screamed at him to turn back, but the map Michael had given him was clear—this was where he needed to be.

He pulled the parchment from his pocket, unfolding it with care. The glowing symbols and lines seemed to pulse faintly, guiding his eyes to a point near the back of the church. An underground passage. That was where he needed to go.

Aleister took a deep breath and stepped forward, the mist swirling around his feet as he crossed the threshold. The air inside was stale, carrying the faint scent of mildew and something far less natural. He raised the lantern, its light casting flickering shadows across the walls. The interior was even more ruined than the outside, with collapsed beams and shattered pews littering the floor. Faded murals of saints and angels clung stubbornly to the crumbling walls, their faces blurred and haunting.

As he moved deeper into the church, his steps careful and deliberate, a faint sound reached his ears. It was distant, almost imperceptible—a whisper. He froze, his heart pounding as he strained to hear. The whisper grew louder, a murmur of voices blending in a chaotic harmony. It came from beneath him, rising through the floor like the groaning of the earth itself.

The passage.

The map had shown the entrance to be near the altar, but the floor there was covered in debris. He began moving the rubble, his hands trembling slightly as the whispering voices grew louder.

After several minutes, his efforts revealed a stone trapdoor, its surface engraved with symbols like those on the map. The whispers stopped abruptly, leaving the silence heavier than before. Whatever was down there, it wasn't waiting to greet him with open arms. He took a deep breath.

"One step at a time," he muttered, gripping the edge of the trapdoor and pulling it open.

The darkness below was absolute, the lantern's light unable to penetrate the void. A set of narrow stone steps descended into the blackness, the air growing colder as it rose to meet him.

This is what Michael wanted? Aleister thought, though he couldn't shake the nagging feeling that he wasn't ready for whatever lay ahead.

He began his descent, the lantern trembling slightly in his hand. Each step took him deeper into the unknown, the weight of the darkness pressing heavier with every breath. The steps spiraled downward, the air growing colder with every step. The flickering light of the lantern illuminated the narrow walls, revealing carvings etched into the stone. The symbols were unfamiliar, their sharp angles and fluid curves seemingly alive as the shadows danced across them. Each step felt heavier than the last, as if an unseen force was trying to pull him back. He gritted his teeth, focusing on the weight of the Ring of Solomon on his finger. Its warmth grounded him, pushing away the whispers of doubt creeping into his mind.

The stairs finally ended, opening into a vast underground chamber. Aleister's breath caught as he raised the lantern, its light barely reaching the edges of the cavern. The ceiling arched high above, supported by ancient pillars covered in more of the strange carvings. The air was damp, carrying the faint metallic tang of blood.

At the center of the chamber stood a stone altar, its surface cracked and stained dark. Surrounding it were scattered remnants of what must have been ceremonial objects—chalices, candles, and fragments of broken statues.

Aleister approached cautiously, his eyes scanning every shadow. The room was unnervingly quiet, the kind of silence that felt alive, as if it were watching him. He stopped in front of the altar, setting the lantern down on its surface. The map in his pocket pulsed faintly, its glow visible even through the fabric. He pulled it out, unfolding it with care, and laid it flat on the altar. The symbols on the map seemed to shift and rearrange themselves, aligning with the carvings on the altar's surface. A faint hum filled the air, and Aleister's pulse quickened.

This is it? he thought.

But the moment of clarity was short-lived. A low growl echoed through the chamber, reverberating off the stone walls and sending chills down Aleister's spine.

He spun around, his hand instinctively moving to the ring. The growl grew louder, followed by the sound of something heavy scraping against the floor. From the shadows, a figure emerged—tall and twisted, its body humanoid but grotesquely malformed. Its eyes glowed with a sickly yellow light, and its mouth was filled with jagged teeth that glistened in the lantern's glow. Aleister took a step back, his heart pounding.

"You've got to be kidding me," he muttered under his breath.

The creature snarled, its clawed hands flexing as it began to move toward him. Each step it took echoed through the chamber, its presence radiating malice. Aleister raised the Ring of Solomon, feeling its warmth intensify.

"Stay back!" he commanded, his voice steady despite the fear gripping him.

The creature hesitated, its glowing eyes narrowing as it regarded the ring. For a moment, Aleister thought it might retreat. But then it let out a deafening roar, the sound shaking the very ground beneath him. Before Aleister could react, the creature lunged. He dove to the side, narrowly avoiding its claws as they raked across the stone where he had just been standing. Scrambling to his feet, Aleister grabbed the lantern and backed toward the altar. His mind raced. The ring was powerful, but it wouldn't be enough on its own—not against something like this.

The creature advanced again, its movements faster this time. Aleister raised the lantern, throwing it with all his strength. The glass shattered against the creature's chest, the oil igniting in a burst of flame. The beast roared in pain, thrashing as the flames licked at its skin. Aleister used the distraction to grab the map and bolt for the stairs. He could hear the creature behind him, its heavy footsteps shaking the ground as it gave chase. The narrow staircase loomed ahead, and Aleister sprinted toward it, his breath coming in ragged gasps.

As he reached the base of the stairs, a sudden burst of light filled the chamber. Aleister turned, shielding his eyes as a radiant blue glow illuminated the room. The creature let out a pained screech, its form dissolving into shadows as the light consumed it. When the glow faded, the chamber was empty, save for the sound of Aleister's ragged breathing. Aleister stared at the spot where the creature had been, his mind racing. The light—it could only have been Michael. He looked down at the map in his hands. The glowing symbols had returned to their original state, their message clear. This wasn't just a step in his journey—it was a test; one he had barely survived.

Taking a deep breath, Aleister turned and began climbing the stairs. The church ruins awaited above, but he couldn't shake the feeling that something—or someone—was watching him. Aleister barely had time to process what had happened in the crypt before another sound snapped him to attention—a low rustling, followed by the crunch of gravel underfoot. He turned sharply, his hand instinctively moving to the Ring of Solomon.

"Who's there?" he demanded, his voice firm despite the unease prickling at his senses.

From the shadows of the graveyard, a figure stepped forward, cloaked and hooded. The moonlight revealed glimpses of intricate tattoos etched into the figure's hands and face.

Its gait was slow and deliberate, the aura around it unsettling.

"Show yourself," he said, his tone edged with warning.

The figure stopped a few paces away, pulling back it's hood. A man stood before him—small and wiry, his face a patchwork of scars and tattoos that seemed almost to writhe in the flickering light. His piercing blue eyes locked onto Aleister with an intensity that felt unnatural.

"Evening," the man said casually, as if they'd just crossed paths on a quiet street.

"What are you?"

"What am I? That's a new one."

"Answer the question."

The man sighed, raising his hands in mock surrender. "Name's Blaze Barton. Demon slayer, light-bringer, all-around pain in the ass to Hell's finest." He grinned, his teeth flashing in the dim light.

"And you must be Aleister Kane—the infamous collector of cursed trinkets."

"How do you know my name?"

"Word travels fast when you've got an Archangel looking out for you. Michael sent me."

"Michael doesn't send people. Especially ones who look like they crawled out of Hell."

Blaze's grin faded, his expression hardening. "Careful, mate. I've spent my life hunting Hell spawn. Don't mistake me for one of them."

Aleister wasn't convinced. "Prove it."

"Alright, then. You want proof? Watch closely."

He raised his hand, and Aleister noticed a faint glow emanating from one of the tattoos on his wrist—a sigil Aleister recognized as a binding mark for exorcism. Blaze muttered something under his breath, and the air around them shifted. From the shadows, a faint growl emerged. Aleister turned and saw a spectral figure—a demon, its form twisted and writhing—emerging from behind a tombstone.

"Your visitor from earlier," Blaze said calmly. "It was hanging around, hoping you'd slip up."

The demon lunged, but Blaze moved quickly, drawing a small dagger from his belt. The blade glowed faintly as he slashed through the air, striking the creature. With a deafening screech, it dissolved into nothingness. Blaze turned back to Aleister, spinning the dagger in his hand before tucking it back into his belt.

"Still think I'm the bad guy?"

Aleister didn't answer immediately. "You're reckless," he said finally. "And I don't need help."

Blaze laughed. "Mate, if you don't need help, then I'm a bloody angel. Face it—you're in over your head. That's why Michael sent me."

Aleister hesitated, his instincts warring with his frustration. "If Michael sent you, then prove you're useful. What's the next step?"

"Glad you asked. First, we need to get you sorted out. You've got power, sure, but it's all tangled up with your past."

"What's that supposed to mean?"

"It means," Blaze said, stepping closer, "you've got baggage. Negative energy, unresolved anger, the whole lot. That ring of yours? It's powerful, but it's only as strong as the heart that wields it. If you want to survive what's coming, you'll need to be cleansed."

"And how do you propose we do that?"

"We go to the Church of Light. You need to be baptized, purified. It's the only way to prepare for the real fight ahead."

Aleister frowned. "The Church of Light? That's a myth."

"Most things are until you find them. Lucky for you, I know exactly where it is. But it won't be easy to get there. The place is well-guarded."

"Guarded by what?"

"Let's just say it's not all sunshine and roses."

"Fine. But if this turns out to be a waste of time, you're on your own."

Blaze extended a hand, his grin returning. "Deal. Now let's get moving. The night's young, and we've got a lot of ground to cover."

Aleister ignored the hand and started walking toward the road. Blaze followed, chuckling softly.

"You're going to love this place. Just wait and see."

Chapter 3

ATTACK OF THE BANSHEES

Blaze studied the map under the moonlight, his expression unreadable as Aleister leaned against a nearby tree. The tension between them hadn't eased, but Aleister couldn't deny Blaze's competence—he seemed to know exactly what he was doing, even if his methods were unconventional.

"How far is this place?" Aleister asked, his voice laced with impatience.

Blaze folded the map carefully and slipped it into his coat.

"Far enough that you don't need to know."

"What's that supposed to mean?"

"The Church of Light is a sacred place. It's not the kind of spot you mark on a map for just anyone to find. Only a handful of us know the way—and that's how it needs to stay."

"So how do you plan to get me there if I can't know where it is?"

A grin spread across Blaze's face, one that Aleister didn't trust in the slightest.

"Simple. You're going to take a nap."

"What?" Before Aleister could protest, Blaze raised a small vial filled with a glowing, amber liquid.

"Relax," he said, shaking it gently. "It's not poison. Just something to make sure you don't remember the route. For your safety and the church's."

"You expect me too just—"

Blaze uncorked the vial, the faint scent of herbs and honey wafting through the air.

"I don't like this any more than you do. But if someone like you—someone not cleansed—knew the way to the church, it'd put the whole place in danger. Now drink up. Or I can force it down your throat, your choice."

Aleister glared at him but snatched the vial, eyeing the contents warily. "You're enjoying this, aren't you?"

"Immensely," Blaze said with a grin. "Now hurry up. We're burning moonlight."

With a deep breath, Aleister downed the liquid, the taste surprisingly sweet. The effect was almost immediate. His vision blurred, the edges of the world fading as a heavy drowsiness overtook him. He staggered slightly, his knees buckling. Blaze caught him before he hit the ground, lowering him gently.

"Sweet dreams, Kane," he muttered before hefting Aleister over his shoulder as everything goes black.

Aleister's awareness returned with a jolt. The cold night air bit at his skin, and his ears filled with the sound of screeches—piercing, otherworldly cries that sent shivers down his spine.

"Wake up!" Blaze's voice cut through the noise. "We've got company!"

Aleister blinked, his vision adjusting to the flickering light of torches Blaze had set up. They were in a clearing surrounded by dense forest, but the shadows were alive—moving, circling.

"What—" Aleister began, but the answer came before he could finish. A figure lunged from the darkness—a pale, skeletal creature with tattered, translucent wings and glowing red eyes. Its wailing scream cut through the air as it swooped toward Aleister.

"Banshees!" Blaze yelled, slashing at the creature with a dagger that glowed faintly with blue light. The blade struck true, and the Banshee dissolved into ash with a shriek.

Aleister had read about them. Studied them. Even heard their wails once before—from a safe distance. But never had he faced them up close. Most people thought Banshees were merely omens—ghostly women who wailed to announce death. That was a lie. Banshees were hunters. Twisted spirits of sorrow and rage, born from souls that died violently—betrayed, murdered, or cursed—and never allowed to pass on. They weren't here to warn of death... they were death. They traveled in shrieking flocks, feeding on the life force of the living, their cries able to shatter bone, rupture organs, and peel sanity away like old wallpaper. One was dangerous. A group? Deadly.

They moved like smoke through the trees—neither fully physical nor spectral—unaffected by ordinary weapons. Only enchanted objects, blessed wards, or divine light could repel them. And worst of all? Once a Banshee marked you with its cry, it would never stop hunting until your soul was claimed.

Aleister staggered to his feet, the fog of sleep still clinging to him. Another Banshee darted toward him; its claws outstretched. He raised the Ring of Solomon, its warmth spreading through his hand as a burst of light repelled the creature.

"Don't let them get close!" Blaze shouted, slashing through another Banshee. "One or two of these things isn't bad, but in packs, they'll suck the life out of you!"

Aleister turned in a circle, his heart pounding. More of the creatures emerged from the shadows, their numbers growing. The air was thick with their wails, a sound that clawed at his sanity.

Blaze moved with precision, his daggers flashing in the torchlight as he struck down one Banshee after another.

"Stay close to the light!" he called, his voice sharp and commanding. "They hate it."

Aleister backed toward the nearest torch, raising the ring again. Another burst of light sent a group of Banshees screeching into the darkness, but more took their place.

"Any bright ideas?" Aleister shouted over the cacophony.

Blaze grinned. "Yeah—don't die!"

Aleister scowled but kept his focus, using the ring to fend off the advancing horde. The fight was chaotic, relentless, and the Banshees showed no sign of letting up. Blaze cursed under his breath, sheathing his daggers.

"Alright, we're doing this the hard way," he muttered, pulling a pouch from his belt. With swift, practiced movements, Blaze scattered a circle of fine white powder around them. He knelt, muttering an incantation under his breath, and the powder flared to life, a glowing barrier forming around them. The Banshees hissed, recoiling from the light, but they didn't retreat. Instead, they swarmed just beyond the circle, their cries growing more frenzied as they clawed at the edges of the barrier.

"We're safe for now," Blaze said, "But this won't hold for-ever. Any ideas?"

Aleister shook his head. The protective circle was strong, but the sheer number of Banshees was overwhelming. They needed something—someone—stronger.

As if in answer, the air above them began to shimmer, a golden light piercing through the darkness.

"What the—" Blaze started, but his words were cut off as a portal materialized within the circle. The portal swirled with radiant energy, its edges sparking like lightning. From within, a figure emerged, stepping gracefully onto the ground.

Aleister blinked, momentarily stunned.

She was breathtaking—tall and statuesque, clad in gleam-ing armor that seemed to radiate its own light. Her dark hair flowed behind her, and her piercing green eyes swept the scene with calm authority. In her hands, she held a sword unlike anything Aleister had ever seen. Its blade shone with a brilliant white light, casting away the shadows and forcing the Banshees to retreat.

"Who the hell is that?" Blaze asked, his voice filled with awe.

The woman's gaze locked onto Aleister.

"I am Victoria, High Priestess of the Order of the Light," she said, her voice firm and melodic. "Protector of the Church and guardian of its secrets."

Before either man could respond, Victoria turned toward the Banshees, raising her sword. The blade flared with light, and a wave of energy surged outward, striking the creatures. The Banshees screamed, their forms dissolving into wisps of shadow as the light consumed them. Within moments, the clearing was silent, the oppressive darkness lifting as if it had never been. Victoria lowered her sword, the light fading as she turned back to Aleister and Blaze.

"You're welcome," she said simply, a hint of amusement in her tone.

Aleister found his voice, though it came out rough. "Thank you. I... wasn't expecting—"

"You weren't supposed to," Victoria interrupted, sheathing her sword. "Your arrival here is no coincidence, Aleister Kane. The Church of Light has awaited you."

"Right, well, that's all very dramatic, but maybe next time you show up *before* we're surrounded by life-sucking banshees."

"Your circle held well enough, demon slayer. But the real trials lie ahead."

"Great," Blaze muttered. "Can't wait."

Victoria ignored him, her attention returning to Aleister. "You must come with me," she said. "The Church of Light is close, but the path is treacherous. The cleansing must be done before your journey can continue."

Aleister hesitated, glancing at Blaze. Despite the stranger's sudden appearance, something about her presence felt undeniably right.

"Lead the way," he said finally.

"Stay close. The light protects us for now, but it won't hold for long."

As they followed her through the forest, Aleister couldn't shake the feeling that this was only the beginning. The woman who had appeared so suddenly, so perfectly, seemed almost too good to be true.

"Who exactly are you?" he asked as they walked.

"I am a servant of the Light, tasked with guarding its sanctuaries and guiding those who seek its power. And you, Aleister Kane, are the first to be chosen in centuries."

The woods were dark and foreboding, the branches overhead twisting like skeletal fingers against the moonlit sky. The further they went, the deeper the shadows became, as though the very forest resisted their passage.

Aleister walked ahead with his lantern, the flickering light barely penetrating the gloom. Blaze trudged behind, muttering quietly to himself, while Victoria moved with effortless grace, as if the forest itself stepped aside for her. Aleister couldn't help but glance at her as they walked. Despite the tension in the air, she seemed untouched by it—calm, poised, and confident. Her armor clinked softly as she moved, but it didn't diminish her presence. Her body was a study of strength and elegance, each step deliberate, her toned figure illuminated faintly by the lantern's light. She was beautiful, yes, but there was something deeper—something perfect about her that felt beyond human. And her scent. Aleister hadn't noticed it before, but now it lingered in the air around her, faint and floral, like lilies carried on a spring breeze. It was intoxicating, a strange contrast to the oppressive decay of the woods surrounding them.

Focus, Kane, he thought, shaking his head. *Now's not the time to admire angelic warriors.* Yet he couldn't deny the pull. There was something about Victoria—an otherworldly aura that drew him in. It wasn't just her beauty or strength, though those were undeniable. It was the way she carried herself, the unwavering determination in her eyes. She felt untouchable, eternal, as if the light itself had shaped her.

"Eyes up, Kane," Blaze's voice cut through Aleister's thoughts, sharp with sarcasm. "You can ogle our shining knight later."

Aleister shot him a glare, cheeks warming slightly. "I wasn't—"

"Sure, you weren't," Blaze smirked, though his gaze darted warily to the shadows. "But if you're done daydreaming, you might want to pay attention. This place doesn't take kindly to distractions."

Victoria turned slightly, her emerald eyes catching the lantern's light as she glanced between them.

"Keep your focus sharp, both of you," she said evenly. "The closer we get to the cemetery, the more it will try to unsettle you."

Aleister nodded, swallowing his embarrassment. He tore his attention back to the path ahead, though the image of Victoria lingered stubbornly in his mind. The forest began to thin, the trees parting like a curtain to reveal the crest of a hill. The group emerged from the woods, and the sight before them stole their breath.

Chapter 4

SOLUM MALEDICTUM

The Cemetery sprawled below, a dark scar on the earth. Its wrought-iron gates hung crooked and rusted, barely holding together. Beyond them, rows of jagged tombstones spread out like broken teeth, many half-buried or shattered. Mausoleums leaned into the earth, their stone facades cracked and covered in creeping vines. Mist blanketed the ground, swirling as though it had a will of its own.

"Bigger than I expected," Blaze muttered, his earlier sarcasm replaced with unease.

As they neared the edge of the hill, Aleister spoke, his voice low.

"Solum Maledictum...Latin for Cursed Ground. I've read about this place."

"Of course you have. Let me guess—lots of doom and gloom?"

"It's more than that," Aleister said, his tone sharper than he intended. "It's a cursed place. A realm where the veil between worlds is thin. The book I read warned that the cemetery feeds on fear and despair. It twists the minds of those who enter, and very few who have walked its grounds ever return."

"The warnings are true," Blaze said. "Solum Maledictum is not bound by the laws of this world. It exists on the edge of the living and the dead—a hunting ground for demons, wraiths, and worse."

Aleister hesitated, his gaze dropping to the ground. He remembered the passage vividly, etched in his mind:

"Beware Solum Maledictum, where the dead don't sleep, and the shadows devour the soul. Only the purest hearts may tread its paths and emerge whole."

"What else did the book say?" Blaze asked.

Aleister exhaled. His breath visible in the cold air. "That the cemetery doesn't just take the living—it takes everything they are. It feeds on your deepest fears, your worst memories. And once it has you, there's no escape."

"Charming. Sounds like my kind of vacation spot."

"It's not a joke," Aleister snapped. "This place... it's alive. It wants us to fail."

"Enough," Victoria said sharply, her voice cutting through the tension. "Dwelling on its dangers will only weaken your resolve. Focus on why we're here, not on what it may do to you."

Aleister fell silent, though his unease didn't lessen. He glanced at Victoria, who strode ahead with unshakable confidence. Despite her commanding presence, he couldn't help but wonder if even she felt the weight of the cemetery's darkness. Aleister's eyes were drawn to the entrance, where two enormous black statues of horses flanked the gates. They stood frozen in mid-charge, their muscular forms unnervingly lifelike. Their eyes were empty voids, but Aleister could feel their presence—a watchful malice that sent a chill down his spine.

"Those statues..." Aleister murmured.

"Guardians," Victoria said, "Forged to protect this place from intruders."

"Are they alive?" Aleister asked, unable to tear his gaze away from their stone forms.

"Not in the way you'd think," Victoria replied. "But if they sense weakness, they will awaken."

"Wonderful," Aleister muttered, glancing toward Blaze. "Anything else we should know?"

Blaze gave a humorless chuckle. "Yeah. Don't look them in the eyes too long. Statues that big don't stay that still for long."

The group descended the hill, the mist growing thicker with every step. The cemetery loomed closer, the gates rising like the paw of some great beast. Aleister couldn't shake the feeling that the shadows were watching, creeping closer with every breath. At last, they reached the gates. Up close, the black horses were even more unsettling, their stone skin smooth yet cold, as if they absorbed the very light around them. Aleister kept his distance, his heart pounding as he caught the faint hum of something ancient—something alive—beneath the surface.

"Let's not linger," Victoria said, her tone sharp. "The longer we wait, the more dangerous this place becomes."

Aleister didn't need to be told twice. He pushed open the gates, the hinges shrieking in protest, and stepped inside. The mist seemed to swallow them whole, and as the gates groaned shut behind them, Aleister couldn't shake the feeling that they'd just crossed into something far worse than they were prepared for. He cautiously monitored his surroundings, the Ring of Solomon faintly glowing on his finger. Beside him, Blaze adjusted the straps of his belt, the faint clink of daggers breaking the quiet. Victoria stood tall, her gleaming armor seeming to repel the very darkness around them, her sword strapped across her back. Her expression was unreadable, but her piercing gaze scanned the graveyard like a hawk.

"This place is cursed," Aleister muttered. "It doesn't feel right. Solum Maledictum has always been a place of great evil. It exists on the edge of this world. A hunting ground for demons who feed on the living."

"Well, fantastic," Blaze said with a dry chuckle. "I've always wanted to visit a jolly place like this."

"Jokes won't help you here, Blaze," Victoria warned. "Keep your weapons ready. The creatures that dwell here are not to be underestimated."

"What exactly are we walking into?" Aleister asked.

"This place is drawn to doubt, fear, and weakness. If you let it, it will consume you."

"Let's get this over with."

They entered the cemetery, the gates groaning shut behind them with a sound like a death knell. The mist thickened, and the air grew colder with every step. It was as though the graveyard itself was alive, watching them. Listening. They moved in silence, their footsteps muffled by the soft, damp earth. The lantern's glow barely pierced the swirling fog. Shadows shifted at the edges of Aleister's vision, vanishing when he turned to look.

"Do you hear that?"

"Hear what?" Blaze asked.

A faint whispering drifted through the air, growing louder as they moved deeper into the cemetery. The voices were impossible to understand—soft, maddening, and inhuman. Victoria's hand hovered over the hilt of her sword.

"Stay close. This is just beginning."

Before Aleister could ask what she meant, a guttural growl split the silence.

From the mist, shadowy figures emerged—twisted forms with glowing red eyes and jagged claws. Demons. Dozens of them.

"Move!" Victoria commanded, drawing her sword in one swift motion. The blade ignited with radiant light, casting a brilliant glow that pushed back the darkness.

"Stay in the light!"

Blaze spun, drawing his daggers. "Well, here's a warm welcome!"

The demons lunged. Victoria's sword struck first, slicing through the closest creature with blinding precision. It let out a screech, dissolving into smoke. Blaze was a blur, his glowing daggers flashing as he fought off another demon. Aleister raised the Ring of Solomon, its light bursting outward, forcing back a group of the creatures. But there were too many. They pressed forward, relentless, their claws raking at the edge of Victoria's light.

"Blaze! Behind you!" Aleister shouted.

Blaze turned just as a massive demon lunged from the fog. It struck him hard, knocking him to the ground. Before anyone could react, two more creatures grabbed him, dragging him toward the shadows.

"Blaze!" Aleister yelled, running toward him.

Blaze struggled, his blades slicing through the air. "Get off me, you bast..."

His voice was cut off as the demons pulled him into the mist.

"Blaze!" Victoria shouted, surging forward, but the shadows swallowed him whole. The silence that followed was deafening.

Aleister stood frozen. His breath ragged. "No... no, no, no."

Victoria moved to his side, her face set in grim determination. "He's not dead."

Aleister turned to her, panic in his voice. "How do you know that?"

She placed a hand on his shoulder.

"Because if he were, this place would have fed on his soul. But they've taken him somewhere likely to their master."

"We have to find him."

"And we will," Victoria said. "But we need information first."

Aleister opened his mouth to argue when a voice, smooth and cold, echoed through the mist.

"Quite the performance," it drawled.

From the shadows stepped a man—tall, impeccably dressed in a dark coat and crimson scarf. His pale skin seemed to glow faintly in the moonlight, and his crimson eyes fixed on them with unsettling calm.

Victoria's hand went to her sword. "A vampire."

The man smiled, revealing sharp fangs.

"You wound me, dear lady. I am Damian Walker, at your service."

"If you're here to fight..."

Damian chuckled softly. "If I were here to fight, you'd already be dead. Fortunately for you, I have no interest in such trivialities."

His smile faded, replaced by a more serious expression. "The man you seek—your friend—is alive, for now. I can help you find him."

"Why would a vampire help us?" Aleister asked.

"Because the demons who took him are trespassers in my domain. They upset the balance. And as much as I loathe meddling in mortal affairs, I despise demons far more."

"What do you want in return?" Victoria asked.

"We'll discuss that in due time. For now, let us focus on retrieving your companion."

Aleister hesitated, doubt gnawing at him. He didn't trust Damian—not for a second. But Blaze's life was on the line, and he couldn't do this alone.

"Fine," Aleister said, his voice firm. "Lead the way."

Damian smiled again, turning toward the mist. "Follow closely. Solum Maledictum is not kind to stragglers."

As the vampire led them deeper into the graveyard, Aleister felt a chill settle over him. Blaze was out there, somewhere. And he would get him back—no matter the cost.

Damian's figure moved like a shadow through the dense fog, his dark coat billowing slightly as he led Aleister and Victoria deeper into the graveyard.

Aleister's voice broke the silence, sharp with urgency. "Who has Blaze?"

Damian slowed, turning slightly to cast a knowing glance over his shoulder. "A formidable adversary. One who thrives in the depths of this wretched place." He paused, his tone tinged with both amusement and disdain. "Her name is Marid."

"Marid..." Victoria murmured. "The mother of shadows."

"I've heard the name. She's—"

"A monster," Damian interjected smoothly. "Once human but consumed by dark pacts and forbidden rituals. She's become something far worse—a creature bound to the darkest circles of Hell yet still tethered to this world."

Aleister's unease was starting to get the best of him. "Why would she take Blaze?"

Damian stopped, turning fully to face them. The dim light illuminated his pale features.
"Blaze made the mistake of killing one of her top demons during one of his... excursions," he explained, "Marid is not the forgiving type. She craves revenge."

"Revenge alone doesn't explain this," Victoria said. "There must be more to this story."

"Ah, you are as sharp as you are radiant," Damian replied with a mock bow. "You're correct, of course. Marid has another reason for taking your friend. She believes he knows the location of the *Staff of Infinite Light*."

Aleister's heart sank. "Does he?"

"Only Blaze can answer that," Damian said, his tone turning serious. "But if Lilith manages to extract the information—and worse, if she gets her hands on the staff—she will become unstoppable. Even the legions of Hell would kneel before her."

"Then we can't let her succeed." Victoria said with conviction.

"Indeed," Damian said with a dry chuckle. "Which is why I am here to assist. Despite my... dietary preferences, I have no love for demons or witches who disrupt the delicate balance of things."

"And what do you gain from this?"Aleister asked.

"Let's just say that keeping Marid in check serves my interests as well as yours. I have no desire to see her rise to power."

"Where is she?" Aleister pressed.

Damian gestured ahead, where the fog seemed to grow thicker, darker. "Beneath the grand crypt, at the heart of this cemetery. That is where she dwells—a labyrinth of tunnels and chambers carved into the earth. Reaching her will be a challenge, and facing her... well, let's just say it will test every ounce of strength you possess."

Aleister's mind racing. "And Blaze?"

"If she hasn't killed him already," Damian said casually, "he'll be alive. For now. She'll want to toy with him first, break him down. She enjoys her games."

"Then let's not waste any more time." Victoria said.

Damian turned toward the path ahead.

"As you wish. But prepare yourselves—Marid's domain is not for the faint of heart."

Aleister exchanged a glance with Victoria, who nodded resolutely. With a deep breath, he followed Damian into the fog, each step carrying them closer to the heart of the cemetery—and into the lair of the Mother of Shadows.

Chapter 5

THE MOTHER OF SHADOWS

The crypt loomed before them. An imposing monolith of stone carved with ancient symbols that seemed to pulse faintly in the dim light. Its facade was adorned with grotesque statues—twisted figures of humans and beasts, their faces contorted in eternal agony. A massive iron gate barred the entrance, rusted but still formidable, as though daring intruders to step closer.

Aleister felt a chill run down his spine as he stared at the gate, the faint whispers of unseen voices brushing against his mind.

"This is it," Damian said, his voice low and almost reverent. "Marid's lair."

Victoria stepped forward, her sword unsheathed and glowing faintly with a soft, golden light. Her expression was calm but determined, her emerald eyes scanning the crypt for signs of danger.

"The air is thick with her presence. She knows we're here."

"Good," Aleister said.

Damian chuckled, his crimson eyes glinting in the lantern's light.

"Brave words. Let's hope you can back them up."

Aleister stepped closer to the gate. The symbols etched into the stone seemed to writhe and twist as he approached, their shapes shifting in ways that made his head ache. He stopped, turning to Victoria.

"Can you sense anything?"

"She's strong," Victoria replied. "The darkness here is old, powerful. Be on guard."

Damian leaned casually against one of the grotesque statues, his tone laced with amusement.

"Oh, she's more than strong. Marid is cunning, unpredictable. She'll have traps waiting for us. And if you're not careful, you might end up as part of her collection."

"Collection?" Aleister asked, glancing at him.

"Souls," Damian said simply. "She keeps them like trophies, bound to her will. You'd do well not to join them."

Aleister turned back to the gate, raising the Ring of Solomon. Its warmth spread through his hand, and a faint golden light emanated from it, illuminating the symbols on the stone. The gate groaned, ancient mechanisms grinding as it slowly began to open. A blast of cold air rushed out, carrying with it the stench of decay and sulfur. Aleister fought the urge to gag as he stepped back, letting the gate swing fully open. Beyond the threshold lay a staircase, carved into the stone and descending into utter darkness. The faint glow of the lantern barely touched the first few steps before being swallowed by the void.

"Lovely," Blaze muttered under his breath. "Can't wait to see the guest accommodations."

"Stay close. The shadows will try to separate us." Victoria said.

Aleister followed her down the stairs, his lantern casting dancing shadows on the rough stone walls. Damian brought up the rear, his movements as silent as the grave. The air grew colder with every step, the oppressive weight of the crypt pressing down on them. Aleister could feel the darkness closing in, not just around them, but inside his mind. Whispers flitted at the edges of his thoughts, soft and seductive, promising power, vengeance, and release. He shook his head.

Focus. This is exactly what she wants.

Victoria paused at the bottom of the stairs; her sword raised as she scanned the chamber ahead. The space was vast, the ceiling lost in shadow. Torches lined the walls, their flames burning an unnatural green. Rows of stone pillars stretched into the darkness, each carved with twisted depictions of agony and despair.

"She's close," Victoria said, her voice low.

Damian stepped beside her, his gaze sweeping the chamber. "Welcome to Marid's domain. Watch your step—she enjoys playing with her food."

Aleister felt the weight of the crypt settle over him like a shroud. Blaze was somewhere in this darkness, and they would find him—but at what cost?

Damian's crimson eyes glinted as he stepped further into the crypt's oppressive darkness. "Marid," he said, his voice echoing off the cold stone walls. "The Mother of Shadows. The Demon Witch. She goes by many names, each one a reminder of the destruction she's left in her wake."

"And you think giving her dramatic titles makes this situation better?"

"It's not about making it better, Mr. Kane. It's about understanding what you're up against. Marid is not just a witch—she's a predator. A master of manipulation. You'd do well to remember that."

"Titles mean nothing if it can bleed like anything else." Victoria said.

Damian chuckled softly. "Oh, my dear high priestess, if only it were that simple."

"Let's focus on finding Blaze before we start worrying about titles. Where is she keeping him?"

Damian's expression darkened. "In her web—beneath the grand crypt. She lures her prey there, binding them in darkness until there's nothing left of who they were. She'll be waiting for us, no doubt."

The group moved deeper into the chamber, the air growing colder with every step. The stone floor beneath their feet began to change, the smooth surface giving way to something rough and uneven. Aleister glanced down, his stomach churning as he realized they were walking on bones—thousands of them, crushed and scattered like dry leaves.

"She's been busy," Damian murmured, his tone almost admiring.

Victoria stopped abruptly, raising her hand. "Wait."

The group froze, the tension thick enough to cut. Aleister strained his ears, the whispers growing louder, almost frantic. Then, from the darkness ahead, a deep, guttural growl rumbled, low and menacing.

"She's sending her pets," Damian said casually. "How predictable."

Victoria sprang forward. Her sword gleaming brighter. "Stand ready."

From the shadows, shapes began to emerge—twisted, hulking creatures with glowing red eyes and jagged claws. Their bodies were a grotesque mix of flesh and bone, their movements jerky and unnatural. Aleister felt his stomach drop as more and more of them appeared, their growls filling the chamber like a symphony of nightmares.

"There's too many," Aleister said, panic creeping into his voice.

"Hold the line. We don't let them separate us."

Damian's fangs glinted as he smiled. "Allow me." In a blur of motion, he leapt forward, his hands extending into razor-sharp claws. He tore through the nearest creature with savage precision, its body disintegrating into ash as it hit the ground.

Victoria charged next, her sword blazing as she cut through the horde with skill and grace. Each strike of her blade sent shock waves of light through the chamber, forcing the creatures back.

Aleister raised the Ring of Solomon, its golden glow bursting outward. The creatures recoiled, hissing and snarling as the light burned their twisted forms. He stepped closer to Victoria, his heart pounding.

"We can't hold them forever!" he shouted.

"We won't need to," Damian called, his voice calm even as he dispatched another creature. "This is just the welcoming committee."

As if on cue, a deafening roar shook the chamber, the ground trembling beneath their feet. The creatures froze, their heads snapping toward the source of the sound. From the darkness at the far end of the chamber, a massive figure began to emerge. The creature was easily twice the size of the others, its body a grotesque mass of muscle and sinew. Its glowing red eyes locked onto them with predatory intent, and it let out another ear-splitting roar.

Victoria moved toward the creature, her sword glowing brighter than ever. "I'll handle this. Keep moving toward the crypt."

"What? No—" Aleister began.

"You have the ring. You're the only one who can face Marid. Go."

"She's not wrong, Mr. Kane. Let the lady work."

Aleister hesitated, torn between the need to press on and the fear of leaving Victoria behind. But as the massive creature charged, there was no time to argue.

"Come on," Damian said, grabbing Aleister's arm. "The crypt is this way."

Aleister cast one last glance at Victoria, her figure blazing like a beacon against the onslaught of darkness. Then he turned and followed Damian into the shadows, his heart heavy with worry—and determination.

The sound of the battle behind them grew faint as Aleister and Damian descended a narrow, winding staircase carved into the stone. The air became thicker, heavier, and Aleister struggled to keep his breathing steady. The Ring of Solomon pulsed faintly, a golden warmth against his skin, but it did little to ease the icy dread creeping through his veins.

Damian led the way, his movements as fluid and deliberate as a predator stalking its prey. His crimson eyes seemed to glow faintly in the darkness, guiding them through the labyrinth of tunnels. Aleister followed close behind, the lantern's flickering light casting shifting shadows on the rough walls.

"She'll know we're coming," Damian said casually, his voice cutting through the oppressive silence.

"How much further?"

"Not far," Damian replied. "But I'd brace yourself. She enjoys making an entrance."

The staircase ended abruptly, opening into a massive underground chamber. Aleister stopped at the threshold, his breath catching in his throat.

The space was unlike anything he'd ever seen. The walls were lined with glowing runes that pulsed with a sickly green light, illuminating the chamber in an eerie glow. Massive stone pillars rose to the unseen ceiling, each one carved with grotesque depictions of torment and despair. The floor was a mosaic of bones, arranged in intricate patterns that seemed to shift and writhe when Aleister looked too long.

At the center of the chamber stood a grand stone altar, its surface slick with some dark, viscous substance. Hanging above it, suspended by chains of black iron, was Blaze. His body was limp, his head slumped forward, and Aleister felt a surge of panic.

"Blaze!" he shouted, rushing forward.

Damian's hand shot out, grabbing Aleister's arm and stopping him in his tracks.

"Don't be so eager," he said, his tone sharp. "This is her web. Every move you make plays into her hands."

"We can't just leave him there!"

"We won't," Damian said. "But if you rush in blindly, you'll end up on that altar next to him."

Aleister looked up at Blaze, his friend's chest rising and falling faintly. He was alive—but for how long? A soft, melodic laugh echoed through the chamber, sending chills down Aleister's spine. The air grew colder, and the green light dimmed, replaced by an ominous crimson glow.

"Well, well," a voice purred, smooth and venomous. "The prodigal mage and his charming entourage. What an unexpected delight."

Aleister turned, his eyes searching the shadows. From the darkness, a figure emerged, draped in flowing black robes that seemed to shift and ripple like liquid. Her skin was pale as moonlight, her sharp features framed by cascading waves of midnight hair. Her eyes burned with an unnatural red glow, and her lips curled into a predatory smile.

"Marid," Damian said, his voice dripping with disdain. "I see you've redecorated the place. I feel it still needs work."

Marid's smile widened as she glided closer, her movements unnervingly smooth. "Damian Walker," she said, her tone mockingly sweet. "Still playing the reluctant hero, I see. Tell me, how does it feel to grovel before mortals?"

Damian's expression darkened, but he said nothing.

"Let him go," he said, his voice steady despite the fear clawing at his chest.

Marid's eyes flicked to him, her smile fading slightly. "And why would I do that, little mage? Your friend has proven quite useful. He knows things—secrets that even you are unaware of."

Aleister's heart sank. "The staff," he said quietly.

Marid's laughter echoed through the chamber, a haunting melody that sent chills down his spine. "Ah, yes. The Staff of Infinite Light. Such a fascinating artifact. So much power, just waiting to be claimed. And your friend—well, let's just say he's been most enlightening."

Aleister's anger grew. "If you hurt him—"

Marid raised a hand, and Aleister froze as an invisible force pressed against his chest, pinning him in place. Her smile returned, cold and cruel.

"Spare me your empty threats, child. You're out of your depth."

Damian stepped up. "Let him go!"

Marid arched an eyebrow, her gaze flicking to Damian. "And what will you do, vampire? Bare your fangs and hope I flinch?"

"I'll do what I must."

The tension in the room crackled like static, the air heavy with the promise of violence. Aleister struggled against the invisible force holding him, his mind racing. He needed to think, to find a way to free Blaze and stop Marid before it was too late. Aleister's breathing was labored as he fought against the invisible force holding him in place. His mind raced, searching for any strategy that wouldn't end in disaster. Blaze hung limply above the altar, the slow rise and fall of his chest a fragile beacon of hope.

Victoria where are you? he thought, his desperation mounting.

"Release him, Marid," Damian said again, his voice cutting through the silence. "Your games are becoming quite tedious."

"You presume to command me, Damian?" She stepped closer, her black robes rippling like liquid shadows. "Have you forgotten your place in the hierarchy of darkness? Or have you grown sentimental in your old age?"

"Sentimental? I'm just tired of cleaning up your messes."

Marid laughed, the sound cold and hollow. "Always the arrogant one. But you've brought me a gift, and for that, I thank you."

Her gaze shifted to Aleister, who still struggled against the oppressive weight holding him down. She studied him, her expression turning thoughtful.

"The mage with the Ring of Solomon," she murmured. "A rare and fascinating relic. And yet... you have no idea of its true potential, do you?"

"I know enough to stop you."

Marid smiled, her sharp teeth gleaming. "Do you? Then by all means, show me."

The pressure holding Aleister suddenly vanished, and he stumbled forward, barely catching himself. Marid stood motionless, her crimson eyes glinting with amusement.

"Go on," she said, gesturing toward the altar. "Save your friend. Or try, at least."

Aleister glanced at Damian, who gave him a faint nod. Aleister raised the lantern and stepped toward the altar, the Ring of Solomon glowing faintly on his finger. The green runes on the walls flickered as he moved, as though reacting to the ring's presence.

As he neared the altar, Blaze stirred, his head lifting weakly.

"Aleister..." he croaked, his voice barely audible.

"I'm here," Aleister said, his voice firm. "Hold on."

The chains suspending Blaze rattled as Marid waved a hand, her smile widening.

"Touch them, and you'll burn," she said lightly. "Unless, of course, you're willing to pay the price."

Aleister hesitated, his gaze flicking to the glowing chains. The runes carved into them pulsed with dark energy, radiating an unnatural heat. He could feel their malevolence even from a distance.

"Stop stalling," Damian said. "You have the ring—use it."

Aleister's heart pounded as he raised his hand, the golden light of the Ring of Solomon intensifying. He focused on the chains, willing the light to push back the darkness.

Marid's expression darkened. "You dare?"

The light from the ring burst outward, colliding with the dark energy of the chains. The runes flickered and dimmed, and the chains began to tremble. Blaze let out a groan as the tension holding him eased.

"No!" Marid hissed, her composure breaking for the first time. She raised her hands, and the chamber shook as the runes on the walls flared to life, casting the room in a sickly green glow.

Damian moved like a shadow, lunging at Marid with his claws extended. She spun to face him, her hand shooting out to conjure a barrier of dark energy. The two collided, the force of their clash sending shockwaves through the chamber.

Aleister gritted his teeth, focusing all his energy on the ring. The golden light grew brighter, pushing back the darkness as the chains holding Blaze began to crack.

"Almost there," he muttered, his voice strained.

Blaze's head lifted again, his eyes fluttering open. "Aleister... behind you..."

Aleister turned just in time to see a hulking shadow lunging toward him. One of Marid's grotesque minions, all claws and teeth, barreled forward with murderous intent. Aleister raised the ring in defense, but the creature was too fast.

Before the creature could reach him, a radiant beam of light sliced through the air, striking the beast and disintegrating it on contact. Aleister turned to see Victoria standing in the doorway, her sword glowing with celestial energy.

"Sorry I'm late," she said. "Did I miss the fun?"

"Victoria!" Aleister called out; his voice filled with relief.

Victoria strode into the chamber, exuding an air of authority. "Focus on Blaze," she said, her eyes locked on Marid. "I'll handle this."

Marid sneered, her crimson gaze snapping to Victoria. "The priestess returns," she said, her voice dripping with venom. "How quaint."

Victoria didn't respond, her sword glowing brighter as she raised it. The two women squared off, the air between them crackling with energy.

Aleister turned back to Blaze, the light from the ring flaring as the chains shattered. Blaze fell, and Aleister caught him, lowering him gently to the ground.

"Got you, my friend." Aleister said.

Blaze gave a weak chuckle, his eyes fluttering shut. "Took you long enough..."

Victoria and Marid faced each other in the center of the chamber, their opposing energies radiating out like waves colliding in a storm. The sickly green glow of the runes clashed with the golden light of Victoria's sword, casting eerie, shifting shadows across the walls.

"You've meddled long enough," Marid hissed, her voice echoing unnaturally. "This place will be your tomb, priestess."

Victoria raised her sword, her expression calm and unwavering. "Your reign ends here, witch!"

Marid's laugh was cold and cruel, reverberating through the chamber. "Bold words for someone so outmatched." She raised her hands, and the air around her crackled with dark energy. Shadows coalesced, forming jagged spears that hovered in the air before launching toward Victoria.

With a fluid motion, Victoria deflected the first wave, her sword cutting through the shadows as if they were tangible.

Meanwhile, Aleister crouched beside Blaze, who had fallen unconscious again. He checked his pulse—weak, but steady. Relief flooded him, but it was short-lived as the ground beneath him trembled.

"Stay with me," Aleister muttered, glancing toward the battle. He could see Victoria holding her own against Marid, but the witch's power was immense.

Damian was circling the room, his crimson eyes fixed on Lilith, waiting for the right moment to strike.

"Damian," Aleister called, his voice low. "Can you distract her?"

The vampire didn't look at him. "I was just waiting for my moment."

In a blur, Damian moved, his claws slashing toward Marid. She spun, her black robes flaring as she conjured a barrier of black shadow. Damian's claws met the barrier with a deafening crack, sparks flying as he pushed against it.

Victoria seized the opening, lunging forward with her sword. Marid barely managed to sidestep, the blade grazing her arm. The witch snarled, her composure slipping as blood, black as ink, dripped onto the stone floor.

"Enough!" Marid roared, her voice reverberating with raw power.

The runes on the walls flared brighter, and the entire chamber trembled. A massive shockwave burst outward, sending Victoria and Damian stumbling back. Aleister braced himself, shielding Blaze as best he could. The air grew colder, and the oppressive energy in the room intensified. Marid floated above the altar now, her arms outstretched as she drew power from the crypt itself.

"You cannot win," she said, her voice a blend of fury and triumph. "I am eternal. This world belongs to me."

Victoria pushed herself to her feet, her sword glowing brighter than ever. "Not while I stand," she said firmly.

Damian joined her, his claws dripping with shadowy remnants of the barrier. "This is getting tedious," he muttered. "Shall we end her?"

Aleister stood, the lantern in one hand and the Ring of Solomon glowing on his other. "We'll end her together."

Marid's eyes snapped to him, her expression twisting into a snarl. "You dare challenge me, mortal? You are nothing."

"Maybe," Aleister said, stepping forward, his voice steady despite the fear clawing at him. "But you'll never get the staff."

Marid let out a guttural scream, the shadows in the room writhing and twisting like living things. "Then I will destroy you and take the ring from your bloody corpse!"

She unleashed a torrent of dark energy, the force barreling toward Aleister. Before he could react, Victoria moved, her sword intercepting the attack. The golden light of her blade clashed with the shadows, creating a dazzling explosion of energy that rocked the chamber.

"Now!" Victoria shouted.

Aleister raised the ring, its golden light flaring as he focused all his will on Marid. The light shot out like a beam, striking the witch and forcing her back. Damian darted forward, slashing at her with inhuman speed, while Victoria pressed the attack with her sword. The combined assault overwhelmed Marid, her screams echoing through the crypt as the golden light consumed her. The runes on the walls flickered and dimmed, and the oppressive energy in the room began to fade. Finally, with one last, ear-piercing shriek, Marid dissolved into a swirling mass of shadow and light, which dissipated into the air. The chamber fell silent, the tension lifting like a shroud.

Aleister stumbled forward. His legs weak beneath him. He reached Blaze and knelt beside him, relief flooding him as he saw his friend still breathing.

Victoria approached. Her armor battered but her expression resolute. "It's over," she said quietly.

Damian dusted himself off, his smirk returning. "Well, that was exhilarating."

Aleister glanced at the altar, the dark stains still glistening in the dim light.

"For now," he said, his voice heavy. "But this is just the beginning."

Chapter 6

THE BLACK VEIL FOREST

The crypt was eerily quiet now, the oppressive energy that had clung to the air finally lifting. The faint green glow of the runes had faded, only the dim light of Aleister's lantern and the golden shimmer of Victoria's sword. The scent of sulfur and decay still lingered, but the weight of Marid's presence was gone.

Aleister knelt beside Blaze, his hand on his friend's shoulder. Blaze's breathing was shallow but steady, and color was slowly returning to his pale face.

"He's alive," Aleister said, relief washing over him. "But he's weak. We need to get him somewhere safe."

Victoria approached, her armor scuffed and bloodied but her movements steady. She sheathed her sword, the golden light fading, and placed a hand on Aleister's shoulder. "You did well. Both of you."

Damian leaned casually against one of the stone pillars, inspecting his claws. "Yes, yes. Heartwarming teamwork and all that. But perhaps we could save the sentiment for after we leave this charming pit of despair?"

Aleister glanced at him. His irritation tempered by exhaustion. "For once, I agree with you."

Victoria nodded. "The Church of the Light isn't far. We can regroup there and ensure Blaze gets the care he needs."

Damian pushed off the pillar. "Ah, the legendary Church of the Light. I've heard tales of its grandeur. Let's hope it lives up to the hype."

Aleister stood. "You're coming with us?"

"Of course. You'll need me for what's ahead, and besides, I've grown rather fond of our little group."

"You're here because you've proven useful. Don't mistake that for trust." Victoria said.

Damian placed a hand over his heart in mock offense. "Your words wound me, my dear."

Aleister ignored their exchange, focusing on Blaze. He slid his arms under Blaze's shoulders, lifting him gently.

"Help me carry him."

Victoria stepped forward, taking Blaze's legs. Together, they began the slow trek back up the winding staircase. Damian followed behind. His movements unnervingly silent. The ascent was grueling, every step heavy with exhaustion and the lingering tension of the battle.

Aleister's thoughts churned as they climbed, his mind replaying Marid's words.

The staff... she was so close to it.

Marid's screams still echoed in my ears. That unholy voice... That cursed lair of rot and shadow... The pain on Blaze's face as her shadow magic tore through him. I had faced demons before—creatures of fire, fury, and trickery. But Marid? She was something else. Older. Deeper. Her power wasn't just dark—it was ancient, woven into the marrow of the world like mold beneath skin.

And if she was just one of them...How many more are waiting for us? How many more times can we do this?

My hatred burns hotter now. For demons. For what they've done to this world. For what they did to my father. To my wife. To Blaze. It doesn't stop. You kill one, and ten more take its place.

Is this a war we're meant to win?

Maybe I'm chasing a ghost. Maybe this staff... this journey... maybe it's all a fool's errand, designed to give me purpose where there is none. What if the demons can't be destroyed? What if this war isn't winnable? What if I'm just a broken man, trying to rewrite a story that ended a long time ago?

I glance at Blaze—pale, barely conscious, tattoos dim. No. Even if it's hopeless. Even if I fall. I'll take every damn last one of them with me.

At last, they emerged into the open air. The cool night breeze was a welcome relief, carrying away the stench of the crypt. The moon hung low in the sky, casting an ethereal glow over the cemetery. The black horse statues at the gates seemed to watch them, their stony gazes unyielding.

"We need to keep moving," Victoria said. "The longer we stay, the more vulnerable we are."

Aleister nodded, adjusting his grip on Blaze. "Lead the way."

The group moved quickly, navigating the twisted paths of the cemetery. The shadows seemed to cling to them, the faint whispers of unseen voices following their every step. Aleister couldn't shake the feeling that they were being watched, though he couldn't see anything beyond the mist.

As they continued down the path, Damian spoke, his tone casual. "So, what's the plan once we reach this fabled church? Pray for salvation?"

Victoria's gaze remained fixed ahead. "The Church of the Light is more than a place of worship. It's a sanctuary, a stronghold against the darkness. But it will require something of us in return."

"What kind of something?" Aleister asked.

"Purity," Victoria said simply. "Before we can proceed, we must be cleansed of all negativity. Only then will the church grant us its blessings."

Damian chuckled softly. "Ah, purity. That should be fun."

Aleister didn't respond, his thoughts weighed down by the journey ahead. The Church of the Light held the next step in their quest, but it also represented another trial—one he wasn't sure he was ready for.

The maze-like paths of Solum Maledictum seemed endless, the oppressive mist clinging to the group like a second skin. Every corner they turned felt the same, every shadow twisting into ominous shapes that seemed to watch their every move. Aleister's grip on Blaze tightened as they navigated the treacherous terrain.

At last, the mist began to thin, and the jagged gravestones gave way to open ground. Aleister squinted into the distance, his heart sinking as the silhouette of an immense, dark forest loomed ahead. The twisted branches of its trees reached skyward like skeletal hands, their dense canopy swallowing any light that dared enter.

Victoria stopped beside him. "The Black Veil Woods," she said softly. "We're close."

Aleister shifted Blaze's weight, his friend groaning softly in his arms. "Close? That place looks like it's waiting to swallow us whole."

"It is," Damian said, his tone almost cheerful. "And if you don't know the way, it will."

Victoria moved forward; her gaze fixed on the foreboding tree line.

"Blaze knows the path. Without him, we'll be lost."

Aleister glanced down at his unconscious friend, panic creeping into his chest. "He's barely holding on as it is. How are we supposed to—"

Blaze stirred, his eyes fluttering open. "Don't... leave me behind," he muttered, his voice weak but resolute.

"We won't," Aleister said quickly. "But we need you, Blaze. You're the only one who knows the way through."

Blaze gave a faint, crooked smile. "Figures... you'd need me for something."

Damian knelt beside them, pulling a flask from his coat. "Here," he said, unscrewing the cap and holding it to Blaze's lips. "This should keep you going."

Blaze took a sip, coughing as the liquid burned its way down. "What... is that?"

"Let's just say it's potent," Damian replied. "You'll thank me later."

Blaze's breathing steadied, and he pushed himself upright with Aleister's help. He glanced toward the forest, his expression grim.

"The Black Veil Woods isn't just any forest. It's alive, in its own way. It'll try to confuse you, trap you. If you stray from the path, you'll never make it out."

"Comforting," Aleister muttered.

"There are markers—subtle ones. Only I can see them. You follow me, step for step. No wandering, no stopping."

Victoria nodded. "Understood."

"Lead the way, then. I've always wanted to get lost in a sentient forest."

"Stay close," Blaze said. "And whatever you do, don't look back."

The group moved cautiously toward the forest, the air growing colder with every step. As they crossed the threshold, the oppressive darkness closed in around them, and the sounds of the outside world faded to nothing. The only sound was the crunch of their footsteps on the leaf-strewn ground.

Aleister glanced at Blaze, who moved with deliberate care, his eyes scanning the trees for signs only he could see.

"You sure about this?" he asked quietly.

"No," Blaze replied. "But it's not like we have a choice."

Victoria stayed close behind, her sword emitting a faint glow that pushed back the darkness just enough to keep them from stumbling. Damian trailed at the rear, his crimson eyes darting to every shadow that moved. The deeper they went, the more the forest seemed to shift around them. Trees bent and twisted, their gnarled branches forming unnatural arches. The path beneath their feet narrowed, winding in ways that made no sense. Aleister felt the weight of the woods pressing in on him, the oppressive silence broken only by the occasional creak of wood or distant rustle of leaves.

"Keep moving," Blaze said. "We're almost—"

A low growl echoed from the darkness, cutting him off. The group froze, their breaths hitching as the sound grew closer.

"What was that?" Aleister whispered.

"Something that doesn't want us here," Blaze said. "Stay together. Don't stop."

Victoria raised her sword, the glow intensifying. "We're not alone."

The growl reverberated through the trees, low and guttural, vibrating in Aleister's chest. He scanned the darkness, but the source of the sound remained hidden, as though the forest itself were toying with them.

"Don't stop. If we hesitate, it'll only get worse." Blaze said.

"Worse?" Damian said. "That's comforting."

Victoria's sword glowed brighter as she took up a protective position beside Blaze. "Eyes forward," she said. "And don't stray."

Aleister focused on Blaze's movements, carefully matching each step. The forest seemed to shift and twist around them, the trees closing in like silent sentinels. The growl came again, closer this time. It was followed by a faint rustling, as though something large were circling them just beyond the edge of the light.

"Blaze... are we sure this is the right way?" Aleister asked.

Blaze didn't answer immediately, his eyes darting between unseen markers on the trees.

"It's the only way."

The rustling grew louder, accompanied by faint whispers that seemed to come from all directions. Aleister's heart raced as the whispers grew clearer, their words indistinct but laced with malice. The forest felt alive, its presence heavy and suffocating.

"We're being hunted," Victoria said. "Stay close."

Damian's claws extended with a soft metallic sound. "By what?"

Blaze's voice dropped to a whisper. "Wraiths. They're part of the forest. Shadows given form."

"Can we fight them?" Aleister asked.

"Not in the way you'd think." Blaze explained. "They feed on fear and confusion. If we lose our way they'll drag us into the darkness."

I'd read about Wraiths in the oldest texts—spirits twisted by pain, hatred, and unfulfilled vengeance. Not ghosts, not demons, but something in between. They were the result of a soul that refused to move on, choosing instead to cling to the darkness. Some were soldiers, cursed to wander battlefields where their blood had been spilled. Others were victims, hollowed out by betrayal or grief. But all of them... *all of them hungered for life.* And worse—they remembered. Not names, not faces. But *feelings.* Anger. Regret. Sorrow so deep it turned to violence. I once read that to face a Wraith is to face a *mirror of your own suffering.* That's how they find you. That's how they feed. They *latch onto the wound inside you* and drink until there's nothing left. I could feel them now—hovering just beyond the mist, whispering in a language I didn't understand but somehow still *felt.* My father's death. The years I spent chasing shadows. Mary's screams in the dark. The Wraiths knew. They always knew.

Victoria raised her sword, the golden glow pushing back the shadows slightly. "Then we don't give them what they want."

A sudden shriek pierced the air, echoing through the trees. The sound was followed by the rustle of branches, the movement impossibly fast.

"Move!" Blaze barked, his voice cutting through the noise. "Stay with me!"

The group broke into a hurried pace, their footsteps crunching against the forest floor. The whispers grew louder, overlapping and chaotic, as if the wraiths were closing in. Shadows danced at the edges of their vision, flickering and shifting like smoke.

Aleister's breath came in sharp bursts, his heart pounding as he struggled to keep up. He caught glimpses of glowing eyes in the darkness, red and malevolent, watching their every move.

"Blaze!" he shouted. "How much farther?"

Blaze didn't answer, his focus entirely on the path ahead. His movements were slower now, his exhaustion catching up to him. Victoria moved closer, her presence a steadying force.

"We need to keep him awake," she said urgently. "If he falters, we're lost."

Aleister reached out, gripping Blaze's arm. "You've got this. Just a little farther."

Blaze nodded weakly; his gaze fixed on a faintly glowing marker carved into a nearby tree.

"There," he said, his voice barely audible. "We're close."

Another shriek tore through the air, and this time, a shadowy figure lunged toward them. Victoria reacted instantly, her sword slicing through the wraith with a burst of golden light. The creature dissolved into smoke, but more shapes began to emerge from the darkness.

"They're swarming," Damian said, his voice low and dangerous. "We need to move. Now!"

The group pressed forward, the path narrowing as the forest seemed to close in around them. The wraiths grew bolder, their attacks more frequent, but Victoria and Damian held them off, their combined strength keeping the creatures at bay. Finally, the trees began to thin, and a faint light appeared in the distance. Blaze stumbled, his legs giving out, but Aleister and Victoria caught him, half-dragging him toward the clearing. As they broke free of the forest's oppressive grip, the wraiths stopped their pursuit, their whispers fading into silence. The group collapsed onto the grass, gasping for breath. The light of dawn was just beginning to touch the horizon, casting a pale glow over the landscape. Ahead of them, rising from the mist, stood a towering structure of gleaming white stone. Its spires reached skyward, radiant and unyielding, a beacon of hope against the darkness.

"The Church of the Light," Victoria said softly, her voice filled with awe.

Aleister stared at the church; his exhaustion momentarily forgotten. They had made it. But as he looked back toward the forest, he couldn't shake the feeling that their journey was far from over.

Chapter 7

THE CHURCH OF
THE LIGHT

The towering Church of the Light loomed before them. Its pristine white stone almost glowing in the early morning light. The air around it felt different—lighter, purer—as though the oppressive darkness of the forest and cemetery could not touch its sacred grounds. The sight of it filled Aleister with a mix of relief and apprehension.

Victoria helped Blaze to his feet. "We're here," she said softly. "You've done well."

Blaze gave a weak chuckle. "Didn't think... we'd make it," he muttered, his voice hoarse.

Damian brushed dirt from his coat, his crimson eyes fixed on the church. "It's... less ostentatious than I imagined."

"It's a sanctuary for those who serve the Light. But it's also a test. The Church doesn't grant its blessings easily."

Aleister's gaze swept over the church, taking in its intricate carvings and radiant spires. "What kind of test?"

"To enter the Church of the Light, you must be cleansed of all negativity—doubt, fear, anger. Only then will it allow you to proceed."

"And what happens if we don't pass?"

Victoria's silence was answer enough.

"Let me guess—if we fail, we die. Well, you guys die. I'm already dead." Damian said jokingly.

"No one has ever failed and lived to tell the tale," Victoria said firmly, cutting through his sarcasm.

Blaze stirred. His voice weak but clear. "So... no pressure."

"We've come this far. There's no turning back now." Aleister said.

Victoria lead the group toward the massive doors of the church. As they approached, the air grew warmer, a soft hum vibrating through the ground beneath their feet. The doors, carved with intricate depictions of angels and celestial battles, seemed to shimmer with an inner light.

Without hesitation, Victoria placed her hand on the door. The carvings glowed brighter, and a deep, resonant tone filled the air as the doors began to open. A soft, golden light spilled out, illuminating the group in its warmth.

"Stay close," Victoria said. "And be ready. The cleansing will test you in ways you can't predict."

Aleister exchanged a glance with Blaze, who nodded weakly. Damian, for once, remained silent, his usually smug demeanor replaced by a flicker of unease.

As they stepped inside, the light enveloped them, and the air grew thick with a sense of divine presence. The interior of the church was vast and awe-inspiring, its walls lined with glowing runes and stained-glass windows that depicted scenes of angelic triumph. At the center of the room stood a fountain of pure, radiant light, its waters shimmering like liquid gold.

Victoria turned to face them, her expression calm but serious. "This is where it begins. Step into the light of the fountain, and it will judge your heart. If you carry darkness, it will purge it. But be warned—the process is not without pain."

Aleister swallowed hard. His gaze fixed on the fountain. He could feel its power from where he stood, a pull that was both comforting and terrifying. "And if we don't?"

"You won't be allowed to proceed," Victoria said simply. "The Church will reject you."

Blaze gave a weak laugh, leaning on Aleister for support. "Well, I've faced worse. Let's get this over with."

"Speak for yourself." Damian said trying to lighten the mood. "I prefer my darkness right where it is, thank you."

"This isn't a choice." Victoria said with a stern voice. "If you want to continue this journey, you must submit to the light."

Aleister took a deep breath as he moved forward. The light of the fountain seemed to grow brighter as he approached, its warmth washing over him. He could feel his heart pounding, every step heavier than the last.

As he reached the edge of the fountain, he glanced back at the others.

"Together?"

Victoria nodded, stepping up beside him. Blaze, with a strained but determined expression, followed. Damian lingered for a moment, his crimson eyes narrowed, before finally stepping forward with a resigned sigh.

One by one, they entered the light.

Aleister stepped into the fountain's golden waters swirling gently around his feet. The warmth enveloped him immediately, sinking into his skin and spreading through his body like a comforting embrace. For a moment, he felt a sense of peace, as if all the weight he carried had been lifted.

Then the pain began.

It started as a faint prickling sensation, like needles piercing his skin. The warmth grew hotter, burning through him, not in a physical sense, but deeper—within his very soul. He gasped, his knees buckling as memories flashed before his eyes. Every mistake, every regret, every ounce of anger and fear he'd ever felt rose to the surface, refusing to be ignored. He saw his father, Lucian, standing tall in his study, only to be struck down by the demon that had haunted Aleister's nightmares for years. He saw Mary, his wife, walking away from him, her face etched with disappointment and pain. He felt the crushing weight of his obsession with revenge, the countless hours spent chasing artifacts, pushing away the people he cared about.

"No..." he murmured, tears streaming down his face. "I didn't mean..."

The light pressed harder, unrelenting, as if demanding more from him. He heard whispers now, voices urging him to let go, to release the burdens that chained him. But could he? Could he truly surrender the pain that had defined his life for so long? Beside him, Victoria stood in the light, her face calm but strained. Her hands gripped the hilt of her sword, the golden glow reflecting off her armor. She, too, seemed to be wrestling with something unseen, her lips moving in silent prayer. Blaze knelt in the water, his tattoos glowing faintly as the light worked its way through him. His jaw was clenched, his breathing shallow, but his eyes remained open, determined. Whatever darkness he carried, he faced it head-on, refusing to let it consume him.

And then there was Damian.

The vampire stood at the edge of the fountain. His crimson eyes narrowed as the light touched him. It burned against his skin, smoke rising where the waters met his body. He hissed, his fangs bared, but he didn't move away. His expression was a mix of defiance and pain, his gaze locked on the light as if daring it to do its worst. The light shifted within Aleister, changing. The pain ebbed slightly, replaced by a warmth that was deeper, purer. He felt something break inside him, as if chains had been shattered. The whispers grew louder, not urging this time, but praising. When he opened his eyes, the light around him had softened, its intensity fading to a gentle glow. He looked down at his hands, trembling but steady, and realized that the darkness he had carried—the anger, the fear—had lessened. Not gone but diminished.

Victoria stepped out of the fountain first. Blaze followed, his movements slow but purposeful, his tattoos glowing faintly as he emerged. Damian lingered for a moment longer, his expression unreadable, before finally stepping out, his coat trailing water behind him.

"Well," Damian said, his tone dry but quiet. "That was quite unpleasant."

Victoria turned to Aleister. "How do you feel?"

Aleister's hands were still trembling. "Lighter," he said finally. "But... not whole."

"That's normal," Victoria replied. "The cleansing removes what holds you back, but it doesn't erase the scars. Those, you'll carry with you."

Aleister nodded, his gaze drifting to the fountain. The waters had stilled, their glow dimming as if the church itself were satisfied.

A soft voice echoed through the chamber, resonant and ethereal. "You have been cleansed. Step forward, seekers of the Light."

The group exchanged glances before moving toward the altar at the far end of the room. It was simple, carved from white stone, but radiated an undeniable power. Above it, a stained-glass window depicted a battle between angels and demons, the forces of light triumphing over the shadows. The soft voice continued to resonate through the chamber, growing stronger as a figure emerged from the radiant light of the altar. Cloaked in robes of shimmering white, the figure exuded an aura of calm and authority. Its face was partially obscured by a glowing hood, but its presence filled the room with a warmth that stilled every fear.

"Welcome, seekers of the Light," the figure said, it's voice both commanding and compassionate. "I am Amadeus, High Keeper of the Order of the Light."

Victoria immediately knelt, bowing her head in reverence.

"High Keeper," she said, her tone filled with respect.

Aleister exchanged a glance with Damian, who raised an eyebrow but remained standing. Blaze, still unsteady on his feet, stepped forward, his gaze locked on Amadeus.

"You're the one I've... felt," Blaze said, his voice rough but steady. "In my dreams."

"The Light has been with you, Blaze Barton, guiding you toward this moment. You hold the knowledge we need to proceed. Step forward and let us awaken what remains hidden."

Blaze hesitated, his exhaustion plain, but Aleister gave him a reassuring nod. Taking a deep breath, Blaze moved to the altar, the golden light intensifying as he approached. Amadeus raised a hand, and a soft glow enveloped Blaze, bathing him in warmth.

"Be still," Amadeus said. "The truth lies within you."

Blaze closed his eyes, his breathing slowing as the light deepened. For a moment, the chamber was silent, save for the faint hum of energy. Then Blaze's eyes snapped open, glowing faintly with golden light.

"I see it," he whispered. "The staff... it's hidden in the Sanctum of Eternity. Buried beneath the Well of Light."

"The Well of Light is sacred ground, guarded by powerful forces. Only those of unwavering resolve can retrieve what lies within."

"We've made it this far. We won't stop now."

"Courage alone will not suffice, Aleister Kane. The path ahead is fraught with trials that will test your body, mind, and spirit. You must all be prepared."

With a wave of his hand, Amadeus summoned a table of gleaming white stone, laden with an array of weapons and tools. Each item radiated a subtle light, their forms elegant yet formidable.

"These will aid you on your journey," Amadeus said.

Amadeus unsheathed a blade that shimmered with the first light of creation itself. Its brilliance spilled across the chamber, I instinctively squinted—not from light, but from truth. The Blade of Dawn didn't just glow... it *remembered*.

"For you Victoria, The Blade of Dawn. A weapon for a true warrior of the Light. Its edge is sharp enough to cut through the shadows of despair."

Victoria stepped forward, taking the blade with a nod of gratitude.

It was said that the blade had been forged from the very first light to touch the earth—the raw essence of dawn, captured before the world knew war. According to legend, the Archangel Uriel carried it during the First Rebellion, when the angels turned against each other and Heaven bled for the first time.

But it was not Uriel who made the Blade infamous. It was a warrior named Seraphiel, one of the few angels who chose to fall not in sin, but in sacrifice. She descended from the heavens, not because of pride, but because humanity cried out in fear—and no one answered. She took the Blade of Dawn with her, defying Heaven's command to stay neutral. Her light burned through the armies of the damned. It is said that where her blade passed, shadow dared not return for a thousand years.

But legend claims she paid the ultimate price. When she stood between a village of innocents and a demon prince who had torn a hole into the mortal realm, Seraphiel struck the demon down—but was mortally wounded in the process. The blade absorbed her final breath, and with it, her spirit. Before her body faded into ash, she whispered a prayer into the hilt:

"May this blade only awaken for the one who carries both light... and love."

And then the sword was gone. Lost to time. Until now.

When Amadeus placed the Blade of Dawn into Victoria's hands, I felt something shift. Not in her... but in the room itself. As if the Church recognized her. As if Heaven remembered her name. She wasn't just a warrior. She was the answer to a prayer whispered by an angel ten thousand years ago.

The room dimmed around us. The torches flickered low. And for a breathless moment... nothing moved. Then the blade came alive. A soft, radiant glow emanated from the steel, not like fire, but sunlight breaking through storm clouds. The symbols etched into the blade's spine blazed golden as if stirred from slumber. The sword vibrated gently in her grip, resonating like it recognized her. Victoria's eyes widened—not in fear, but in a strange, overwhelming *familiarity*. Like part of her had held this weapon before... in another life.

"By the Light..." Blaze whispered from beside me.

He took a step forward, awe overtaking his usually steady features. "That's it. That's really it."

"You've seen it before?" Aleister asked.

Blaze nodded slowly, not taking his eyes off the weapon.

"No... but I've been searching for it most of my life. Stories. Fragments. The Archangel's relic. Lost after Seraphiel fell. Everyone thought it was a myth."

He exhaled. Voice low. "Until now."

Victoria's grip tightened around the blade. Her gaze distant—focused inward. And then she whispered, almost to herself:

"I know this light..."

"For you, Aleister," Amadeus continued, "the Lantern of Truth. It will illuminate the hidden paths and reveal what seeks to deceive."

When Amadeus was gifting relics, I was expecting a weapon. What he handed me was something far stranger. An old lantern—wrought from a dark, weathered metal that felt far heavier than it looked. The glass was etched with runes I didn't recognize, and inside... no flame. Just a faint, swirling glow. Like a memory that refused to die. At first glance, it was unimpressive. But the moment my fingers curled around its handle; I felt a divine charge. Not in my arms. Not in my body. But in my soul.

I had read of it in only the most obscure grimoires. A relic said to have been forged by Gabriel himself from the breath of God. It was not created to reveal lies in men—it was made to pierce the blackest abyss.

When the heavens first waged war against the hell born legions, they needed a way to fight the shadows—not with steel, but with clarity. With revelation. This lantern does not expose your secrets. It exposes theirs. Demons cloaked in false flesh must reveal their true form. Haunted woods, cursed tombs, and forgotten catacombs—no darkness can hide in its presence. It turns night into judgment. A small sun, born from divine fury.

They say the last time it was lit fully, it blinded an army of specters, forced a legion of demons into retreat, and revealed a traitor standing among a holy order. But it doesn't burn endlessly. Its flame must be earned. It responds to the soul of the one who holds it. If there is doubt, it flickers. If there is fear, it dims. If there is hate...It goes out.

Amadeus met my eyes when he handed it to me and said only this: "It will only shine for the one who still believes there's something worth saving."

I looked down into the small glow and felt the warmth against my fingers.

And for a moment, I did believe.

"Blaze," Amadeus said, turning to the demon slayer. "You already carry your weapon—your body is marked with the sacred runes of protection. But I grant you this." He held out a vial of shimmering liquid. "The Tears of Eternity. Use them wisely."

Blaze accepted the vial, his grip firm despite his weariness.

Inside the vial, suspended like liquid starlight, swirled a colorless tear that shimmered with every hue of the soul.

I had heard of them only once buried in a forgotten scroll locked beneath a Vatican archive. Legend says they were born from the Weeping Angel of the Ninth Veil—a celestial guardian who watches over the souls of fallen warriors. She weeps not from sorrow, but from remembrance. From the love she still carries for every life lost in the war between Heaven and Hell. Her tears are not for healing flesh... but for restoring the soul. Just one drop can rekindle hope in the hopeless. Cleanse the corrupt. Return clarity to a mind drowning in despair. But it's more than that. The Tears weaken the grip of evil. To a demon, even one drop is like swallowing sunlight. To a corrupted soul, it is a mirror too painful to bear. They say if the tears are placed upon cursed ground, it will push back the darkness and make it holy again—if only for a time. And Blaze...He held it like it might break him. Not with fear, but reverence. Like he knew it wasn't just for the fight ahead... but for something he hadn't told us. Something he'd been carrying for a long time.

Amadeus looked him in the eyes.

"You will know the moment to use it. Do not waste it on wounds of the flesh. Save it for the soul that matters most."

Blaze nodded once. Said nothing. And tucked the vial into a secret pocket in his coat. And I could tell...He already knew who it was for.

Finally, Amadeus turned to Damian. "And you, Damian Walker. Though you walk a shadowed path, the Light has not forsaken you." He handed him a small, ornate dagger. "The Dagger of Apollo. It will pierce even the most resilient darkness."

Damian smiled, turning the dagger over in his hands. "Not bad."

The dagger was slender, curved at the edge like the crescent moon, its blade forged from something more brilliant than silver—sunlight hardened into steel. At its center, an obsidian stone pulsed faintly, as if drawing in shadow only to kill it.

The Dagger of Apollo.

I had read of it in a book I wasn't supposed to touch—a forbidden tome sealed in the archives beneath the Vatican. The blade was said to be forged by Apollo himself, not as a weapon of war... but of divine correction.

In the earliest days, when monsters still roamed the earth unchecked, there were things even the gods feared. Creatures born from the blackened corners of creation—things that refused to die.

The dagger was created to cut through illusion, to strike not the body, but the soul. A demon could be ten feet tall, armored in bone and fire, but if struck by this blade in its true form, it would fall. Not fade. Not retreat. Fall—permanently.

But the blade came with a curse. It could only be wielded by someone caught between light and shadow—a soul torn by duality, never fully belonging to either realm.

And now it was in the hands of Damian Walker—a vampire, yes—but something more. A man who walked between what he was and what he wanted to be. A creature of the night fighting for the light. The dagger didn't resist him. It welcomed him.

He looked down at it like it was a mirror.

And for the first time since we'd met, I saw something in Damian's eyes I hadn't expected: Purpose. Not revenge. Not survival.

But *purpose.*

Amadeus stepped back. His hands raised as the golden light of the altar flared once more. "Know this: once you possess the Staff of Infinite Light, its power will remain with you for only three days. After that, it must return to the Well of Light to recharge. During this time, no Angelic force can aid you. The battle will be yours alone."

The weight of the words settled over the group, the gravity of their mission sinking in.

"We'll do what we have to," Aleister said firmly. "We won't fail."

Amadeus nodded. "Then may the Light guide you."

The golden glow around them began to fade, the High Keeper's form dissolving into the air. As the chamber returned to stillness, Aleister turned to the others, his resolve unmistakable.

"Let's get moving," he declared. "Our mission is unmistakable." With renewed purpose, the group emerged from the Church of the Light, the weight of their mission heavy, yet their resolve unshaken.

The glow of the Church of the Light faded behind them as the group made their way along a narrow, winding path through the countryside. Blaze leaned heavily on Aleister for support, his steps uneven but determined.

"There's a town not far from here," Blaze said, his voice strained. "Small place, but they've got a healer. She's helped me out before."

Victoria nodded. "A healer would be invaluable right now. And a bit of rest wouldn't hurt any of us."

Damian adjusted his coat. "A town, you say? I wouldn't mind something stronger than holy water."

Blaze let out a weak chuckle. "There's a pub there, too. Old place, but it's got decent drinks."

"You're sure this healer can help?" Aleister asked.

Blaze nodded. "If anyone can, it's her."

The journey was slow but uneventful, the quiet countryside a welcome change from the oppressive atmosphere of the Black Veil Woods. As they crested a small hill, the town came into view—a quaint cluster of stone buildings nestled in a valley, smoke curling lazily from chimneys.

The group descended into the town. The cobblestone streets quiet in the late afternoon sun. Blaze directed them to a modest house near the edge of the village, its wooden door marked with a carved sigil that Aleister didn't recognize.

"This is it," Blaze said, leaning against the door frame. "Her name's Meridien. She'll patch me up."

Victoria knocked firmly on the door. Moments later, it creaked open to reveal a petite woman with piercing blue eyes and silver hair that framed her sharp features. She crossed her arms, her gaze landing on Blaze.

"Well, if it isn't Blaze Barton," she said, her tone a mix of amusement and exasperation. "What trouble have you stumbled into this time?"

Blaze gave her a faint grin, his usual bravado dulled by exhaustion.

"You know me, Meridien. Trouble's just part of the charm."

Meridien stepped aside, motioning him inside. "Come on, then, before you bleed out on my doorstep."

Blaze hesitated at the threshold, turning to the group. "You don't have to stick around," he said, his voice unusually soft. "Go into town. There's a pub called *The Golden Stag* not far from here—good food, better drinks. You could use a break."

"Are you sure? We can wait—"

"I'm sure," Blaze interrupted. "I'll be fine. Meridien's the best healer there is. Besides..." His gaze moved to her briefly before returning to Aleister. "She's not much for an audience."

Victoria said nothing, her sharp eyes catching the subtle exchange. She nodded, stepping back.

"We'll head into town. Take the time you need."

Blaze nodded his thanks, turning to follow Meridien into the house. As the door closed behind him.

"Well, well. It seems our fearless demon slayer has a softer side."

"Let's go."

The trio made their way into the heart of the town. They soon found The Golden Stag Pub Blaze had mentioned, a cozy establishment with wooden beams and a warm hearth. The hum of conversation and the scent of hearty food greeted them as they stepped inside. Settling into a corner table, they ordered food and drinks, the atmosphere a welcome reprieve from the tension of their journey. Aleister found himself relaxing for the first time in days, the warmth of the fire and the camaraderie of his companions easing his weary mind. As the barmaid brought their drinks, Damian leaned back in his chair, swirling his glass.

"So," he said, his crimson eyes gleaming with mischief. "Do we think Blaze and our charming healer have... history?"

Victoria sipped her drink, her expression unreadable. "It's none of our concern."

"Oh, come on. Didn't you see the way he looked at her? That wasn't just gratitude."

Aleister shook his head, though a small smile tugged at his lips. "Blaze doesn't strike me as the sentimental type."

"Everyone's sentimental about something," Damian said, raising his glass. "Even demon slayers."

Victoria set her drink down, her tone shifting. "We should use this time to prepare. Once Blaze is ready, we'll need to move quickly."

The conversation turned to strategy, their moment of levity giving way to the seriousness of their task. But in the back of his mind, Aleister couldn't help but wonder about Blaze and Meridien. Whatever history they shared, it was clear Blaze had left a part of himself in this town—and perhaps, in her care.

Chapter 8

THE GOLDEN STAG

The warm glow of the hearth cast flickering shadows across the wooden beams of The Golden Stag. The faint hum of conversation and the occasional clink of glasses filled the air, a soothing backdrop to the crackle of the fire. Aleister sat at the corner table with Victoria and Damian, the comforting weight of a tankard in his hand. For the first time in what felt like ages, they weren't running or fighting for their lives.

Still, the tension of their mission lingered, unspoken but present.

Victoria was the first to break the silence. "Once Blaze is rested, we'll need to head straight for the Well of Light. Time isn't on our side."

Damian leaned back in his chair. His eyes gleaming with amusement. "Ah, yes. Straight to business as usual. You two really know how to enjoy an evening off."

"This isn't a vacation, Damian. Lives are at stake."

"And yet', Damian said, "we're sitting in a cozy pub, sipping ale and pretending the world isn't about to end. I'd say that calls for a bit of levity, don't you think?"

"Levity?" Aleister asked.

Damian leaned forward. "Let's not pretend we're all just cogs in this little divine machine. We're people, with stories. And if we're going to march headfirst into doom together, I'd like to know who I'm dying with."

Victoria slammed her drink down. "You think this is a game?"

"No," Damian said, his tone softening. "But even you must admit, we could use a moment to breathe. To be... human." His gaze moved to Aleister, a sly grin spreading across his face. "Or mostly human, in some cases."

"Fine. You want stories? Why don't you start?" Aleister said.

Damian's grin widened. "Gladly." He leaned back, his fingers tapping rhythmically on the edge of his drink.

"Let's see... Where to begin? Ah, yes. I was born a very long time ago, in a quaint little village that no longer exists. My family was poor but happy. That is, until some enterprising demon cult decided our village was the perfect place to perform a summoning ritual."

Aleister exchanged a glance with Victoria, who remained silent but attentive.

Damian continued. "Long story short, they didn't get their demon, but they did get a very angry vampire. He wiped out the cult—and everyone else in the village for good measure. Including me." He took a sip of his drink, his gaze distant. "I woke up three days later, buried in a shallow grave. Turns out, vampires don't always finish what they start."

"And you chose to become one of them?" Victoria asked.

"Chose?" Damian laughed bitterly. "Hardly. The first years were... messy. I hated what I was. What I had to do to survive. But eventually, I realized I could use it—turn the curse into something useful. So here I am, drinking with a demon slayer, a priestess, and a ceremonial magician. Life's funny, isn't it?"

"And what drives you now?" Aleister asked.

"Revenge, mostly. Against the demon who started it all. And maybe a little redemption, though I don't hold my breath for that."

The table fell silent for a moment, the weight of Damian's words settling over them. Victoria broke the silence, her tone softer than usual.

"Your turn, Aleister. What drives you?"

"Revenge, I suppose. My father was killed by a demon when I was a child. It set me on this path—collecting artifacts, learning everything I could about the occult. For years, I thought I could make the world safer, rid it of evil. But..." He trailed off, his gaze distant. "It cost me everything. My marriage. My peace of mind. And now, I'm not even sure if it's enough."

Victoria's expression softened. "It's not just about revenge, though, is it?"

"No. It's about protecting what's left. And maybe... finding a way to fix what I broke."

Damian raised his glass. "To broken souls and questionable redemption."

Victoria raised her glass. "To the fight ahead."

Aleister joined them, the clink of glasses a quiet promise in the dim light of The Golden Stag.

The warmth of the pub felt almost surreal, a brief reprieve from the ever-present darkness that loomed over their journey. For a moment, Aleister let himself sink into the atmosphere—the laughter of other patrons, the flicker of the hearth, the faint scent of roasted meat wafting through the air.

"Anyone else care to share their tragic backstory, or shall I regale you with another?"

Victoria rolled her eyes. "It's not a competition, Damian."

"No," he agreed, leaning forward, "but if it were, I'd be winning."

"What about you, Victoria? You've been awfully quiet."

Victoria stiffened slightly. "There's not much to tell."

Damian arched an eyebrow, his expression playful but curious.

"Oh, come now. A priestess of the Light with your skill set doesn't end up here without a story."

Victoria hesitated, her gaze dropping to her glass. For a moment, Aleister thought she might brush them off, but then she spoke, her voice steady but tinged with emotion.

"I was born into the Order of the Light. My parents were devoted servants, dedicating their lives to the fight against darkness. They trained me from the moment I could walk, preparing me for a life I didn't choose. When I was twelve, my parents were killed during a demon incursion. I saw it happen. I tried to help, but I wasn't strong enough." She looked up, her emerald eyes fierce. "That's when I swore, I'd never be weak again. I devoted myself to the Light, to becoming the warrior my parents wanted me to be."

"And now you lead others." Aleister said, his respect for her deepening.

"I don't lead," she said quickly. "I guide. The Light leads."

"Modesty doesn't suit you, Victoria. But I suppose it's admirable."

She ignored him, turning her gaze to Aleister. "And what about you? What keeps you going?"

"The thought that I might be able to fix what's broken. My wife... Mary. She left because I let my obsession with revenge take over. I don't blame her. But now, knowing she might be in danger, I—" He stopped, shaking his head. "I can't fail again. I must make this right."

"You will. The Light doesn't choose people lightly." Victoria said.

Damian leaned back in his chair. His grin replaced with something more thoughtful.

"Well, aren't we just a merry band of tortured souls?"

"What about you, Damian? I'm sure your full of fantastic stories."

"Oh, I've got plenty," Damian said with a sly grin. "But you'd never believe half of them. Suffice it to say, I'm here because I have nowhere else to be. And if I can annoy a demon or two along the way, all the better."

Victoria shook her head, a faint smile tugging at her lips. "You're insufferable."

"And yet, you tolerate me," Damian said with a wink.

The group fell into a companionable silence, the tension of their journey momentarily eased. Aleister glanced around the room, taking in the faces of his companions. They were an unlikely group—each with their own scars, their own demons to fight. But for the first time, he felt a flicker of something he hadn't felt in years: hope.

The pub's lively atmosphere buzzed around them, but at their table, a comfortable quiet had settled in again. Aleister leaned back in his chair, letting the warmth of the fire and the ale soothe his nerves.

Damian broke the silence, his tone lighter this time. "You know, for a group of supposed heroes, we're surprisingly dour. We should try laughing more. Builds morale."

"Do you have a joke, Damian? Or just more charming anecdotes about your undead misadventures?"

"I'm full of surprises, my dear. But alas, my humor is lost on the righteous."

Aleister chuckled, shaking his head. "You're relentless, I'll give you that."

Damian leaned forward, his expression growing more serious. "Jokes aside, this... thing we're doing? It's big. Bigger than any of us. And while I enjoy the company, we all know this isn't ending with us riding off into the sunset."

Victoria nodded solemnly. "The Light's work is never finished. But that's why we're here—to make sure it continues."

"It's not just about the Light, though, is it? It's about the people we've lost. The ones we're trying to save." Aleister said.

"Touching," Damian said, though his tone wasn't mocking. "This place has charm," his voice light as his crimson eyes scanned the room. "Rustic. Almost makes you forget about the hordes of demons waiting to devour us."

Victoria sipped her drink, her tone sharp. "I haven't forgotten. And neither should you."

"I'd never dream of it," Damian replied. "But perhaps we could pretend, just for tonight."

Aleister's gaze drifted to the pub's door as it creaked open. A figure entered, cloaked in shadow, it's movements precise yet unobtrusive. The hood of its cloak remained up, obscuring its face, but a faint glimmer of a pendant caught Aleister's eye as it moved toward the bar. Something about the figure felt... off. Not immediately threatening, but wrong. As if it didn't quite belong.

Damian's voice pulled him back. "What's caught your eye, Kane?"

Aleister's gaze lingered on the stranger. "That pendant. It's... familiar, but I don't recognize the symbol."

Victoria followed his gaze. "It could be nothing."

"Or it could be something," Damian added, his grin fading slightly. "You're not the only ones searching for the Well of Light, remember."

The stranger ordered a drink, its movements calm and deliberate. It didn't glance around the room or seem to notice the group, but Aleister couldn't shake the sense of being watched. As the figure paid for its drink, its sleeve lifted slightly, revealing a glimpse of a tattoo on the figure's wrist—a dark sigil Aleister recognized instantly. His stomach churned. He'd seen that sigil before, etched into the bindings of cursed tomes and whispered about in ancient texts. It was a mark of allegiance to the demonic.

Victoria's hand moved subtly to her sword. "We can't let it follow us."

"Not here. Not now. We don't know who they are or what they want."

Damian leaned forward. His voice low. "But we can't ignore them. If they're connected to the demons, they can't be allowed to know where we're going."

The stranger finished his drink quickly, setting the glass down with precision. Without a glance at the room, he turned and exited the pub, the door swinging shut behind him.

"Good," Damian said, his tone light but his eyes serious. "Less time to scheme."

Whoever the stranger was, its presence wasn't coincidence. The sigil had confirmed that much. But they couldn't afford a confrontation now—not with Blaze still recovering and their next steps uncertain.

"We leave at first light," Aleister said firmly. "And if it's still following us, we deal with it then."

Victoria nodded, her gaze lingering on the door.

Damian raised his glass. "To vigilance, then. And to making sure our uninvited friend doesn't overstay his welcome."

Aleister didn't raise his drink this time, his mind too preoccupied. The brief reprieve of the pub had been shattered by the reminder of the dangers waiting outside its walls. The road ahead would be perilous, but now, it seemed, their enemies weren't content to wait for them to arrive.

Chapter 9

INTO THE
UNKNOWN

The morning sun painted the small town in hues of gold and amber as Aleister, Victoria, and Damian approached Meridien's modest home. The chill of the night had faded, replaced by the warmth of a new day. Birds sang softly in the distance, their melodies a stark contrast to the heavy thoughts weighing on Aleister's mind.

As they reached the carved wooden door, Aleister noticed that the sigil etched into it glimmered faintly, as though alive with some unseen energy. He exchanged a glance with Victoria, who nodded silently before rapping her knuckles against the wood.

Moments later, the door creaked open, revealing Meridien. She looked tired, but her piercing blue eyes were as sharp as ever.

"You're early," she said, stepping aside to let them in.

Blaze was seated in a chair by the hearth, his coat draped over the backrest and a steaming cup of tea in his hands. His tattoos seemed to glow faintly in the morning light, and though he still looked pale, he gave them a weak smile as they entered.

"Look who's decided to check in on me," Blaze said, his voice raspy but lighter than the day before. "I was starting to think you'd forgotten about me."

Victoria crossed her arms. "You're hard to forget, Blaze."

Damian stared intently at Blaze, leaning against the door frame. "You look almost human again. Meridien must work miracles."

"She's good, I'll give her that. Though she's not much for bedside manners."

Meridien rolled her eyes, placing a bowl of herbs on a nearby table. "And you're as charming as ever, Blaze. Try not to undo all my work the moment you leave."

"How are you feeling? Can you travel?" Aleister asked.

Blaze took a deep breath, setting his tea aside.

"I'll manage. We don't exactly have the luxury of waiting around, do we?"

"He'll be fine if he doesn't overdo it. The magic I used to heal him won't last forever, so keep an eye on him."

Aleister nodded, his respect for her evident. "Thank you, for everything."

Meridien's gaze lingered on Blaze for a moment longer before she turned away, busying herself with the herbs on the table. Blaze stood, pulling on his coat with a wince but managing to mask the pain.

"Alright," he said, his usual bravado creeping back into his voice. "Let's get this show on the road."

As they stepped outside, the air was crisp, carrying the faint scent of pine and earth. Blaze paused, glancing back at Meridien, who stood in the doorway.

"Take care of yourself," he said.

Meridien gave him a faint smile. "You too."

The group began their journey, the town quickly fading into the distance as they entered the wilderness. Damian broke the silence as they walked, his tone playful.

"So, Blaze, should we ask about the history between you and our lovely healer, or is that strictly classified?"

"Not a chance, vampire."

"Let's just concentrate on the journey ahead, shall we?" Victoria said.

Aleister glanced at Blaze. "Do you remember anything else? From the cleansing?"

Blaze's expression grew serious. "I don't know where exactly it is yet, but I can feel it. Like a pull in the back of my mind. Once we're close, I'll know."

Aleister nodded. "Then we'll trust you to lead the way."

The group pressed on, the forest growing darker and denser as they moved further from the town. Though the sunlight still filtered through the trees, there was an unshakable feeling of being watched. The journey to the Well of Light had begun, and the shadows were already closing in. The path grew narrower as the forest thickened around them. The towering trees seemed to press closer, their branches intertwined to form a canopy that dimmed the sunlight into a pale, eerie glow. The group moved in silence. Their footsteps muffled by the moss-covered ground. Aleister glanced at Blaze, who led the way with cautious determination. Though Blaze's injuries were mended, his movements were still measured, each step deliberate. Aleister couldn't help but feel some concern.

"You sure you're up for this?" Aleister asked quietly.

"Worried about me, Kane? I didn't think you cared."

"Just don't collapse halfway to the Well. We're kind of depending on you."

Blaze chuckled, though it was short-lived. "Don't worry. I've got a stubborn streak that keeps me upright when I shouldn't be."

Damian fell into step beside them, his crimson eyes scanning the shadows. "You're not the only one with stubborn tendencies, Barton. I'd wager we all have a bit of a death wish, considering the company we keep."

Victoria, walking slightly ahead, turned her head just enough to catch Damian's smirk. "Speak for yourself. Some of us are here because we believe in something greater than ourselves."

Damian placed a hand on his chest in mock offense. "Oh, I believe in something greater, Victoria. Myself."

Victoria ignored him, her focus returning to the path. "We should stay alert. This part of the forest is known for its tricks. The shadows aren't always empty."

"She's right. This place is crawling with things that would love to see us fail."

"What kind of things?"

Blaze glanced back at Aleister. "You'll know them when you see them. And when you do, don't stop moving."

They continued forward, the forest growing quieter with each step. Even the faint rustling of leaves and the occasional bird calls had faded, leaving only the sound of their breathing and footsteps. As they rounded a bend, the trees thinned slightly, revealing a clearing up ahead. Blaze stopped abruptly, holding up a hand to signal the others. They froze, their eyes following his gaze.

At the center of the clearing stood an ancient stone obelisk, its surface covered in weathered runes. A faint, unnatural glow emanated from the markings, casting the area in an eerie light. Surrounding the obelisk were scattered bones, some old and brittle, others disturbingly fresh.

"Well, that's inviting," Damian muttered, his tone unusually subdued.

Victoria stepped closer, her hand on the hilt of her sword. "It's a marker. A warning to those who enter this part of the forest."

"A warning from what?" Aleister asked.

"The forest itself. It's alive, in a way. And it doesn't like visitors." Blaze warned.

As if on cue, the wind picked up, rustling the leaves with a low, mournful wail. The shadows around them seemed to deepen, shifting in ways that made Aleister's skin crawl.

"Stay close," Blaze said. "And whatever you do, don't look back."

The obelisk loomed over them, its glow pulsating faintly, as if alive. The air grew colder, and the faint sound of whispers reached Aleister's ears, though he couldn't discern their source. As they moved past the obelisk, the forest seemed to close in around them, the trees leaning closer, their branches clawing at the air. Aleister glanced at Victoria, who was scanning their surroundings with sharp eyes. Damian's usual smirk was gone, replaced by a rare seriousness. Blaze led them with steady steps, his tattoos faintly glowing in the dim light. His presence was a grounding force, a reminder that they weren't entirely at the mercy of the forest. But as they pressed deeper into the woods, Aleister felt a chill race down his spine. That familiar sensation had returned—the unsettling feeling that something, or someone, was watching them. Victoria's hand hovered near the hilt of her sword as she scanned their surroundings, her every movement calculated and deliberate. Blaze, though still recovering, led the way with his usual determination, his tattoos faintly glowing in the dim light. Damian brought up the rear, his sharp eyes darting between the shadows.

"You feel it, too?" Aleister asked Blaze in a low voice.

Blaze nodded. "We're being followed. Have been for a while now."

"How many?"

"Too many."

A faint rustle echoed through the woods, followed by another, closer this time. Aleister raised the Lantern of Truth, the light cut through the shadows revealing nothing but the tangled roots and twisted branches of the forest.

"They're toying with us."

Then, from the darkness, came a deep, guttural voice.

"You've come far enough."

Aleister froze as figures emerged from the trees. Their forms shrouded in black armor that seemed to absorb the light. Their eyes glowed a sickly yellow, and their movements were unnatural, as if the bodies they inhabited were puppets. The air grew colder, the stench of sulfur wafting toward the group.

The leader stepped forward. His face partially obscured by a twisted helm.

"Aleister Kane!" he said, his voice reverberating unnaturally, as though a thousand voices spoke in unison. "Your journey ends here!"

"Who are you?" Aleister said.

The warrior tilted his head, a grotesque mockery of curiosity. "We are the damned, the forsaken souls who serve the master of the Nine Hells. We come with a message."

Victoria stepped forward, her sword drawn, the blade gleaming with a faint light. "Speak and then leave!"

The leader laughed, a sound that echoed through the forest like nails on glass.

He turned his glowing gaze to Aleister. "The master knows of your quest. He knows of your search for the *Staff of Infinite Light*. You will stop this foolishness, now."

Aleister squared his shoulders, his voice defiant. "And if I don't?"

The warrior's smile widened, revealing jagged, unnatural teeth.

"Then Mary dies."

Aleister's blood ran cold. "What?"

"You heard me, mortal," the leader hissed, stepping closer. "Your precious wife is already in the master's grasp. Her life hangs by a thread, and it's a thread we will gladly cut if you continue your foolish quest."

Victoria placed a hand on Aleister's arm. "Don't listen to them. It's a trick."

The warrior's eyes moved to Victoria, his grin widening. "Oh, it's no trick, priestess. She's his now. And if Kane values her life, he will end his little quest."

Aleister's heart was pounding in his chest.

"How do I know you're telling the truth?"

The warrior laughed again. "You don't. But would you risk it?"

"We're not afraid of you or your master. If you want to stop us, you'll have to try harder than idle threats." Blaze said.

The leader's grin faded, replaced by a snarl. "You've been warned. The master's mercy is limited. Continue this path, and you will bring destruction upon everything you hold dear."

The warriors dissolved into the darkness, leaving the group standing in tense silence. The forest seemed to breathe around them, the oppressive atmosphere pressing down as if the shadows themselves were watching.

"Shadow Knights," Aleister said quietly, the name leaving a bitter taste in his mouth. "I've heard of them, but I thought they were just stories."

"They're as real as the demons they serve." Blaze said.

"What do you know about them?" Aleister asked.

"Shadow Knights aren't born—they're made. Men who've fallen to darkness, possessed by demons too powerful to control. They're twisted into something worse than human and less than demon. Bound forever to the will of the Nine Hells."

Aleister's stomach turned at the thought. "Why use mortals at all? Why not just send demons?"

"It's about sending a message. Shadow Knights aren't just enforcers—they're symbols. A reminder that no one is safe from possession, that even the strongest can be broken and turned."

"And they follow Asmodeus?" Victoria asked.

"Always. They're his personal army. If they're here, it means Asmodeus is paying attention."

Aleister's breath caught in his chest. "And if they're telling the truth…"

Blaze turned to him, his expression hard. "You can't let them get in your head, Kane. The Shadow Knights don't just deliver messages—they plant seeds. Doubt. Fear. That's how they work. Don't let them win."

Aleister nodded slowly, though his mind raced. Mary. Her name echoed in his thoughts, the warriors' warning a constant drumbeat against his resolve.

"If they have her…"

Blaze stepped closer putting his hand Aleister's shoulder.

"Then we'll get her back. But we can't lose sight of the bigger picture. The staff is the key to stopping them—and stopping Asmodeus."

Victoria glanced toward the path ahead, her sword still in hand. "We need to move. If they're watching us, they won't be far."

Aleister forced himself to focus, the weight of Blaze's words grounding him.

"Let's move," he said, his voice steady despite the storm raging inside him.

As they continued through the woods, the oppressive silence returned, broken only by the faint rustle of leaves underfoot. The Shadow Knights warning hung over them like a shroud, but Aleister forced himself to push forward. His steps were heavier now, his thoughts darker, but his resolve burned brighter than ever.

Chapter 10

THE STAFF OF INFINITE LIGHT

The forest was eerily quiet, the oppressive weight of unseen eyes pressing down on the group. The Shadow Knights were out there, watching, waiting. Aleister scanned their surroundings, each flicker of shadow a stark reminder of the lurking danger. Blaze halted suddenly. His gaze sharp.

"We're not alone," he said quietly. His tattoos began to glow faintly, casting an otherworldly light against the trees.

"What's the plan, Blaze? They're following us, and we can't lead them to the staff."

Blaze took a deep breath, his mind clearly working through the problem.

"We'll split up," he said finally. "But not in the way they think."

"Care to elaborate, or should we just guess?" Damian said.

Blaze ignored him, turning to Aleister. "I'll cast a spell to create the illusion that we're all still together. To anyone watching, it'll look like the group hasn't changed. Meanwhile, we'll split into two real groups. One will head for the staff, and the other will draw the Shadow Knights away."

"Can you do that? Create an illusion that strong?" Aleister asked.

"I can. But it'll take a lot out of me, and we'll need to move quickly once it's in place. The illusion won't last forever."

Victoria nodded. "Then let's make it count. Who goes where?"

Blaze's gaze swept over the group. "Aleister, you're going with me. The staff is tied to you. If you're not there, we won't be able to claim it."

"Then I'll lead the decoy group, and Damian can accompany me." Victoria said.

Damian crossed his arms. "Oh, fantastic. The vampire and the warrior priestess, off to play bait."

"Exactly," Blaze said, his tone blunt. "You'll head east, toward the river. Keep moving and keep them guessing. We'll head west, toward the staff."

Aleister's stomach churned at the thought of splitting up, but he nodded. "Alright. Let's do it."

Blaze knelt on the ground, his tattoos glowing fiercely as he began to chant in a low, steady voice. The air around them seemed to shimmer, the forest growing unnaturally quiet. The glow from his tattoos spread outward, forming a faint, translucent dome around the group.

The illusion took shape slowly, a perfect replica of the group standing together, their movements synchronized and natural. Aleister stared at his duplicate, a strange sense of detachment washing over him.

"It's incredible," Victoria said quietly. "They'll never know the difference."

Blaze's voice was strained as he finished the spell, his breathing labored. "It'll hold long enough. But we need to move. Now."

Victoria and Damian exchanged a glance, then turned to Aleister and Blaze. "Good luck," Victoria said, her tone steady. "We'll meet again."

With that, Victoria and Damian disappeared into the shadows, their steps silent as they headed east. Blaze motioned for Aleister to follow, and the two turned west, their pace quick and deliberate.

The illusion shimmered behind them, its presence reassuring and unnerving all at once. Aleister couldn't help but glance back, his mind racing with worry for Victoria and Damian. But Blaze's voice pulled him back to the present.

"Focus, Kane," Blaze said, his tone firm. "They'll be fine. Right now, we need to stay ahead of the Shadow Knights"

Aleister nodded.

The forest grew darker as they pressed on, the path ahead twisting and uncertain. The staff was close, but so was the danger.

"Are you alright?" Aleister asked, glancing at Blaze with concern.

Blaze waved him off, his voice rough. "I'll manage. Just... keep your eyes open."

Aleister slowly scanned his surroundings. The faint glow from the lantern was a fragile barrier against the encroaching darkness, and he couldn't help but feel the weight of the Shadow Knights's warning pressing down on him. The image of Mary haunted him, her face flickering in his mind like a fading photograph.

They pushed forward in silence, the forest growing denser. The path twisted and turned, and Blaze led the way with a precision that belied his exhaustion. Every so often, he would pause, his tattoos glowing faintly as he muttered under his breath, checking the direction.

"How much farther?" Aleister finally asked, his voice low.

Blaze stopped, leaning against a tree to catch his breath. "Not far," he said, his tone grim. "But we're being watched. I can feel it."

Aleister's heart sank. "The Shadow Knights?"

Blaze shook his head. "No. Something else."

Before Aleister could ask, a sudden chill washed over him, the air growing frigid. The faint sound of whispers reached his ears, indistinct and echoing, as if carried on an unnatural wind.

Blaze straightened, his tattoos flaring brighter. "Get ready," he said, his voice sharp. "We're not alone."

The whispers grew louder, taking on a sinister, mocking tone. Shadows shifted and writhed at the edge of the Lantern's light, and Aleister caught glimpses of movement—distorted figures, their forms flickering like static.

"What are they?" Aleister asked, his voice barely above a whisper.

"Wraiths," Blaze replied, his tone dark. "Souls twisted by darkness, bound to this place. They're drawn to the staff's power."

There was a time I thought they were just a myth—stories told in whispered circles of occult scholars; tales used to scare initiates away from delving too deep.

But Wraiths are real.

They aren't demons. They aren't ghosts. They're what's left when a soul dies in torment and refuses to move on but isn't damned enough for Hell or pure enough for judgment. They're liminal creatures—hungry for identity, desperate to feel again. But they don't consume flesh. They feed on memory.

A Wraith doesn't kill you with claws or flame. It draws out your mind, one thought at a time—starting with your hope, your joy, your will to fight. You'll forget your name before you forget the pain.

Blaze stiffened beside me.

"We can't let them touch us," he muttered. "Not even for a second."

I knew why.

Once a Wraith latches on, it shows you your worst regrets, your darkest fears, and your greatest failures—until you start to believe them.

Until you become one. They don't want to kill you. They want to replace you.

The first wraith lunged from the shadows, its form a tattered, translucent figure with hollow eyes that glowed an eerie blue. Blaze stepped forward, his tattoos blazing as he raised a hand. A burst of light erupted from his palm, striking the wraith and sending it shrieking back into the darkness.

Aleister raised the Lantern of Truth, its light flaring brighter as the wraiths closed in. They recoiled from the glow, their inhuman screeches piercing the silence.

"Keep them back!" Blaze shouted. His voice strained as he conjured another burst of light.

The wraiths circled them, their movements erratic and disjointed. One lunged at Aleister, its claw-like hands reaching for him. He swung the lantern instinctively, the light searing the creature and forcing it to retreat with a wail.

Blaze stumbled, his tattoos flickering as his strength waned.

"I can't hold them all off," he said through gritted teeth.

Aleister stepped closer, positioning himself beside Blaze.

"Then we do it together."

The two fought side by side, the Lantern of Truth and Blaze's tattoos illuminating the forest in bursts of radiant light. The wraiths' numbers began to dwindle, their forms dissipating one by one until only silence remained.

Aleister lowered the lantern, his breaths coming in ragged gasps. Blaze leaned heavily against a tree, his tattoos dimming as he caught his breath.

"They'll be back," Blaze said, his voice hoarse. "We need to keep moving."

Aleister nodded. The encounter had shaken him, but it also reminded him of what was at stake. The staff was close, and they couldn't afford to falter now.

As they pressed on, the forest began to thin, revealing a rocky outcropping in the distance. Blaze paused as he surveyed the terrain.

"That's it," he said, pointing to a narrow path that wound its way up the rocks. "The staff is beyond there."

The rocky outcropping loomed ahead, its jagged edges stark against the faint glow of the approaching dawn. Aleister and Blaze climbed in silence, each step deliberate, their senses sharp. The path was narrow, winding perilously close to sheer drops on either side. The air grew colder, carrying a faint hum that seemed to vibrate through Aleister's chest.

At the top of the ridge, the path opened into a small plateau. In the center stood a stone archway, weathered and ancient, its surface etched with intricate carvings that seemed to shift under the faint light. Beyond the arch, a narrow bridge stretched across a deep chasm, its surface shimmering as though made of liquid light.

Blaze stopped.

"The Bridge of Radiance," he murmured, his voice tinged with awe. "We're here."

Aleister stepped closer. The archway radiated a quiet power, its carvings depicting battles between angels and demons, with the *Staff of Infinite Light* at the center of it all.

"What is this place?" Aleister asked, his voice hushed.

Blaze gestured to the bridge. "It's the final barrier. Only those deemed worthy can cross it. The unworthy…" He trailed off, his gaze fixed on the shimmering surface of the bridge. "Well, let's just say they don't make it far."

"And if we're not worthy?"

Blaze glanced at him, a faint smirk tugging at the corner of his mouth. "Then this is a very short chapter in our story."

The faint hum grew louder as they approached the archway, the carvings glowing softly as if coming to life. Blaze hesitated, his gaze narrowing as he studied the bridge.

"This is it," Blaze said, his voice steady despite the tension in his posture. "The staff lies on the other side. But if the Shadow Knights are following us, they'll be close."

Aleister nodded. "Then we need to move quickly."

Blaze stepped through the archway first and tested the bridge. The surface rippled under his foot but held firm. He glanced back at Aleister and nodded.

"It's safe—for now."

Aleister followed. The chasm below seemed endless, a swirling void of light and shadow that pulsed with an eerie rhythm. Each step felt heavier than the last, the hum growing louder as if resonating with his very soul. Halfway across, the bridge trembled, a low growl echoing from the void below. Aleister froze.

"What was that?"

"A guardian. Keep moving."

Before Aleister could respond, a massive shadow rose from the chasm, its form shifting and writhing as it emerged. The creature was unlike anything he had ever seen, its body a mass of tendrils and glowing eyes, each one fixed on them with a predatory intensity.

Blaze moved faster, his tattoos blazing with light.

"Stay close to me."

The creature roared, the sound reverberating through the chasm and sending shock waves across the bridge. Blaze raised his hands, chanting in a low, commanding voice as his tattoos pulsed with power. A barrier of light formed around them, pushing back the creature's tendrils as they lashed out.

Aleister held the Lantern of Truth high, its light flaring brighter as the creature recoiled.

"What is this thing?" he shouted over the roar.

"A test," Blaze replied, his voice strained. "The bridge doesn't let anyone cross without proving their worth."

The creature lunged, its tendrils striking the barrier with a force that shook the bridge. Blaze staggered, his energy faltering.

"I can't hold it much longer!"

Aleister's mind raced. The Lantern of Truth pulsed in his hand, its glow intensifying as if responding to his determination. Taking a deep breath, he stepped forward, placing himself between Blaze and the creature. The light from the lantern erupted, a brilliant beam that struck the creature square in its core. The shadowy form writhed and shrieked, its tendrils dissolving into the void. The bridge steadied, the hum fading into silence as the creature vanished.

Blaze straightened, his breathing ragged but his expression triumphant.

"You did it."

Aleister lowered the lantern, his hands trembling.

"What now?"

Blaze gestured to the end of the bridge, where a small pedestal stood bathed in light. Atop it rested the *Staff of Infinite Light*, its surface gleaming with an ethereal glow.

"We claim it," Blaze said, his voice filled with reverence. "And prepare for what comes next."

The pedestal glowed faintly, the light radiating from the *Staff of Infinite Light* casting long shadows across the bridge. Aleister hesitated, his breath catching in his throat as he stared at the staff. Its surface was smooth, almost fluid, as if it were alive. Runes etched along its length shimmered with a faint golden light, their patterns shifting and dancing like fireflies in the dark.

Blaze stepped beside him, his tattoos dimming now that the guardian was gone.

"This is it," he said, his voice reverent. "The power we need to end this."

Aleister's hand trembled as he reached for the staff. The moment his fingers brushed its surface, a surge of energy shot through him. He gasped, his knees buckling slightly under the weight of the power coursing through his veins.

Images flooded his mind—visions of battles fought in ancient times, angels wielding the staff against legions of demons. He saw glimpses of the Well of Light, its radiant energy pulsing in harmony with the staff's power. And then, he saw Mary. Her face was pale, her eyes wide with terror as she reached for him, her voice a whisper in the storm of visions.

"Aleister!" Blaze's voice cut through the haze, pulling him back to the present. "Are you alright?"

Aleister steadied himself, his grip tightening on the staff. The energy surged again, this time more controlled, settling into a steady rhythm that seemed to resonate with his heartbeat.

"I'm fine," he said, his voice stronger than he expected. "The staff... it's incredible!"

Blaze nodded. "It's not just power. It's responsibility. The staff responds to the heart of the one who wields it. If you falter, it will falter."

Aleister took a deep breath, the weight of the staff both literal and symbolic. He turned to Blaze.

"This is what we've been searching for. But it's only the beginning."

Blaze's gaze darkened. "You're right. Now that we have it, the real fight begins."

A faint tremor rippled through the ground, and Aleister glanced back at the bridge. The shimmering surface had begun to fade, the protective light dimming as the energy of the staff shifted to him.

"We need to move," Blaze said. "The staff's power won't go unnoticed. Every demon within miles will feel it."

They turned toward the path ahead. The forest loomed once more, its shadows deepening as if aware of the power now in their possession.

"Blaze," Aleister said, his voice low. "This staff... it's more than just a weapon. It's alive."

"It's connected to the Light. To the very essence of creation. But don't let that overwhelm you. Right now, it's a tool. Use it wisely."

As they descended from the plateau, the weight of their mission pressed heavier on Aleister. The staff pulsed in his hand, a steady reminder of the responsibility he now carried. The visions of Mary lingered in his mind, her face a beacon of hope and pain. He had the power to change everything—to save her, to end the war, to bring light where there was only darkness. But with that power came the fear of failure, the knowledge that one misstep could doom them all.

Chapter 11

HUNTED BY KNIGHT

The forest was eerily silent, the kind of quiet that set Victoria on edge. Damian walked silently beside her. Even he seemed to sense the tension in the air.

"This is your idea of fun, isn't it?" Damian finally broke the silence.

"What part of this feels like fun to you?"

Damian shrugged, his crimson eyes scanning the dark woods.

"The part where we're likely being stalked by demons, of course. Keeps things interesting."

Victoria's focus remained on their surroundings, every nerve alert for the slightest sound. The Shadow Knights were out there, and while Blaze's spell might have confused them for a time, it was only a matter of when—not if—they would catch up.

"You don't talk much, do you?" Damian said, his tone more curious than teasing.

"I talk when I have something to say," Victoria replied.

"And what's your story, then?" Damian pressed. "You're clearly not just a sword-wielding priestess. There's something... different about you."

"My story isn't important. Not now."

"Humor me," Damian said, his smirk returning faintly. "If we're about to die horribly, I'd like to know who I'm dying with."

"I was trained by the Order of the Light. My life is dedicated to protecting the balance between Heaven and Hell. That's all you need to know."

"Straight to the point," Damian mused. "I like that."

Before Victoria could respond, a rustling sound to their left made her stop in her tracks. Damian's hand went to the hilt of his dagger, his movements smooth and deliberate.

"They're here," Victoria said quietly, her voice steady despite the unease prickling at her skin.

The rustling grew louder, and from the shadows, the first of the Shadow Knights emerged. Their armor was black as obsidian, their hollow eyes glowing with an unnatural light. They moved with an eerie grace, their weapons gleaming faintly in the dim light.

"Ah, there they are," Damian muttered. "I was beginning to think they'd gotten lost."

Victoria stepped forward, her sword at the ready.

"Stay close. We can't let them separate us."

The Shadow Knights advanced, their movements calculated and predatory. Victoria struck first, her blade meeting the warrior's sword with a deafening clash. The force of the impact sent a jolt up her arm, but she held firm, her training kicking in instinctively.

Damian moved beside her, his dagger flashing as he parried another attack. The Shadow Knights fought with a ferocity that was almost otherworldly, their strikes precise and relentless. Despite their skill, Damian's agility and sharp wit kept him one step ahead, his movements almost a dance as he countered each blow.

"They're stronger than I expected," Damian said, his tone light despite the sweat beading on his brow.

Victoria didn't respond, her focus entirely on the battle. Her sword glowed faintly with the light of her faith, each strike pushing the Shadow Knights back. But for every warrior she struck down, another seemed to take its place.

"We can't keep this up," Damian said, his voice strained. "They're trying to wear us down."

Victoria's gaze flicked to their surroundings, searching for an opening. "We need to retreat. Regroup."

"And here I thought you enjoyed a good fight," Damian quipped, though his breath was labored.

Victoria ignored him again, her focus shifting to a narrow path that branched off from their current position.

"There. It's too tight for them to follow us in numbers."

Damian followed her gaze, nodding.

"Lead the way, oh fearless leader."

With a final, powerful strike, Victoria created a brief opening in the Shadow Knights ranks.

"Go!" she shouted, her voice commanding.

The two of them darted toward the path, their footsteps quick and deliberate. The Shadow Knights hesitated, their movements slower as they calculated their next move. The narrow trail forced the warriors to follow in single file, giving Victoria and Damian a moment to catch their breath.

"Remind me to thank Blaze for his brilliant spell," Damian muttered, his tone dripping with sarcasm.

Victoria allowed herself a faint smile.

"If we make it out of this alive, I'll let you buy the first round."

The narrow path twisted and turned, the walls of dense foliage pressing close on either side.

The Shadow Knights were forced to slow their pursuit, their numbers reduced to a single-file line. Still, the oppressive sense of being hunted loomed over Victoria and Damian like a storm cloud. Damian glanced over his shoulder, catching glimpses of the warriors' glowing eyes through the gaps in the trees.

"They're not giving up, are they?"

"They won't stop until we're dead," Victoria replied, her tone grim. "Keep moving."

The path began to widen slightly, the trees giving way to jagged rocks and uneven terrain. Victoria led the way, her sword ready, her sharp eyes scanning the area for any advantage. Damian followed closely, his dagger in hand, his usual smirk replaced by a focused determination.

"Up ahead," Victoria said, pointing to a cluster of boulders that formed a natural chokepoint. "We can make a stand there."

Damian raised an eyebrow. "A stand? You mean fight?"

"You have a better idea?"

"Not at the moment," Damian admitted, his grin returning faintly. "Let's see what you've got, priestess."

They reached the choke point and turned to face the approaching Shadow Knights. The warriors advanced with a relentless precision, their dark armor glinting faintly in the dim light.

"Stay behind me," she said firmly.

"Not a chance," Damian replied, his dagger spinning deftly in his hand. "You'll need me."

The first of the Shadow Knight lunged forward, its blade aimed directly at Victoria. She deflected the strike with a graceful parry, her counterattack swift and precise. The warrior staggered back, but another quickly took its place, forcing her to stay on the defensive.

Damian darted in and out of the fray, his movements almost serpentine. He struck with precision, his dagger finding gaps in the Knight's armor. Despite his usual bravado, there was a quiet efficiency to his fighting style—a reminder that, for all his quips, he was a skilled and deadly opponent.

"They're testing us," Victoria said, her voice steady despite the strain of the battle.

Damian nodded, his breath coming in quick bursts.

"Trying to see how long we can hold out. Charming."

The fight intensified, the Shadow Knights attacks growing more coordinated. Victoria and Damian moved in unison, their blades a seamless dance of offense and defense. The glow of Victoria's sword clashed with the dark energy emanating from the warriors, the air crackling with the force of their blows.

Despite their skill, the Shadow Knights numbers were overwhelming. Victoria's strikes became slower, her breaths heavier. Damian's movements lost some of their fluidity, his quips replaced by grim silence.

"We can't keep this up," Victoria said, her voice strained.

"Then we don't," Damian replied, his gaze darting toward a narrow crevice between two large boulders.

"Through there. It's too tight for them to follow."

Victoria hesitated, her instinct to fight warring with the reality of their situation. Finally, she nodded.

"Go."

Damian darted toward the crevice, slipping through with practiced ease. Victoria followed, her sword scraping against the rock as she squeezed through the narrow gap. The Shadow Knights reached the choke point moments later, their progress halted by the impassable barrier.

On the other side of the crevice, Damian leaned against a rock, his breath coming in ragged gasps.

"Well, that was invigorating."

"We're not out of danger yet."

As if to underscore her point, a low, guttural growl echoed through the air. Victoria turned sharply, her sword ready, as a pair of glowing red eyes appeared in the shadows ahead.

"Oh, come on," Damian muttered, straightening. "Can't we catch a break?"

From the darkness emerged a massive, wolf-like creature, its fur bristling with dark energy. Its fangs glinted as it snarled, its eyes locked onto Victoria and Damian with a predatory intensity.

"An Umbra Claw," Victoria said, her voice low. "They've sent one of their pets."

Damian sighed, his dagger glinting faintly. "Of course they have."

Long ago, when the first warriors of the Shadow Knights were possessed by high-ranking demons, the unholy transformation proved too unstable for most mortal hosts. Many went mad. Others perished. But a few... changed.

They were the strongest war-beasts of Hell, blended with men who had lost all traces of humanity. Their bodies twisted, reshaped by infernal rites, becoming something entirely new—four-legged monstrosities with the mind of a hunter and the soul of a predator. Their flesh is wrapped in sinewy darkness, ever shifting. Their eyes burn with the residual fire of demonic possession, and their jaws can tear through enchanted steel.

But their true weapon is their howl.

The Black Howl is said to carry through both physical and spiritual realms, stripping courage from the living and summoning fear-born memories to the surface. Those who hear it say it echoes with the cries of those the hound has already devoured body and soul.

To the Shadow Knights, the Umbra Claw are more than weapons—they are sacred companions, kept in chains of bone and command, fed only on the light of their fallen enemies. Only the highest of the possessed may command them, and even then, not for long. Their loyalty is to the darkness itself.

The hound lunged, its powerful jaws snapping inches from Victoria's blade. She sidestepped, her counter strike grazing its side. The creature howled. Its movements unnaturally fast as it turned to attack again.

Damian circled to its flank, his dagger striking at its legs. The hound snarled; its focus divided between the two of them. Despite its size, it moved with a terrifying agility, its attacks relentless.

Victoria's sword glowed brighter, the light searing the hound's dark energy with each strike. Damian's movements were a blur, his dagger finding weak points in the creature's defenses. Together, they fought with a coordination born of necessity, each move calculated to exploit the hound's openings.

Finally, with a powerful strike, Victoria drove her sword into the hound's chest. The creature let out a final, piercing howl before dissolving into shadow, its dark energy dissipating into the air.

Victoria lowered her sword, her breaths heavy. Damian wiped the blood from his dagger, his usual smirk returning faintly.

"Well," he said, his tone light. "I'm just having the time of my life."

"We need to keep moving."

"Ok, back to it." Damian said.

The forest thinned as the hours wore on, the oppressive shadows giving way to patches of moonlight filtering through the trees. Victoria and Damian moved cautiously, the weight of their battle against the Shadow Knights still heavy on their shoulders. Though they had escaped for the moment, the presence of their relentless pursuers lingered like a shadow in their minds.

"They'll catch up eventually," Damian said, his tone light but his expression serious. "And next time, they'll come prepared."

Victoria nodded, fatigue pulling at her muscles.

"We need to stay ahead of them. If we reach higher ground, we might gain an advantage."

Damian glanced up at the steep incline ahead. "You do love making me work for it."

They began the climb, the uneven terrain slowing their pace but providing a better vantage point. As they reached the crest, Victoria paused, scanning the forest below. Her sharp eyes caught movement—a faint flicker of shadows moving against the moonlight.

"They're still tracking us," she said, her voice low.

Damian leaned against a tree; his breathing steady but labored.

"They're persistent, I'll give them that."

"We can't keep running. They'll wear us down." Victoria said.

"So, what's the plan? Heroic last stand?"

"Not yet," Victoria replied. "We need to find somewhere defensible."

As if in answer to her words, a crumbling structure came into view in the distance—a long-abandoned watchtower, its silhouette stark against the night sky. It was little more than a ruin, but it offered shelter and, more importantly, a single point of entry.

"There," Victoria said, pointing to the tower. "We'll make our stand there."

"I like the way you think, priestess."

They hurried toward the tower, their movements swift and deliberate. The Shadow Knights presence grew more pronounced, the faint sound of their armor clinking against the underbrush growing louder with each passing moment. By the time they reached the base of the tower, the Knights were nearly upon them.

Victoria and Damian positioned themselves at the narrow entrance, their weapons ready. The first of the Shadow Knights appeared, stepping into the moonlight with their dark armor gleaming ominously. Victoria struck first, her sword a blur of light as it clashed against the warrior's blade. Damian moved with a predator's grace, his dagger finding its mark with deadly precision.

The battle was fierce, each strike a test of their resolve. But the Shadow Knights numbers were overwhelming, and it wasn't long before fatigue began to take its toll. Victoria's strikes became slower, her breaths heavier. Damian's movements lost some of their agility, his usual quips replaced by grim silence.

Finally, the inevitable happened. A Shadow Knight warrior slipped past Victoria's defenses, striking her sword from her hand. Before she could recover, another delivered a crushing blow to her side, sending her to the ground.

Damian lunged to defend her, his dagger flashing in the moonlight. But he was outnumbered, and a powerful strike to his chest sent him sprawling. The Knights closed in; their glowing eyes filled with dark triumph.

Victoria struggled to rise, but a heavy boot pressed her back down. She looked up to see one of the Knights looming over her, it's voice a low, menacing growl.

"You're coming with us," the warrior said. "The King of Demons wishes to meet you."

Damian coughed, blood staining the corner of his mouth.

"Lovely. I always wanted an audience with royalty."

Victoria glared at him. "Now's not the time, Damian."

"Humor helps with the pain," Damian muttered, wincing as one of the Shadow Knights bound his hands.

The warriors secured their captives and began the march through the forest, their movements silent and methodical. Victoria and Damian exchanged a glance, their unspoken determination clear.

The Knights moved in a disciplined formation, their footsteps unnervingly silent despite the rocky forest terrain. Victoria and Damian were bound with thick iron chains that seemed to hum faintly with dark energy, suppressing any strength or power they might summon. The faint glow of Victoria's divine light had dimmed entirely, and Damian's usually quick movements were sluggish.

"You know," Damian said, his voice a low murmur as he stumbled along. "I always imagined if I got captured by demon warriors, there'd be more fanfare. Maybe a dark parade or at least a sinister speech."

"Save your breath. We need to conserve our energy."

"Conserve energy for what? The grand execution?"

"No," Victoria said, her voice steady despite the exhaustion pulling at her. "For when the opportunity to escape presents itself."

The Shadow Knights leader, a tall figure in ornate black armor, glanced back at them, his hollow, glowing eyes piercing through the thick air.

"Silence," he growled, his voice like gravel scraping over steel.

Damian raised his bound hands in mock surrender.

"See? No sense of humor."

They continued deeper into the forest, the shadows growing darker and denser with each step. The air grew heavier, charged with an ominous energy that prickled Victoria's skin. She could feel it—the presence of an ancient evil growing stronger with every mile they traveled. Finally, the forest opened into a wide clearing.

Acheron.

Once a grand cathedral, it now rose like a corpse left standing, stitched together by chains and black stone. Massive, rusted iron spikes jutted out of its spires like broken bones, and its great bell tower—cracked down the middle—hung low over the landscape like a noose made of shadow. The stained glass was shattered, replaced with jagged obsidian panes that bled faint red light from within. The front doors, once carved with holy symbols, were now engraved with demonic glyphs, and each step leading to the entrance was lined with skulls fused into the stone, whispering as if still aware. The land around it was barren, a black scar where nothing grew—a wound on the world.

"I can feel the Divine Light screaming beneath it." Victoria whispered.

Faint red light pulsed from cracks in the structure, illuminating the surrounding area with an unnatural glow. The air here was thick with the stench of sulfur, decay and blood.

"Charming place. Really sets the mood."

The Shadow Knights marched them toward the makeshift prison, the ground beneath their feet transitioning from soft earth to cold, jagged stone. The entrance to Acheron was a gaping maw, its jagged edges resembling the teeth of a great beast. Two enormous demon statues flanked the entrance, their eyes glowing faintly as the group approached.

Inside, the temperature dropped sharply, the walls of the prison emitting a faint, bone-chilling mist. The doors of Acheron closed behind them with a deep, final thud, like the sealing of a tomb. The air was thick and wet, saturated with death, decay, and something more ancient—old blood, layered over centuries, sunk deep into stone that once knew only prayers. The Shadow Knights led them down a narrow spiral staircase carved from obsidian. Torchlight flickered unnaturally, as if struggling to remain lit in the suffocating darkness. Each step groaned under their boots with a voice of its own, stone lamenting its sacred betrayal. As they descended, whispers filled the air—soft, desperate voices in a language neither of them recognized. They echoed through the walls, not loud, but constant—like memories trying to claw their way back to the surface.

"This place... it's alive," Damian murmured. His body trembled, not from fear—but rage. "Every stone remembers what it used to be."

Victoria's focus was on the lightless door at the bottom of the stairs, where two more Shadow Knights stood guard—massive brutes in horned helms, gripping chained staves forged from corrupted angelic weapons. The door opened not with a creak, but a shriek. They were shoved into a narrow corridor lined with iron-barred cells, most of them empty—but not all. From some, soft weeping. From others, guttural growls, long since stripped of language.

"This is where they break you," Victoria whispered. "Not your body. Your soul."

Acheron wasn't just a prison. It was a processing depot for prisoners of war. Captured angels, divine warriors, and even humans were held here before being sent to Hell—to serve as slaves, or worse, to be converted into demons through rituals that stripped them of their essence.

At the end of the corridor, the cells widened into a holding chamber—a wide, circular room beneath the cathedral's altar. In its center stood a stone table, ringed with rusted restraints and soaked in dry blood.

In the shadows stood a tall figure—draped in tattered crimson robes, a bone-white mask etched with runes of dominion and torment. He stepped forward, and the torches dimmed.

The Warden of Acheron.

His voice was sand against steel.

"You are the first to enter this place and still carry the Light within you. It will be... interesting... to see how long that lasts."

He gestured, and Damian was dragged toward the table.

Victoria lunged, but one of the Umbra Claw hounds snarled and bared its teeth, forcing her back.

"Tell me where the others are," the Warden said, addressing Victoria. "Tell me where the Staff is."

She met his gaze without flinching.

"Burn."

The Warden tilted his head.

"Eventually," he said. "But not before you beg me for it."

Damian strained against the rusted restraints as they clamped over his wrists and ankles, the iron hissing as it touched his skin. The Warden moved slowly—ritualistic, not hurried—a predator that knew the kill was inevitable.

Victoria was forced to her knees, chained to a wrought-iron pillar facing Damian. She could do nothing but watch.

The Warden raised a hand, fingers gnarled like charred roots and uttered a phrase in the Tongue of the Abyss. The torchlight flared blue. Dark glyphs ignited across the stone floor, forming a circle beneath the table.

Damian arched his back as a shock of phantom pain hit him—not physical, but psychic, like needles threading into the deepest memories of his soul.

"Let us begin with truth," the Warden murmured.

The glyphs brightened. In the air above Damian's chest, an image flickered to life—a memory pulled from deep within him. It was Damian... as a child.

Clutching the body of his dying sister. Crying out into the night as her blood soaked his hands. Powerless.

Damian's eyes widened, pain twisting his features.

"No... no, don't—"

"Pain is the path to clarity," the Warden intoned. "All truth comes through suffering."

Another memory surfaced.

Damian, newly turned, slaughtering a coven of demons with primal fury. Screaming her name. Weeping as he drove a blade into his own reflection, hating what he had become.

"Stop this!" Victoria shouted.

"I am only helping him remember," the Warden said.

He turned to her, lowering his hood slightly revealing nothing beneath the mask but darkness, a void that seemed to stare directly into her soul.

"Now you," he said.

The glyphs shifted, crawling toward Victoria. She closed her eyes and braced herself.

It was the battlefield. Her brother, Elias. Falling. Screaming her name. Her hands had been too far away—her sword too slow. She reached, but her light had dimmed. He died in darkness.

The Warden whispered behind her.

"Your guilt shines brighter than your faith, Priestess. What good is your light if it only flickers when it is needed most?"

Victoria didn't speak. Her knuckles white with fury.

"Tell me where Aleister Kane is," the Warden said, soft as ash. "Or I will show him what you hide from even yourself."

Victoria lifted her head, eyes burning with defiance. "You'll have to break me first."

The Warden nodded, almost respectfully.

"And so, I shall."

Chapter 12

ACHERON PRISON

The forest was quiet, too quiet. Aleister felt the weight of the staff in his hand as they pressed forward, Blaze walking just ahead of him. It glowed faintly, its ethereal light casting long shadows that danced against the trees. Despite the victory of claiming it, Aleister couldn't shake the feeling of dread growing in his chest.

Blaze stopped abruptly, scanning the path ahead.

"Something's wrong," he said.

"What is it?"

Blaze turned to him. "Victoria and Damian. I can't sense them anymore."

A chill ran down Aleister's spine.

"What do you mean? They were supposed to draw the Shadow Knights away."

Blaze shook his head. "Something's happened."

Aleister's mind raced. Victoria was a warrior, capable and unyielding. Damian, for all his arrogance, was sharp and resourceful. For them to fall silent meant something far worse than a minor skirmish.

"What do we do?" Aleister asked, his voice steady despite the storm of emotions brewing inside him.

Blaze hesitated. "We should stay on course. The staff—"

"We can't just leave them. If they've been captured..."

Blaze sighed, running a hand through his hair.

"I don't even know where they are. The Shadow Knights could've taken them anywhere."

Aleister's thoughts flashed to the encounter with the Shadow Knights. Their warning about Mary, the weight of their threat—it all felt too connected.

"They didn't just take them randomly. They're bait."

Blaze frowned. "For you?"

"For the staff," Aleister said. "But yes, me too. Asmodeus knows I won't abandon them."

Blaze paced for a moment.

"If we go after them, we risk losing everything. The staff, our mission... everything."

Aleister stepped closer. "We lose everything if we don't. You think the Shadow Knights will stop with Victoria and Damian? They'll come for us, for the staff, for everyone we care about. This fight isn't just about the staff anymore."

Blaze stopped pacing, his eyes meeting Aleister's. There was a flicker of understanding there, a shared determination.

"Fine," Blaze said finally. "We find them. But if this is a trap—and it will be a trap—we go in prepared."

Aleister nodded. "Agreed."

Blaze took a deep breath. "I'll need to track them. Give me a moment."

Aleister watched as Blaze knelt on the ground, his hands glowing faintly as he muttered an incantation. The light from his tattoos spread across the forest floor, forming intricate patterns that pulsed with energy. After a moment, Blaze stood, his expression grim.

"They're being held at Acheron Prison," he said. "It's a prisoner depot not too far from here."

Aleister felt a surge of determination.

"Let's not waste any more time. We must save our friends."

Blaze gave him a wary look. "It's not going to be easy. Acheron is heavily guarded."

"Then we'll make it work. I'm not losing anyone else."

Aleister's determination was undeniably inspiring, yet Blaze's experience told a different story. Acheron harbored far more sinister threats than mere demon guards. There was a malevolent presence that Blaze kept hidden, a dark force that truly terrified him

.

The journey toward the Acheron Prison was grueling. The forest grew darker with every mile, the air heavier, almost suffocating. The faint glow of the Staff provided some comfort, but its light was fragile against the encroaching shadows. Blaze moved with purpose, his tattoos glowing faintly as he navigated the treacherous terrain.

Aleister's thoughts raced as they pressed forward. Images of Victoria and Damian flashed through his mind, their fates uncertain.

"We need to talk strategy," Blaze said, breaking the tense silence. He didn't stop walking, but his tone was sharp and direct.

"Acheron isn't just a prison. It's alive with dark magic."

"So how do we get in?"

Blaze hesitated, his tattoos flickering.

"There's a back entrance—an old tunnel system beneath the prison. It's dangerous, but it's our best shot. The Shadow Knights won't expect us to come that way."

Aleister nodded. "What kind of danger are we talking about?"

"The tunnels are filled with traps—both physical and magical. And there's a guardian. A creature bound to the area, tasked with protecting it from intruders."

"What kind of creature?" Aleister asked.

Blaze didn't answer immediately. When he did, his voice was low.

"A soul eater. It feeds on fear, doubt, and regret. If you let it get in your head, you're finished."

Aleister's stomach churned at the thought, but he pushed the fear aside. "We'll deal with it. Whatever it takes."

Blaze gave him a sidelong glance. "You're more determined than I thought."

"I've lost too much already. I won't lose them too."

Blaze nodded, a flicker of respect in his eyes. "Alright. Let's keep moving. The sooner we get there, the better."

As they approached the edge of the forest, the landscape began to change. The trees thinned, replaced by jagged rocks and barren earth. In the distance, the Acheron prison loomed, its dark silhouette hovered over the land like a dark sentinel. The faint red glow emanating from its cracks cast an eerie light over the desolate terrain.

"We're close," Blaze said.

The wind howled through the jagged landscape as Blaze and Aleister crouched behind a crumbled stone wall overlooking the eastern face of Acheron Prison. The faint smell of sulfur and rot riding every gust of air.

Blaze's tattoos flared slightly across his chest.

"They're still alive," he muttered, squinting toward the structure. "But not for long."

Aleister adjusted the strap on his satchel, the Lantern of Truth tucked safely inside.

"The front is suicide."

Blaze nodded. He pointed toward a slope behind the cathedral. Overgrown with dead ivy and thorn-choked roots, the earth gave way to a partially sunken archway, half-buried in rubble. A back entrance, long forgotten.

"That's an old catacomb entrance," Blaze said. "Sanctuary architects used them centuries ago—to remove bodies from sacred ground before burial."

Aleister narrowed his eyes. "How do you know it's still passable?"

"I don't. But death doesn't seal doors. Fear does. Once we're inside, stay close to me. The traps are designed to disorient and separate intruders. If we get split up…"

They moved quickly; their steps silent as they crossed the rocky terrain. The closer they got to the entrance, the stronger the oppressive energy became. By the time they reached the entrance, Aleister's chest felt tight, as if the air itself were trying to push him back.

Blaze placed a hand on Aleister's shoulder. "This is your last chance to turn back."

Aleister shook his head. "I'm not going anywhere."

Blaze's lips quirked into a faint smile.

They stepped into the archway, the darkness swallowing them whole. The light from the staff flickered, struggling against the suffocating shadows. Blaze's tattoos flared brighter, casting eerie patterns on the walls as they descended into the tunnels. The air grew colder, the faint sound of whispers echoing through the passageways. Aleister peered through the darkness, his senses on high alert. He could feel the presence of the soul eater, a gnawing unease that clawed at the edges of his mind.

"Remember," Blaze said. "Don't let it get in your head. Focus on the goal."

Aleister nodded. They had come too far to turn back now. The darkness in the tunnels seemed alive, shifting and breathing like a living entity. They lit only a single orb of pale blue flame—Blaze's magic—soft enough not to draw attention, bright enough to catch the edge of hidden dangers.

The tunnel walls were tight and cold, lined with forgotten relics, broken icons, rusted swords. The air tasted like dust and dried blood. Carved into the stone were ancient warding symbols—many of them desecrated others twisted into curses. The deeper they went, the clearer it became: this tunnel was no mere passageway.

"These tunnels aren't for moving bodies anymore," Aleister said softly. "They're for trapping them."

"Stay close," Blaze said. "The traps are up ahead."

Aleister nodded, his eyes scanning the walls. The carvings here were ancient, demonic sigils etched deep into the stone. They pulsed faintly, as though reacting to their presence.

Blaze stopped suddenly, raising a hand to signal silence. He knelt, examining the floor with a practiced eye.

"Pressure plates," he muttered. "Step wrong, and the whole tunnel collapses."

Aleister peered over his shoulder, his heart sinking as he saw the faint lines of the trap Blaze had spotted. The plates were nearly invisible, blending seamlessly with the surrounding stone. Blaze began to trace a safe path with his fingers, his tattoos flaring as he muttered an incantation.

"Follow exactly where I step," Blaze instructed. "No deviations."

Aleister nodded, his pulse quickening as Blaze began to move. Each step was deliberate, the tension in the air palpable. Aleister followed closely; his senses heightened.

They were halfway across the trapped section when Aleister faltered, his foot slipping slightly.

"Focus, Kane." Blaze said.

Aleister steadied himself, taking a deep breath.

"I'm fine," he said, his voice a little rattled.

They continued their careful progress; the tension filled the foul air. When they finally reached the other side of the trap, Aleister let out a breath he hadn't realized he was holding.

"Good work," Blaze said, clapping him on the shoulder. "But it's only going to get harder from here."

The tunnel ahead sloped downward, the air growing colder with each step. A deep, guttural growl echoed through the stone as they advanced. Blaze stopped, his tattoos flaring brighter as he drew a protective sigil in the air.

"It's close," Blaze said, his voice low. "The soul eater."

"What do we do?"

"We don't run. If we show fear, it'll tear us apart."

The growl grew louder, and from the shadows emerged a massive, shifting form. The soul eater's body was a swirling mass of darkness, its glowing eyes fixed on them with predatory intent. Its presence was suffocating, the air thick with despair and malice.

I had read about them once. Only once. And even then, the page had been torn from the book—not removed, torn—as if the author had changed their mind about letting the world remember what they'd recorded.

The *Soul Eater.*

A name spoken only in whispers among occultists and ceremonial magicians, who'd dared to conjure ancient grief into form. Not a demon. Not a ghost. Something else. Not born of Hell... but shaped by it. They were said to be remnants—the hollowed-out spirits of once-divine beings who had failed in their duty to the Light. Fallen not through sin, but through despair. Angels who didn't rebel—only broke. Their punishment wasn't damnation...It was emptiness. To become a Soul Eater is to forget your name, your purpose... even your form. You become a hunger given shape. And your only instinct is to consume what you lost—souls, memory, light. They don't kill the body. They starve the soul—draining your essence until only a shell remains. You lose yourself in layers. One memory at a time. Your name. Your purpose. Your love. Gone. And when you finally scream, it's not your voice that comes out. It's theirs.

"Stay behind me. Use the staff only if I fall." Blaze commanded.

The soul eater lunged, its form stretching and warping as it attacked. Blaze raised his hands, a barrier of light erupting from his tattoos and forcing the creature back. It howled, its voice a piercing wail that shook the tunnel.

Aleister watched, his heart pounding as Blaze fought to hold the creature at bay. The staff pulsed in his hand, the light growing brighter as if urging him to act.

"Blaze!" Aleister shouted. "It's reacting to the staff!"

Blaze gritted his teeth, the strain evident in his posture. "Then use it! But be careful!"

Aleister raised the staff high. Light erupted in a blinding flash, striking the soul eater and sending it shrieking into the darkness. The oppressive energy lifted slightly, the air becoming easier to breathe.

Blaze staggered, his tattoos dimming as he leaned against the wall.

"Nice work," he said, his voice hoarse. "But that won't keep it down for long."

Aleister helped him to his feet. "Then we keep moving."

"Lead the way, Kane."

Together, they pressed on. The tunnel began to widen as they moved deeper, the walls slick with moisture that seemed to seep from the oppressive darkness itself. The faint echoes of their footsteps bounced off the stone, distorted as though the tunnel itself were alive and watching. The faint light of the staff flickered the shadows around them clawing hungrily at its glow. Blaze's tattoos had dimmed after the encounter with the soul eater, leaving Aleister to lead the way. The warmth and energy of the staff steadying his nerves.

"You did well back there," Blaze said, breaking the silence.

Aleister glanced at him, surprised by the unexpected compliment. "You mean with the soul eater?"

"You didn't let the fear take you. That's not easy, even for someone with experience."

Aleister let out a dry chuckle. "I didn't feel fearless."

"Fearless isn't the goal," Blaze replied. "Fear is natural. It keeps you sharp. It's how you use it that matters."

Aleister nodded, the weight of Blaze's words settling over him. He knew fear all too well—fear of failure, of losing the people he cared about, of succumbing to the darkness he fought so hard to resist. But Blaze was right. Fear wasn't the enemy. Giving into it was.

When they reached the end of the tunnel, Blaze held up a hand, signaling for Aleister to stop.

"This is it," Blaze said, his voice low. "Once we go up, there's no turning back."

Aleister took a deep breath, his gaze fixed on the staircase. "Victoria and Damian... they're here?"

Blaze nodded. "I can feel their presence. Weak, but alive."

Aleister's chest tightened. The thought of them suffering filled him with both anger and resolve.

"Then let's get our friends back."

They ascended the spiral staircase, the air growing heavier with each step. The walls seemed to close in around them, the glow of the staff dimming as the oppressive energy of the prison intensified. By the time they reached the top, Aleister's breathing was labored, his body trembling from the weight of the atmosphere. Now, deep in the bowels of Acheron, they reached a narrow stone corridor veiled in mist. A single iron gate stood at the end—slightly ajar, light flickering beyond.

Blaze stopped and gestured to Aleister to kill the light from the staff. Aleister obeyed. Darkness swallowed them. They approached the gate silently, leaning into the crack. Inside was a circular chamber, walls ringed with black iron chains, old angelic runes defiled by blood. At its center stood the interrogation altar, and behind it, looming like a spider in its web, stood the Warden of Acheron.

Victoria and Damian were chained on opposite sides of the room, their heads slumped, blood trailing from lips and temples. The Warden raised a burning dagger and approached Victoria once more.

"We will peel away the Light from your soul like flesh from bone."

Aleister's eyes widened, his face contorted with a mix of terror and anger.

I can't lose her. Not her.

Blaze leaned in. "We charge in now, and we all die."

Aleister nodded. "So, what's the play?"

Blaze scanned the room. "See the chain glyphs above the altar? If I sever those with a disruptor rune, it'll short the entire sigil grid in the room."

"How long will that give us?"

Blaze shrugged. "Ten seconds. Maybe less."

"That's enough."

They retreated slightly behind the gate. Blaze opened his satchel and pulled out a folded parchment inscribed with glowing silver runes—the disruptor. He whispered a binding chant as he etched a symbol into the air with his dagger.

Aleister braced the staff of Infinite Light against the wall.

"When the grid drops, I'll blind the room with a flare. You get Victoria."

Blaze whispered the last word of the incantation and hurled the disruptor parchment into the room. It hit the wall above the Warden's head and detonated in a flash of silvery light, severing the arcane current running through the chains and floor. The chamber screamed—every glyph flared and died.

Aleister burst through the gate, raising the staff, and unleashed a pulse of divine light so bright it blinded the room, forcing the Shadow Knight guards to stumble backward.

Blaze sprinted through the shadows like a dagger in flight, reaching Victoria and cutting her down with one swipe of his blade.

"Took your sweet time," she rasped.

"You're welcome," he muttered, lifting her up.

Aleister freed Damian, who staggered but stayed upright.

"Can you walk?"

"I can stagger with style. That count?" Damian replied sarcastically.

As the light dimmed, the Warden recovered—enraged, his bone mask cracked, black ichor leaking from his mouth.

"You will not leave this place!"

But they didn't wait. Blaze hurled a smoke bomb into the corridor behind them as they escaped through the tunnel.

"They'll expect us to flee the way we came," he said. "So, we take the old aqueducts beneath the sanctum."

"Where do they lead?" Victoria asked, coughing.

"Out," Blaze answered. "I hope."

They ran through the tunnels, the aqueduct path winding like a serpent beneath the ruined cathedral. The air was damp and thick with mildew, the ceiling dripping fetid water as their boots pounded through shallow pools. They didn't speak. Just moved. Until they didn't.

A low growl echoed through the dark ahead, followed by the sound of iron scraping stone. Something massive stirred in the shadows. From the black, a figure emerged, towering, hunched, its body wrapped in rotted ceremonial robes. Its face was a blackened skull, eyes like burning coals sunk deep into sockets. Around its neck hung chains made from angel bones—twisted into wards of desecration.

Azareth the death Angel.

Even the name left a bitter taste on the soul. Not Asmodeus. But close. Aleister had read the name once, buried deep in a forbidden text—one written in faded ink and sealed in human skin. The scribes didn't speak it aloud. They feared it would draw his gaze.

Once, long ago, Azareth had been Seraphim—a flame-winged commander of celestial legions. A being of unmatched resolve. He was known as the Torchbearer of Conviction, the one who lit the way through doubt for the armies of Heaven.

But something changed.

He questioned the mercy of Heaven... and its silence in the face of suffering. When the first rift cracked between Light and Shadow, Azareth didn't follow Lucifer. He didn't rebel for power. He fell because his faith burned out. And when a Seraph's faith dies... so does everything else inside them. What was left became a thing of hunger. A husk of divinity draped in bone and shadow. A devourer of hope. A grave for what he once believed.

The thing before Aleister now wasn't an angel. Not anymore. It was a warning. Of what happens when light forgets why it shines.

"Go! Lead them out of the tunnels." Aleister said, stepping forward. "I'll handle this."

"With that?" Blaze motioned to the Staff.

Aleister didn't answer. He held the Staff of Infinite Light aloft, its golden inlay pulsing with brilliance. He felt the surge of divine power flow through him—warmth, purpose, legacy.

The tunnel groaned beneath their feet as Azareth stepped fully into view—ten feet of bone, fire, and absence. The air burned cold around him. His every movement whispered of something that once knew holiness but now only remembered hatred.

Aleister didn't hesitate. "In the name of the Light, be banished!"

He struck the ground with the staff. A shock wave of holy energy surged forward, slamming directly into Azareth's chest. The tunnel shook. Dust rained down. The light seared into the stone. But Azareth... didn't move. He looked down at the blackened scorch mark smoldering across his ribs, then slowly raised his head—those hollow eye sockets glowing with slow-burning mockery.

"Do you think that light still remembers you?" he hissed, his voice like dry wind across bone. "It didn't save me. It won't save you."

Aleister gritted his teeth and struck again—this time a vertical arc of power that crashed into Azareth's shoulder and side, sending shards of stone flying. Still nothing. Azareth stepped forward, lifting a hand wreathed in shadows, preparing to unleash a torrent of soul-rending fire.

Blaze slammed his hands into the stone floor, activating a glowing sigil shield that erupted in a dome of burning runes around them just as Azareth's attack struck. Blaze held the barrier just long enough to keep the group from being obliterated by Azareth's soul-scorching fire. But cracks were already forming in the glowing sigil. His arms trembled, sweat mixing with ash.

"I can't hold him much longer!" Blaze yelled.

"We need to stop him here!" Aleister shouted, raising the staff again.

But Victoria's voice cut through the chaos, firm and commanding:

"Aleister! You can't defeat him—not yet! You must bring the tunnel down!"

Aleister froze for a split second, hesitation locking in his chest.

Damian staggered up beside him, bleeding but steady.

"She's right! If we fight, we die. If we fall back and regroup... we live."

Aleister's grip tightened around the staff, frustration burning behind his eyes. But he knew they were right.

"Let's bury this son of a bitch!"

He slammed the staff into the floor again, this time channeling all the divine force he could muster not into attack—but into collapse. A brilliant white beam smashed into the above rafters of muck and cobwebs. The stone above groaned, then cracked.

Victoria pulled Damian back as Blaze reinforced the shield for one final surge of protection. The ceiling gave way with a thunderous roar, boulders crashing down in a violent wave that slammed into Azareth and sealed the tunnel behind them. The dust was thick, but the path ahead was clear—narrow, winding, broken, but leading out.

Blaze lowered the flickering sigil, chest heaving.

"That was close."

Aleister looked back once, the collapsed tunnel still glowing faintly red.

"He's not dead, is he?"

"No," Victoria said quietly. "But neither are we."

The group emerged from the tunnels into the cold night air, their breaths visible in the icy mist. Aleister collapsed onto a nearby boulder, the staff resting across his knees. His chest heaved as he tried to process what had just happened.

Blaze crouched beside him. His tattoos dimmed.

"That staff should've destroyed him," he said, his voice tight with frustration.

Victoria sat nearby, wincing as she adjusted her battered armor.

"What went wrong?"

Aleister stared at the staff, its faint glow pulsing weakly.

"It's not enough," he said quietly. "I thought... I thought it would work."

"Asmodeus was right. The staff is powerful, but we're missing something. A key piece of the puzzle still eludes us. We need to find Doctor Crowe's journals—they must have the answers." Blaze said.

Damian leaned against a tree, his usual smirk absent.

"So, what? We find the journals and hope they tell us what to do?"

Blaze nodded thoughtfully. "It's our only chance. Without them, the staff is merely a beacon in the darkness. But I know someone who might know where they are."

Aleister closed his eyes, the weight of his failure pressing down on him. But even as doubt gnawed at him, a spark of determination remained.

"Then we find the journals," he said firmly. "All of them. Whatever it takes."

The group exchanged weary nods, the resolve in their eyes unspoken but clear. Their journey was far from over, and the path ahead was fraught with danger. But they had no choice. The fate of humanity—and Aleister's own soul—depended on it.

Chapter 13

THE WITCHES WAY

The town of Evermere's distant lights shimmered like faint stars against the backdrop of the encroaching night. Aleister walked with the staff tucked securely in his grasp, his thoughts a turbulent mix of frustration and determination. The defeat at Acheron Prison still weighed heavily on him, but it only strengthened his resolve to find the missing Journals of Doctor Crowe.

Victoria walked alongside him, her steps steady despite the bruises and scrapes from their earlier ordeal. Damian trailed behind, uncharacteristically quiet, while Blaze led the group, his tattoos glowing faintly in the twilight.

"Are you sure about this witch, Blaze?" Aleister asked, breaking the silence.

"She's our best shot. If anyone knows about the journals, it's her."

"And what's her price?" Damian asked, his tone skeptical. "Witches don't work for free."

"She'll help. Let's just say I've done her a few favors in the past."

"You've got quite the network, Barton."

"You don't survive in this line of work without making a few connections."

As they approached the edge of the town, the group fell silent. The streets were quiet, the glow of lanterns casting long shadows across the cobblestone paths. It was a small, unassuming place, the kind of town that seemed untouched by the horrors of the outside world. But Aleister knew better. Evil could find its way into even the most peaceful corners of existence.

Blaze led them to a modest cottage on the outskirts of town. The windows were shuttered, and smoke curled lazily from the chimney. The scent of herbs and incense lingered in the air, a faint hint of something more potent beneath it.

"This is it," Blaze said, stopping at the gate.

Aleister studied the house, his unease growing. "What should we expect?"

Blaze's smile didn't reach his eyes. "Let's just say she's not your average witch."

He pushed open the gate, and the group followed him to the door. Blaze knocked twice, the sound echoing in the still night. A moment later, the door creaked open, revealing a woman with striking green eyes and long, silver-streaked hair. She wore a flowing robe adorned with intricate patterns, her presence both commanding and enigmatic.

"Blaze Barton," she said, her voice smooth but laced with curiosity. "It's been a long time."

"Luna," Blaze replied. "I need your help."

Her gaze shifted to the group, lingering on Aleister and the staff in his hands. A faint smile played on her lips.

"I see you've brought friends. And something... extraordinary."

Aleister stepped forward.

"We're looking for the Journals of Doctor Crowe."

Luna's expression darkened. "A dangerous quest. Do you understand the risks?"

"We do," Aleister said firmly. "But we don't have a choice."

Luna studied him for a moment, her gaze piercing. Finally, she stepped aside, motioning for them to enter.

"Come inside. Let's talk."

The group filed into the cottage, the warm glow of the fire casting flickering shadows on the walls. Shelves lined with jars of herbs, crystals, and other mystical items filled the space, creating an atmosphere both inviting and mysterious.

Luna gestured for them to sit at a wooden table near the hearth. She took a seat across from them, her green eyes sharp and calculating.

"So, you seek the lost journals. Tell me why."

Aleister hesitated, glancing at Blaze before speaking. "The Staff of Infinite Light... it's incomplete. Without the knowledge in the journals, we can't use it to its full potential. We need it to stop Asmodeus, the king of nine hells."

Luna leaned back, her expression thoughtful. "The journals are not easy to find. Doctor Crowe went to great lengths to ensure they would never fall into the wrong hands."

"Do you know where they are?" Blaze asked.

"I know of their last known locations. But accessing them will not be easy. They're hidden in places of great significance, protected by ancient magic and guardians."

"What places?"

"The Hidden Library of Shadows, for one. But finding it is a quest in itself."

The name sent a shiver down Aleister's spine. The library was the stuff of legend, a sacred place said to hold knowledge lost to time. If the journals were there, it would be a monumental challenge to retrieve them.

Luna rose, moving to a shelf where she retrieved a small, ornate box. She placed it on the table, opening it to reveal a map etched with intricate symbols.

"This will guide you to the library. But be warned—the path is treacherous, and the guardians will not show mercy."

Aleister reached for the map. "We'll find it. Whatever it takes."

Luna's gaze softened, a flicker of admiration in her eyes.

"You carry a heavy burden, Aleister Kane. Be sure you are prepared for what lies ahead."

Luna's green eyes flickered with a mix of caution and intrigue as she tapped a finger on the map.

"The Library of Shadows," she said, her voice heavy with reverence. "It is not merely a place of knowledge. It is a sanctum where the light of truth and the darkness of secrets converge."

Aleister's gaze fixed on the intricate symbols etched into the map. The name alone sent a shiver through him.

"How do we find it?"

"The path is not marked in the conventional sense. The map will guide you, but only if you can decipher its markings. And even then, the library is guarded by wards and entities that will test your worthiness."

Blaze studied the map, as he traced a finger over one of the symbols.

"These sigils... they're older than anything I've seen. This won't be easy."

"It's not meant to be," Luna said. "The library was hidden to protect the knowledge within. Only those deemed worthy can access it."

Damian leaned casually against the table.

"And who decides worthiness? Some mystical gate-keeper?"

Luna turned to him, her lips curving into a faint smile.

"In a manner of speaking. The library's guardians are ancient, and they do not judge lightly."

Victoria, who had been quietly observing, stepped forward.

"Do we have any idea what kind of guardians we're dealing with?"

"They are shadows, living extensions of the library itself. They'll test your strength, your resolve, and your purity of purpose. If you fail... you will become one of them."

The room fell silent, the weight of her words settling over the group.

"We've faced far worse," Aleister said. "We can handle whatever it throws at us."

"I hope so, for your sake."

She placed a small vial on the table, its contents a swirling silver liquid. "Take this. It is an elixir of clarity. When the time comes, it will help you see the path forward."

Aleister picked up the vial, studying it closely before slipping it into his pocket. "Thank you."

"Be careful, Aleister Kane. The journey ahead will test you in ways you cannot yet imagine."

Blaze stood, rolling up the map and tucking it into his coat.

"We'll be ready."

The group rose, the weight of their mission heavier than ever. As they made their way to the door, Luna called out, her voice halting them in their tracks.

"One more thing."

They turned, and her gaze locked with Aleister's.

"The library will reveal truths, not just about the staff, but about yourselves. Be prepared to face what you might not want to see."

The group exchanged glances, their thoughts unspoken but aligned. How much worse could it get? With that, they set off to face their next set of seemingly endless challenges.

They decided to camp just outside the town, the flickering firelight casting long shadows across their faces. Aleister sat apart from the others, the staff resting against his shoulder as he stared at the rolled-up map in Blaze's hand.

"Do you think we'll make it?" Victoria's voice broke the silence as she approached.

"We don't have a choice." Aleister said

Victoria sat beside him.

"Luna said the library would test us. Do you think you're ready for that?"

"I don't know. But I know I can't fail. Not now."

Victoria studied him for a moment before speaking.

"You carry a lot on your shoulders, Aleister. But you're not alone in this."

Her words struck a chord, and Aleister nodded, the faintest hint of gratitude in his eyes.

"Thank you."

As the fire crackled and the night deepened, the group prepared for the journey ahead, each of them grappling with their own fears and uncertainties. The path to the Library of Shadows was shrouded in mystery, but one thing was clear—they would need more than courage to succeed.

The morning came too quickly, the pale light of dawn casting a cold, gray hue over the camp. Blaze was the first to rise, his movements efficient as he packed his gear and checked the map Meridien had given them. His tattoos glimmered faintly in the dim light, a testament to the power coursing through him, but even he seemed weighed down by the task ahead.

Aleister stood at the edge of the camp, staring out at the dense forest that stretched before them. The map in Blaze's hands had revealed the general direction, but the precise path was still unclear. The forest, much like the Library of Shadows itself, seemed alive, shifting and twisting with an unnatural energy that set Aleister's teeth on edge.

"You ready for this?" Damian's voice broke the silence, his usual levity tinged with a rare seriousness.

Aleister glanced at him. "I don't think anyone's ever ready for something like this."

Damian smirked faintly, adjusting the blade at his hip.

"Fair enough. But hey, at least we've got the dream team."

Victoria joined them, her armor polished and gleaming despite the previous day's trials.

"Dream team or not, we need to stay focused. The library isn't going to welcome us with open arms."

Blaze approached, rolling up the map and tucking it into his coat.

"She's right. This isn't just a library—it's a sanctum of power. It'll do everything it can to keep us out."

Aleister turned to face the group.

"Then we don't give it the chance."

With a collective nod, they gathered their belongings and set out, the forest swallowing them as they ventured deeper into the unknown. The air grew colder the farther they went, the faint sounds of wildlife gradually fading until only the crunch of their footsteps remained. The dense forest seemed to press in around them as the group moved cautiously through the undergrowth. The air was thick with tension, every rustle of leaves or snap of a twig setting them on edge.

"We've been quiet for too long," Damian said, breaking the silence. "How about someone tells a joke? You know, lighten the mood before we get eaten by a tree or something."

Victoria's lips twitched in a barely concealed smile.

"If humor is your coping mechanism, Damian, I think you'll need more than jokes where we're going."

"Hey, laughter's a weapon too. Not everything has to be swords and spells."

Aleister, walking a few steps behind, spoke up.

"Do you think we'll find the journals in time? If Asmodeus gets wind of where we're heading..."

"The Shadow Knights already know we're searching for the journals. That's why they're on our trail. They can't get to the Library of Shadows without us, but if we make a mistake..."

Victoria nodded. "Then we have to make sure we don't."

The conversation lulled as the group pressed forward, their path winding through dense thickets and towering trees. Aleister found his gaze drifting to Victoria, her figure moving gracefully despite the rugged terrain. He caught the faint scent of something floral, clean and sharp, that seemed out of place in the forest.

His mind wandered. How was she so composed? So... perfect? Her movements were precise, her armor gleaming despite their trials. There was an unshakable strength in her, a determination that mirrored his own, yet he felt drawn to something more—a warmth he hadn't allowed himself to feel in years.

"You okay back there, Aleister?" Victoria's voice jolted him from his thoughts, her gaze meeting his.

He cleared his throat, trying to mask his embarrassment. "Yeah. Just... thinking."

Damian chuckled. "Thinking, huh? Careful, Kane. Thinking too much can get you into trouble."

Aleister shot him a withering look. "You'd know all about trouble, wouldn't you?"

Damian raised his hands in mock surrender. "Touché."

Blaze suddenly stopped, holding up a hand.

"Quiet," he said, his voice low and tense.

The group froze, their eyes scanning the forest. The atmosphere had changed—the air felt heavier, colder. Aleister could sense it too, a subtle but unmistakable shift in the energy around them.

"What is it?" Victoria asked, her hand on the hilt of her sword.

Blaze's tattoos flared briefly. "We're not alone."

They moved cautiously forward, their senses on high alert. The trees thinned, revealing a clearing bathed in an eerie light. At the top of a hill, silhouetted against the sky, stood a lone figure on horseback. The horse's eyes glowed red, and its rider seemed to meld with the shadows, an ominous presence that sent a chill down Aleister's spine.

"What in the hell..." Damian muttered, gripping his blade.

Another rider emerged beside the first, then another. Slowly, more figures appeared, their numbers growing until the crest of the hill was filled with shadowy forms. An army of demons.

Aleister's heart pounded as he raised the Staff of Infinite Light, its glow cutting through the unnatural darkness. "This isn't good."

"That's an understatement," Blaze muttered, his tattoos glowing brighter. "They're blocking our path."

Victoria stepped forward, her sword gleaming in the faint light. "We can't let them stop us. Not here."

As the demonic army began to descend the hill, Blaze turned to the group. "Stick together. Don't give them any openings."

But Victoria had other plans. She raised her sword high, its blade catching the light as she closed her eyes. Her voice rang out, clear and commanding. "In the name of the Light, I summon the warriors of Heaven!"

A piercing light shot from her sword into the sky, splitting the clouds. A moment later, the heavens answered with a trumpet blast. Angelic figures descended, their wings spreading as they formed a line opposite the demonic army. Their presence filled the clearing with a radiant energy that pushed back the shadows.

Aleister watched in awe as the angels and demons faced off, the tension crackling like a storm about to break. He tightened his grip on the staff, bracing himself for the chaos to come.

And then, the battle began.

Chapter 14

A HEAVY BURDEN

The clash of steel and the unearthly cries of demons filled the clearing, a cacophony of chaos as the Shadow Knights charged into the ranks of the angelic warriors. Swords clanged, light clashed with shadow, and the air pulsed with divine and infernal energy. The earth beneath their feet trembled as the forces of Heaven and Hell collided in a battle that shook the very fabric of the forest.

Aleister watched as angelic warriors soared through the air, their swords cleaving through the ranks of demonic soldiers. But for every demon that fell, another seemed to take its place, their numbers seemingly endless. Aleister could only watch, his face expressionless, his mind wondered as the battle started to rage.

I've read of celestial wars in ancient texts—poems penned in blood and starlight, scriptures written by the mad and the blessed. But nothing... nothing prepares you for the sound of angelic wings tearing through the sky like thunder. Or for the sight of shadow and flame crashing down upon them. I should be in awe. I should be inspired by the Light. But all I feel is hate. Lucian Kane died while I hid behind a door, clutching a ring I didn't understand. That day carved a hole in me so deep I've never stopped falling. And my Mary? If she's dead, then I swear on what little remains of my soul—I'll destroy the gates of Hell with my bare hands! I'll drag every last demon into the abyss with me! Let Heaven wage its war. I'm not here to save the world. I never was. I'm here to end this malevolence, this cycle that steals the ones we love and leaves us shattered, consumed with grief and fury. I don't know where you are, Mary. I don't even know if you're alive... but if I have to carve through every demon in every realm to find you—I will.

Victoria, a few paces behind Aleister, watched not the battle—but *him*. She could feel it—the anguish in his soul. It radiated from him like heat. It was the same pain she had once carried. The same darkness that had nearly consumed her. Quietly, she stepped beside him. Her voice was low, calm... but heavy with history.

"I know what it's like... to hate so much it hollows you out."

Aleister didn't turn to her.

"Do you?" he said, coldly. "Did you lose your father to a demon? Or wonder every day if the one you love is still alive or lying in some pit being torn apart for spite?"

Victoria's gaze stayed on the horizon, where two angels circled a Shadow Knight in a blaze of holy fire.

"No," she said. "But I lost someone who was my light. My brother, Elias."

Aleister blinked, tension easing slightly at her tone.

"I was there when he died. I failed him. I let my fear dull my sword, and by the time I reached him—he was gone. The light I swore to protect... vanished."

She paused, voice cracking just slightly.

"For a long time, I hated everything. Myself. Heaven. Even the Light. I wandered through battlefields hoping something would take me. That the pain would finally end. But it didn't."

Aleister turned now, his expression shifting.

"What changed?"

Victoria finally looked him in the eye.

"Love...I remembered that Elias didn't die for revenge. He died protecting something. Someone. And if I wanted to honor him, I had to live... and fight with light in my heart, not darkness."

A silence fell between them as another angel fell from the sky.

"I still grieve him," she whispered. "But grief doesn't have to turn into hate, Aleister. It can become strength—if you let it."

Aleister lowered his head. The storm inside him didn't vanish, but it... softened. Slightly.

"I don't know if I can come back from where I am," he said quietly.

"Then don't come back," she said. "Just walk forward. And I'll walk with you."

Victoria extended her hand.

Aleister hesitated. But then, slowly—he took it. Her fingers were warm, steady, anchoring him like a lifeline. They stood there amid the roar of angels and demons, the light of Heaven battling the darkness—yet for a moment, it was just the two of them. Broken souls, standing upright despite everything that was happening.

"One step at a time," she said, her voice soft but certain. "Together."

Aleister gave a faint nod.

"This isn't going to end well," Damian muttered, his blade drawn but held at his side. His eyes darted between the chaos and their path forward.

Victoria, standing tall with her sword still glowing faintly from her summoning, turned to the group.

"We're not here to fight this battle."

Blaze's tattoos flared as he scanned the surrounding area. "She's right. If we stay, we'll be dragged into a fight we can't win."

"You're suggesting we just leave?" Aleister said.

"We're not running. We're advancing. This battle is a distraction, and we need to use it to our advantage. If the Shadow Knights are focused on the angels, they won't be able to follow us."

Damian smirked, sheathing his blade.

"Now you're speaking my language."

Aleister hesitated, glancing back at the battle. The angels fought valiantly, their light pushing back the tide of darkness, but he knew Victoria was right. Their mission wasn't to win this battle—it was to reach the Library of Shadows and unlock the staff's full potential.

"Fine," he said. "Let's move."

Victoria nodded, her sword still in hand as she led the way.

"Stay low and keep quiet. We can't afford to draw attention."

The group slipped away from the chaos, moving swiftly but cautiously through the undergrowth. The sounds of battle grew fainter with each step, though the occasional echo of a trumpet blast or demonic roar reminded them of the war raging behind them.

Blaze paused briefly to consult the map.

"This way," he whispered, pointing to a narrow path that wound through the trees.

The forest seemed to shift around them, the oppressive atmosphere growing heavier as they ventured deeper. Aleister couldn't shake the feeling that the shadows were watching, waiting for a moment of weakness.

"Do you think the angels will win?" Damian asked, breaking the tense silence.

"They're not fighting to win. They're fighting to buy us time."

"Some consolation," Damian muttered, though he quickened his pace.

Aleister scanned the trees. "Let's hope it's enough."

As they pressed on, the forest grew darker, the trees twisting into unnatural shapes. The path became harder to follow, and Blaze's tattoos flared brighter as he muttered incantations under his breath to guide them.

"We're getting close," he said, his voice low. "I can feel it."

The shadows seemed thicker here, their movements more deliberate. He glanced at Victoria, who moved with practiced precision, her eyes scanning the path ahead. Then, a low growl cut through the silence.

The group froze, their hands moving instinctively to their weapons. From the darkness emerged a pair of glowing red eyes, followed by another, and another. A pack of shadowy creatures stepped into the faint light of Blaze's tattoos, their forms indistinct but menacing.

"Looks like the Shadow Knights left us a parting gift," Damian said, drawing his blade.

Victoria raised her sword, its glow illuminating the creatures. "Stay together. Don't let them separate us."

The creatures circled, their growls growing louder. Aleister raised the staff, its light flaring to push back the encroaching darkness. The creatures hesitated, their glowing eyes narrowing, but they didn't retreat.

"They're testing us," Blaze said, his voice tense. "Seeing if we're weak enough to take."

"Then let's show them we're not," Victoria said, stepping forward.

The growls deepened into a bone-chilling chorus, reverberating through the dense forest. The shadowy creatures moved closer, their forms shifting unnaturally as though the darkness itself animated them. Aleister held the Staff higher, its glow pushing the shadows back momentarily, but the creatures seemed emboldened, testing the strength of the staff's radiance.

"We can't let them pin us down here," Victoria said, stepping in front of the group, her sword gleaming as she prepared to strike. "Blaze, can your spells hold them off?"

Blaze's tattoos flared brighter as he chanted an incantation under his breath. A faint barrier of shimmering light appeared around the group, forcing the creatures to stop their advance. The beasts snarled, as they circled the perimeter.

"This will hold them," Blaze said, his voice strained, "but not for long. Whatever these things are, they're strong."

Damian twirled his blade in his hand, his usual bravado returning. "Guess we'd better make it quick, then."

Aleister glanced at Blaze. "Can we fight them?"

"Not without exhausting ourselves," Blaze replied. "And we'll need our strength for what's ahead."

Victoria surveyed the shadowy forms, her expression grim. "Then we don't fight. We move."

The creatures began testing the barrier, lunging at it with clawed limbs and snarling ferociously. Blaze winced, his tattoos dimming slightly as he maintained the spell. "They're wearing it down."

"We don't have much time," Aleister said. "Blaze, can you guide us out of here?"

Blaze nodded, sweat beaded on his forehead.

"I can keep the barrier up long enough for us to break through their line. But we'll have to move fast."

Victoria took position at the front, her sword glowing brighter.

"On my mark, we run. No hesitation. Stay close."

The group tensed, preparing for the dash.

The creatures growled louder, their attacks on the barrier growing more frenzied.

"Now!" Victoria shouted.

The barrier flared as Blaze channeled his energy, creating a momentary surge that knocked the creatures back. The group sprinted forward, weaving through the snarling beasts. Victoria led the charge, her sword slashing through a shadowy creature that lunged at them. Its form dissipated into smoke, but another quickly took its place.

Aleister swung the staff, its light cutting through the darkness and driving the creatures back. Damian moved with surprising agility, his blade slicing through the shadows as he kept pace with the group.

"Keep moving!" Blaze shouted. The spell was taking its toll, and the creatures were relentless.

The group reached a narrow pathway that wound through the trees. Victoria stopped briefly, glancing back to ensure everyone was still with them.

"This way!" she called, leading them down the path.

The creatures gave chase, their guttural growls echoing through the forest. The path twisted and turned, the dense trees providing brief moments of cover. Aleister's heart pounded as he ran, the staff's light barely keeping the shadows at bay.

"We can't outrun them forever," Damian said, his breath coming in short bursts.

Victoria glanced at Blaze, who was visibly struggling to maintain his pace.

"How much longer can you keep that spell up?"

"Not long," Blaze admitted, his voice tight. "But we're close. The forest is thinning."

Aleister's eyes darted ahead, and he saw it too—a faint glimmer of open space beyond the trees.

"We're almost there!"

The group burst through the tree line into a wide clearing bathed in moonlight. The sudden openness was disorienting, the shadows seeming to hesitate as they reached the edge of the forest.

Blaze dropped to one knee, his tattoos fading as the barrier spell collapsed. He gasped for air, his exhaustion evident.

"That's it... I'm tapped."

The shadowy creatures stopped at the edge of the clearing, growling and pacing but unwilling to enter. Aleister glanced back.

"Why aren't they following?"

Victoria scanned the clearing.

"This place... it feels different. Like something's keeping them out."

Damian sheathed his blade, his breathing heavy. "Maybe they're afraid of the light."

Blaze managed a weak laugh, pushing himself to his feet.

"Or maybe something worse lives here."

Aleister didn't respond, his attention drawn to the center of the clearing. There, rising from the earth like a jagged wound, was a massive stone structure. Its surface was etched with glowing symbols, faintly pulsing in the moonlight.

"The entrance to the next trial," Victoria said, her voice quiet but certain.

Aleister moved forward, his exhaustion momentarily forgotten. The Staff pulsed in his hand, as though responding to the structure.

"The Library of Shadows..."

"Not yet." Blaze said shaking his head. "This is just another test."

Victoria placed a hand on Aleister's shoulder.

"We'll face it together. But first, we rest. Whatever's inside... we'll need our strength."

The campfire crackled softly, casting flickering light across the group as they sat in uneasy silence. The clearing felt too open, too exposed, yet the oppressive weight of the forest beyond was even worse. Aleister sat closest to the fire. His gaze fixed on the flames but his mind far away. Victoria cleaned her blade meticulously, the rhythm of her movements steady and calming. Blaze leaned back against a fallen log. Exhaustion evident on his dirty face. Damian sharpened his dagger absentmindedly, his usual smirk absent.

But Aleister couldn't sit still. His fingers drummed against his thigh as his thoughts churned. He saw Mary's face every time he closed his eyes, heard her voice in the silence between the crackling of the fire. The uncertainty of her safety gnawed at him, fueling his frustration and helplessness. Finally, he stood abruptly, the movement drawing the attention of the others. Without a word, he stepped away from the fire, pacing just beyond its glow.

"Are you alright?" Damian asked, his voice wary.

Aleister didn't answer. Instead, he clenched his fists and turned his gaze skyward.

"Michael!" he shouted, his voice echoing into the night. "Show yourself!"

The others exchanged uneasy glances.

"Aleister, what are you doing?" Blazed said. Rising to meet Aleister.

Aleister ignored him.

"You're always watching, aren't you? Always there when it suits your purpose. Well, I need answers, and I need them now!"

The fire flared suddenly, its light growing brighter as a familiar blue glow descended into the clearing. The group shielded their eyes as the radiant form of the Archangel Michael appeared, his presence filling the air with an overwhelming sense of peace and power.

Michael's gaze fell on Aleister.

"Why have you summoned me, Aleister Kane?"

Aleister's frustration started to boil over.

"You know why. Mary. I need to know she's safe. You brought me into this fight—now prove to me that she's not paying the price for it!"

Michael regarded him silently for a moment before speaking.

"Your wife, Mary, is safe for the moment. I have placed my protection around her, shielding her from the darkness that seeks her. But I cannot show you more than this."

"That's not enough. I need to see her. I need to know she's alive." Aleister demanded.

Michael's gaze softened, his voice gentle but firm.

"Aleister, you must trust in me. Mary is safe. But your focus must remain on the task before you. If you falter, her safety—and the safety of countless others—will be lost."

Aleister took a step back, his emotions warring within him. He wanted to believe Michael, to trust in his words, but the weight of his fears and doubts was crushing. He turned away, muttering under his breath.

"I just want her back..."

Michael's glow dimmed slightly.

"Your love for her is your strength, Aleister. Hold onto it, but do not let it cloud your purpose."

With that, the blue light faded, leaving the group in the dim firelight once more. Victoria stood, watching Aleister closely.

"Are you alright?"

Aleister didn't respond immediately. Finally, he nodded, though his shoulders remained tense.

"I'll be fine."

The camp fell into an uneasy silence as the others settled in for the night. Aleister lay on his bedroll, staring up at the sky, his mind too restless for sleep. The reassurance Michael had offered felt hollow, a bandage over a gaping wound. He closed his eyes, but instead of rest, a strange pull began to take hold. A faint whisper echoed in his mind, calling his name. He sat up abruptly, scanning the clearing. The others were asleep, their forms faintly illuminated by the dying fire. The whisper came again, stronger this time, and his gaze was drawn to the edge of the clearing.

Without thinking, he rose and followed the sound, his feet carrying him deeper into the forest. The trees seemed to part before him, revealing a faint path that hadn't been there before. The whisper grew louder, more insistent, guiding him through the twisting darkness.

Finally, he emerged into a clearing where a massive, ancient castle loomed. Its towers reached into the sky, their edges crumbling with age. The air around it was thick with a malevolent energy, and Aleister's heart pounded as he approached. The massive iron doors creaked open as he neared, revealing a dimly lit hall. At the far end revealing a courtyard bathed in dim, flickering light. The air was thick with decay, and every breath felt heavy. In the center of the courtyard stood a massive statue of a fallen angel. Its stone wings were broken, its face locked in a frozen expression of anguish. The base of the statue was covered in dark vines that seemed to pulse with a life of their own. He couldn't shake the feeling that he was being watched, the oppressive atmosphere pressing down on him with every step.

Suddenly, the courtyard grew colder. A deep, guttural laugh echoed through the air, sending a chill up Aleister's spine. The vines covering the statue's base began to writhe, and the statue's face shifted, its stone lips parting as it spoke.

"Welcome, Aleister Kane," the voice rumbled, unmistakably that of Asmodeus. The statue's eyes glowed with a sinister red light, its features contorting into a mocking smile.

"How does it feel to walk willingly into my domain?"

Aleister froze, his grip on the staff tightening.

"Show yourself, Asmodeus. Stop hiding behind parlor tricks."

The statue chuckled, the sound reverberating through the courtyard.

"Why should I waste my strength? This form serves me well enough."

Aleister glared at the animated face.

"What do you want?"

The statue leaned forward slightly. Its movements impossibly fluid for stone.

"You amuse me, mortal. Always so defiant, so full of purpose. Do you truly believe you can win this war? That you can defeat me?"

"I don't just believe—I know," Aleister retorted sharply. "And I'll do whatever it takes to bring you and your minions to ashes."

The statue's grin widened.

"Such conviction... but so naïve. You can't kill me, Aleister. I am eternal, a force beyond your comprehension. This quest of yours? Futile. It will end in despair, just like it did for your father."

Aleister's breath hitched at the mention of Lucian, but he didn't falter.

"You're wrong. I'll stop you. I'll stop all of this."

"Oh, you'll try. But even now, your strength wanes. Your precious wife—Mary, was it? How long do you think she'll remain safe while you chase shadows?"

Aleister stepped closer, the staff flaring with light.

"Leave her out of this."

The statue's face twisted into a sneer.

"You can't protect her, Aleister. Not from me. I am always watching, always waiting."

Asmodeus's laughter echoed through the courtyard, but as it faded, Aleister noticed something—the statue's presence, its connection to Asmodeus, felt tethered to the castle itself. A realization struck him: Asmodeus could only watch him here, on unholy ground. The knowledge gave him a flicker of hope, but the weight of the demon's words still pressed heavily on him.

"This isn't over," Aleister said, his voice steady despite the turmoil inside.

"No, mortal. It is far from over."

And with that, the statue solidified into cold stone. The stench of sulfur dissipated, leaving Aleister once again in a state of frustration and anger. As he exited the castle, the cold night air hit him like a wave. He felt drained, the weight of the encounter with Asmodeus pressing heavily on his shoulders. He stopped just beyond the gates, taking a deep breath to steady himself.

"Are you alright, Kane?" Blaze's voice broke the silence.

Aleister turned to see the demon hunter leaning casually against a tree, his tattoos glowing faintly in the darkness. Despite his relaxed posture, there was a sharpness in Blaze's eyes—a readiness to act if needed.

"You followed me," Aleister said, his tone more surprised than accusatory.

"Of course I did. You think I'd let you wander into a place like that alone? Someone's gotta keep you alive."

"You heard him, didn't you? Asmodeus. He said I can't kill him."

Blaze pushed off the tree and walked over.

"He's right. You can't kill him. But you don't need to."

"What are you talking about?"

Blaze placed a hand on Aleister's shoulder.

"You're looking at this the wrong way. This isn't about killing Asmodeus—it's about banishing him. Sending him and his minions back to the pit where they belong."

"And you think that's enough?"

"It's more than enough," Blaze said. "You send him back, you weaken his hold on this realm. You protect the people he's trying to destroy. That's the win, Kane. And don't let him tell you otherwise."

"He wants me to fail?"

"Exactly. That's why he's trying to mess with your head. Don't let him."

For a moment, Aleister said nothing. Then he straightened, gripping the staff with renewed determination. "Alright. Let's get back to camp."

Blaze smirked. "That's the spirit."

The forest seemed quieter than usual as Aleister and Blaze made their way back to camp. The night air felt heavier, charged with the echoes of Aleister's encounter with Asmodeus. Blaze walked a step ahead, his glowing tattoos dimming now that they were away from the castle.

"You're awfully quiet, Kane," Blaze said, breaking the silence. "Usually, you've got a lot more to say after something like that."

"Just trying to process. Everything he said... it got to me."

Blaze stopped.

"That's exactly what he wanted. Don't let him get in your head. Asmodeus thrives on fear and doubt. The second you give in to it, you're playing his game."

"Easier said than done."

"That's why you've got me around—to remind you that you don't have to carry it all alone."

They continued walking, the distant glow of the campfire finally coming into view. As they approached, Aleister felt a tiny bit of guilt for leaving the others without explanation. Victoria and Damian were seated by the fire, their heads snapping up the moment the two men emerged from the darkness.

"About time you came back," Damian said, though there was more relief than irritation in his voice. "What happened?"

Victoria stood.

"We were about to come looking for you."

Aleister hesitated, unsure of how much to share. "I... needed some time to clear my head. Blaze found me before I got into too much trouble."

Damian raised an eyebrow. "You, in trouble? Never."

"Let's just say the big guy had a chat with someone he wasn't prepared for." Blaze said.

"Asmodeus?" Victoria Asked.

Aleister nodded, sitting down heavily by the fire. "He's toying with us and with me. He knows we're getting close to something important, and he wants to stop me at all costs."

Victoria sat beside him.

"Then that means we're on the right track. If he's this desperate to break you, Aleister, it's because he knows you're a threat."

Aleister gazed into the fire, the flickering flames reflecting the turmoil in his mind.

"He said I can't kill him. That this whole quest is pointless."

Victoria placed a hand on his arm, her touch grounding him.

"You may not be able to kill him, but you can stop him. And that's what matters."

The group fell into a contemplative silence, the fire crackling softly as they each processed the weight of their mission. After a few moments, Damian broke the quiet with a low whistle.

"So," he said, leaning back against the log. "Anyone else feel like we're marching straight into a death trap?"

Blaze chuckled, though it lacked his usual humor.

"Wouldn't be the first time."

Chapter 15

THE LIBRARY OF SHADOWS

As dawn began to break, the group gathered their belongings and prepared to continue their journey. The faint light of the rising sun painted the forest in shades of gold and green, a stark contrast to the oppressive darkness they'd faced the night before.

Blaze unrolled the map they'd been using and traced their route.

"The Library of Shadows is still a couple of days away. But the closer we get, the harder it's going to be to stay under the radar."

"The Shadow Knights won't give up. They'll be waiting for us." Victoria said.

Damian yawned and started to stretch. "So, what's the plan? Fight our way through or sneak past?"

Blaze tapped the map thoughtfully.

"Sneaking past would be ideal, but with how persistent they've been, I doubt we'll avoid them completely."

The forest seemed to hold its breath as the group pressed forward, their footsteps muffled by the soft earth. The morning light filtered through the dense canopy above, but it offered little comfort. The air was thick with tension, the weight of their mission pressing heavily on them all.

Blaze led the way, the map in one hand and a small compass in the other. His tattoos pulsed. A subtle reminder of the protective spells woven into his flesh. Victoria walked beside him, her sword resting against her shoulder, ever vigilant. Aleister and Damian followed closely.

"Anyone else feel like we're being watched?" Damian muttered.

Blaze glanced over his shoulder. "We probably are. The Shadow Knights aren't exactly subtle when they're tracking someone."

"How much further until we reach the Library of Shadows?" Aleister asked.

Blaze consulted the map again.

"If we keep up this pace, we'll reach the outer perimeter by nightfall. But getting in won't be as simple as just walking up to the door."

"What kind of obstacles are we looking at?" Victoria asked.

Blaze hesitated, his gaze lingering on the map.

"The library is protected by ancient wards—powerful magic designed to keep out anyone unworthy. We'll need to pass a series of trials to prove we're worthy of entering."

Damian groaned. "Great. I love a good trial by death."

"What kind of trials?" Aleister asked.

"Could be anything. Physical, mental, spiritual. The library's magic is unpredictable. It tests what it needs to, and it doesn't play fair."

As the day wore on, the forest grew darker, the trees twisting into unnatural shapes. The air grew colder, and the faint sound of whispers seemed to drift through the shadows. Aleister couldn't tell if the whispers were real or a product of his imagination, but they set his nerves on edge.

Blaze suddenly stopped, holding up a hand.

"Wait."

The group froze, their eyes scanning the dense undergrowth around them. The whispers grew louder, and the air seemed to vibrate with an unseen energy.

"What is it?" Victoria asked, her voice low.

Blaze muttered an incantation under his breath.

"Something's close. Something... old."

Damian drew his blade, his usual bravado replaced with caution.

"Any chance it's friendly?"

"No, this one wants to do us harm." Blaze said.

The whispers echoed into a deafening roar as the ground beneath them trembled. A massive fissure split the earth ahead, and from the darkness emerged a figure cloaked in shadow. Its form was indistinct, shifting like smoke, but its presence was undeniable.

"A Sentinel," Blaze said. "The library's first line of defense."

The shadowy figure loomed before them; its glowing red eyes fixed on the group. It spoke in a deep, resonant voice that seemed to echo within their very souls.

"Who dares approach the Library of Shadows?" the Sentinel asked.

Aleister stepped forward.

"We seek the knowledge within. We mean no harm."

"The library does not grant its secrets lightly. Only those who prove themselves may enter."

Blaze glanced at the others.

"Here we go."

The Sentinel raised a hand, and the forest around them seemed to dissolve into darkness. The ground shifted beneath their feet, and when the light returned, they found themselves standing in a vast, featureless expanse.

"What the hell just happened?" Damian asked, his blade at the ready.

"The first trial," Blaze said. "Stay alert."

The Sentinel's voice echoed around them.

"To proceed, you must confront the shadows within. Reveal your greatest fear or be consumed by it."

Aleister felt a cold chill as the air around them grew heavy. Shadows began to coalesce in front of each of them, taking on familiar shapes and forms. Aleister watched as a figure stepped forward, its features identical to his own.

The Shadow Aleister smiled, its expression cold and mocking.

"You can't save her, you know. No matter how hard you try, you'll always fail."

Aleister's heart was pounding relentlessly.

"You're wrong."

The Shadow laughed, the sound made his hairs stand on end.

"Am I? You couldn't save your father. You couldn't save Mary. And you won't save anyone else!"

Aleister stood his ground. "I may have failed before, but I won't stop fighting. I won't let fear control me."

The Shadow's smile faded, and it began to dissolve into smoke. Aleister felt a surge of relief, but the weight of the trial was far from over.

Victoria, Blaze, and Damian each faced their own shadows, their struggles playing out in silence. The Sentinel watched impassively, its red eyes glowing faintly as it observed their progress.

One by one, the shadows faded, leaving the group standing in the empty expanse once more. The Sentinel's voice echoed around them.

"You have passed the first trial. But the path ahead remains treacherous. Proceed, if you dare."

The ground shifted again, and the group found themselves back in the forest. The Sentinel had vanished, but its presence still lingered.

Blaze let out a shaky breath.

"That was... unpleasant."

Damian sheathed his blade. "Speak for yourself. I kind of liked it."

"Are you alright?" Victoria asked.

Aleister nodded. "Let's keep moving. We're not done yet."

The group pressed forward, the forest around them eerily silent, as if the trees themselves watched their every move. Aleister led the way, his encounter with his own shadow still echoing in his mind. Yet, he had resolved not to let it break him. Mary was out there, and he would find a way to save her.

What's next? Trial by fire? A horde of demons? Maybe a talking riddle monster?" Blaze said.

"I'd say don't tempt fate, but I have a feeling we're in for worse." Victoria said.

Damian cracked his knuckles. "I say let them throw whatever they want at us. I haven't had a good fight in hours."

Aleister's focus was locked on what lay ahead. As the trees began to thin, they revealed a landscape unlike anything he had ever seen before. Rising from the earth was an immense stone structure, stretching endlessly in both directions—massive black walls carved with ancient runes, pulsing with a faint, eerie glow. The structure twisted and coiled like a living thing, forming a labyrinth of towering corridors. The air crackled with arcane energy, an invisible pressure settling over them.

"The Library of Shadows," Blaze murmured, awed despite himself.

Aleister stepped closer, running his fingers over the stone. The energy pulsing beneath the surface sent chills up his spine.

"It's alive."

Victoria placed a hand on the wall. "Not just alive sentient."

"Let me guess. Another trial?" Blaze commented sarcastically.

As if in response, the walls groaned and shifted. A deep, resonant voice spoke from nowhere and everywhere at once.

"Knowledge is not freely given. It's earned. Prove your wisdom or be lost within these halls for eternity."

The walls rumbled, and a narrow passage opened before them.

"Of course. A maze. Why does it always have to be a maze?" Blaze remarked with his usual dry humor.

Aleister exchanged glances with Victoria and Blaze. There was no other way forward.

"Stay close," Aleister said. "And whatever happens, don't get separated."

They stepped inside, the passage sealing behind them with an ominous thud. The air inside the labyrinth was thick with dust and magic. The corridors twisted in ways that defied logic, leading them down impossible paths that looped back onto themselves. Shadows clung to the walls, whispering in languages Aleister didn't recognize.

Blaze ran his hand over the inscriptions.

"This isn't just a library—it's a prison."

"For what?" Victoria asked.

"For knowledge that was meant to be forgotten." Blaze said.

Aleister scanned the area with a little more urgency.

"Then we need to find what we came for before we end up part of the collection."

They pressed on, the only light coming from the staff and Blaze's glowing sigils. The whispers grew louder, the shadows shifting at the edges of their vision.

Then the path split into three.

"Of course," Damian muttered. "A choice."

The walls pulsed, and the disembodied voice spoke again.

"Three paths, three choices. Choose wisely or be lost within the abyss."

Aleister studied the paths. One led into total darkness. The second flickered with faint, shifting lights. The third was lined with doors—hundreds of them.

"We don't have time for riddles," Victoria said.

Aleister closed his eyes, focusing on the staff's glow.

"The answer is in the journals. We need to find them."

Blaze turned toward the path with doors.

"Libraries have archives. If the journals are here, they're locked away. This is our best bet."

Damian exhaled. "I swear, if one of those doors leads to a death trap, I'm blaming you."

Blaze grinned. "Wouldn't be the first time."

They chose the path of doors and stepped forward, the corridor shifting behind them, sealing their fate. The hallway stretched endlessly, lined with ancient doors, each marked with strange sigils.

Aleister reached for one, but before he could touch it, the sigil glowed red-hot, and the door slammed open on its own. A powerful gust of wind roared out, nearly knocking them off their feet.

From the darkness within, a figure stepped forward—a ghostly librarian draped in black robes, its hollow eyes glowing faintly.

"You seek knowledge," it intoned. "But knowledge has a cost."

The figure extended a skeletal hand, pointing at Aleister.

"Prove your worth, seeker of truth. Answer correctly, and you may proceed. Answer falsely, and your soul will remain here... forever."

Aleister's pulse quickened. He had prepared for battles, ambushes, even demons—but riddles?

Blaze patted him on the shoulder. "No pressure."

The librarian's hollow voice filled the chamber.

"I have no beginning, yet I end all things. I am silent as the grave, yet in my presence, all tremble. None can escape me, though many seek to delay me. What am I?"

Aleister swallowed hard. The others stayed silent, letting him answer.

His mind raced. No beginning but ends all things. Silent, but feared.

"...Death," he said.

The librarian tilted its head. Then, slowly, it nodded.

"You may pass."

The door creaked open, revealing a massive chamber beyond.

And at the center of the room, resting on a pedestal, was a weathered book bound in dark leather.

One of *The Lost Journals of Doctor Crowe.*

Aleister stepped forward, his hands trembling as he reached for the journal. The air around it pulsed with power. The moment his fingers brushed the cover, a surge of memories flooded his mind—visions of Father Crowe, of battles fought long before his time. The journal was more than just a record. It was a legacy.

As he opened it, the first words on the page sent a chill down his spine.

"To those who seek the Staff of Infinite Light—know this: The power you wield is only half the battle. Without the key, the staff is nothing."

Aleister's blood ran cold. The key. The missing piece.

Blaze peered over his shoulder.

"What does it mean?"

Aleister turned to the group, his face deep in thought.

"The staff alone isn't enough. We need something more."

"Damian groaned. "You mean we came all this way, fought through hell, and we still don't have what we need?"

Aleister closed the journal. "No. But we have the knowledge to find it."

"Then we move. Before something else in this place decides we don't belong here." Victoria said.

As they turned to leave, the shadows stirred once more. The library wasn't done with them yet.

Chapter 16

THE PRICE OF KNOWING

The moment Aleister closed the journal, the entire chamber trembled. A low, guttural hum reverberated through the walls, and the air thickened with unseen energy.

"We need to move," Victoria said.

"Yeah, I don't think the library wants us taking this book." Blaze said as his tattoos began to flare.

Aleister tucked the journal under his arm as he scanned the room. The way they had entered was gone—vanished into the shifting stone. In its place, the walls contorted, forming an intricate maze of twisting corridors. The whispering shadows that had lurked in the periphery now swirled into tangible forms—faceless figures with hollow eyes, their limbs elongated and jagged. The library had sent its guardians.

"Fantastic. We're stealing from a sentient labyrinth. This just keeps getting better." Damian said as he readied his blade.

One of the shadowy figures lunged. Victoria swung her blade, cleaving it in two. Instead of dying, the figure splintered into more wraith like forms, each slithering forward like living smoke.

"They don't die!" she warned.

"Then we run!" Blaze exclaimed.

The ground shifted beneath them, threatening to split apart. Aleister turned sharply, scanning for any exit. His gaze locked onto a spiraling staircase in the far corner of the room, leading up into the dark.

"There!" he shouted, already moving.

The others followed, cutting through the shifting shadows as they ran. The library groaned, the walls twisting, trying to close them in. The stairway spiraled upward, narrow and uneven. The higher they climbed, the stronger the resistance. Winds howled through the corridors; spectral figures clawed at their arms. Aleister focused on the staff, letting its light push the darkness back.

"We're almost there!"

Blaze reached the top first, slamming his shoulder into a heavy wooden door. It didn't budge.

"It's locked!"

Aleister pushed forward, pressing his hand to the center of the door. The *Staff of Infinite Light* pulsed, reacting to the ancient magic. A voice echoed in his mind.

"Knowledge stolen is knowledge lost. Knowledge earned is knowledge kept."

He felt the journal thrum in his grip. The price for their exit had to be paid. Without hesitation, he tore a page from the journal, the parchment crumbling to dust in his hands. The door groaned in response, its ancient mechanism unlocking with a deep thud.

"It worked! Go!" Aleister shouted.

The group burst through the door, stumbling onto cold, solid ground. The moment the last of them passed through, the entrance behind them slammed shut, sealing the Library of Shadows once more.

Silence.

The wind howled through the desolate landscape before them. They were standing on the edge of a steep ravine, the jagged cliffs stretching endlessly into the darkness.

Blaze doubled over, catching his breath.

"Well... that was awful."

Damian sheathed his blade. "Agreed."

"What the hell was that about? Why did the library let us go?" Victoria asked.

Aleister lifted the journal, his fingers still tingling from the magic.

"It took a price. A piece of knowledge in exchange for our escape."

"And what exactly did we lose?" Blaze asked.

Aleister opened the book, flipping through the pages. His stomach dropped. An entire passage was missing. It had been about the *key*. Victoria cursed under her breath.

"The library erased it!"

"We have part of the answer... but not all of it." Aleister said.

"So, what now?" Damian asked.

Aleister looked out over the ravine. Somewhere out there, the missing piece of their puzzle still waited to be found.

"All we can do is keep going," he said. "We find the key."

Behind them, the whispers of the library faded into the wind, but its presence lingered—a silent reminder that knowledge was never given freely.

The wind howled through the ravine, carrying with it the eerie whispers of the Library of Shadows, though the place itself had vanished behind them. Aleister stared at the journal in his hands, frustration knotting his stomach. The missing passage—it was the key, the answer they had fought so hard to find, and now it was gone.

Victoria stepped beside Blaze, her golden hair whipping in the wind. "We're missing something. The library wouldn't have erased it completely."

Blaze scoffed, pacing near the cliff's edge.

"Oh yeah? You want to go back inside and ask nicely for a do-over?"

Damian ran a hand through his dark hair, studying the vast ravine before them.

"Arguing isn't going to get us across. Unless one of you has a bridge hidden in your pocket, we should focus on finding a way forward."

Aleister closed the journal, forcing himself to push aside the loss for now. He turned his attention to the gorge ahead. The ravine stretched for miles, an endless chasm of jagged rock and mist. Far below, a river of black water churned, the sound barely reaching their ears. The other side was shrouded in thick fog, obscuring whatever lay beyond.

Blaze crouched, running his fingers through the dirt.

"There's something unnatural about this place."

Victoria nodded. "I can feel it too. This isn't just a ravine—it's a boundary."

"A boundary between what?" Aleister asked.

Damian studied the darkness below.

"Between worlds."

The weight of his words settled over them. Blaze's tattoos flared briefly as he muttered an incantation, testing the energy around them. He stood, dusting off his hands.

"There's magic here. Old magic. This place is meant to keep something in—or keep us out."

Victoria scanned the area, then her gaze landed on a series of ancient pillars protruding from the cliffside, half-buried in the earth. Runes were etched into the stone, barely visible beneath centuries of wear.

"There," she said. "That's a crossing point."

Aleister approached the first pillar, brushing dirt away from the runes.

"It's a summoning inscription. A bridge should be here."

Blaze smirked. "Great. All we must do is summon an ancient bridge in a cursed ravine between worlds. Should be easy."

"You're the spell guy, Blaze. Get to it." Damian said in his usual sarcastic manor.

Blaze rolled his eyes but crouched beside Aleister, examining the runes. "I'll need time. This kind of magic is... tricky."

"Then we hold the line until you're done."

Victoria unsheathed her sword. "Agreed."

As Blaze began his incantation, the air around them grew colder. The runes pulsed with a dim, eerie light, responding to the ancient magic being awakened. The ground trembled, and a low growl rumbled through the mist below. Something was waking up.

Dark shapes slithered through the mist, rising from the depths of the gorge. Eyes like burning coals glowed in the darkness, and the air filled with the sound of rustling wings.

Damian's grip on his weapon tightened. "Tell me that's just the wind."

"They were waiting." Aleister said.

The mist parted, revealing monstrous creatures—twisted forms with elongated limbs and gaping maws filled with jagged teeth. They moved like shadows, slipping between realities, their forms flickering between substance and smoke.

Victoria raised her sword. "We don't have time for this."

Blaze, still muttering his spell, hissed through gritted teeth. "I'm working as fast as I can!"

The creatures lunged. Aleister swung the staff, its light slicing through the nearest beast. It shrieked and dissolved into mist but more took its place. Damian moved with deadly precision, his blade flashing in the dim light, while Victoria held the line, striking down anything that got too close.

Blaze's chanting reached a crescendo. The runes flared, and suddenly, from the abyss below, a bridge of dark stone began to rise, stretching toward the other side.

"It's working!" Blaze shouted.

Aleister glanced back. The bridge was forming, but it wasn't done yet. "We just need to hold them off a little longer!"

The creatures, sensing their time running out, became more aggressive. One leapt toward Blaze, claws outstretched. Aleister reacted instinctively, thrusting the staff forward. A blast of light erupted, incinerating the creature before it could reach him.

Blaze exhaled shakily. "You're gonna make me cry, Kane."

"Less talking, more running!" Damian shouted.

The bridge groaned under its own weight as it solidified, spanning the vast ravine.

"Move!" Aleister commanded.

They ran, their boots thudding against the ancient stone. The creatures howled in rage, the mist swirling violently around them. As they neared the halfway point, the bridge began to crack.

"It's not stable!" Blaze shouted.

Victoria grabbed Aleister's arm, shoving him forward.

"Run, damn it!"

They sprinted, the structure crumbling beneath them. Just as they reached the other side, the bridge gave way entirely, collapsing into the abyss below.

Aleister stumbled forward, catching himself on his knees. He turned back, watching as the creatures shrieked from the other side, trapped and unable to follow.

Damian panted, wiping blood from his face.

"Well. That really sucked."

Victoria straightened, sheathing her sword.

"At least we made it."

Blaze flopped onto his back, exhausted. "Next time, let's just find a normal bridge."

Aleister slowly stood, turning his gaze toward the foggy landscape ahead. "No turning back now."

The others followed his gaze. Beyond the mist, their next destination awaited.

Chapter 17

WHISPERS

The mist curled around them like ghostly tendrils, obscuring their surroundings in an eerie, shifting haze. Now that they had crossed the ravine, the landscape was completely unknown. The ground beneath their feet was damp and uneven, the air thick with an unnatural stillness.

Aleister extended the Staff in front of him, its faint glow cutting through the fog.

"Stay close," he warned.

Victoria walked beside him, eyes scanning the shadows for movement.

"I don't like this. It's too quiet."

Blaze rubbed his temples, his tattoos flickering faintly.

"There's something... wrong with this place. Like it's watching us."

"Great. More cursed terrain. Why can't these lost artifacts ever be hidden in a cozy little cottage?"

Aleister ignored the banter, his mind focused on the journal and the missing passage. *The key. They had to find it. But where?*

The mist shifted, and a whisper drifted through the air.

"...Aleister Kane..."

He froze.

The others stopped immediately, sensing the change in his posture.

"You heard that too, right?"

Damian swallowed hard.

"Yeah."

The whisper came again, soft and elongated, spoken by a voice that was neither male nor female, neither human nor entirely otherworldly.

"...Come... find me..."

Victoria stepped closer to Aleister.

"This could be a trap."

Blaze scoffed. "Could be? I'd bet my last silver dagger it is."

Damian was skeptical.

"If something's calling us, it means it wants us to come to it. Which means we have the advantage.

Aleister considered the words carefully. The whisper hadn't felt like Asmodeus, nor did it carry the same oppressive weight as the Shadow Knights. It was something else—something ancient. Something tied to the knowledge they sought. Taking a deep breath, Aleister turned toward the sound. The mist gradually thinned as they moved forward, revealing the outlines of ruined structures buried in the earth. Towering stone pillars jutted from the ground at odd angles, covered in deep cracks and intricate carvings that had long since been worn by time. The architecture was nothing like any of them had seen before ancient and alien, almost as if it didn't belong to this world. Aleister traced his fingers over one of the symbols. The moment his skin made contact, a pulse of energy rippled through the air.

The whisper returned. "...Closer..."

A faint glow appeared in the distance, flickering between the ruins like a dying ember.

"I hate this already." Damian said.

Victoria turned her attention on Aleister.

"You're leading this. What do you want to do?"

Aleister hesitated for only a moment. Then, he walked toward the glow. The others followed without question. As they stepped deeper into the ruins, the ground beneath them began to shift. Faint golden markings emerged along the cracked stone, illuminating a circular platform at the heart of the ruins. The glow they had been following hovered just above it—small, no larger than a candle flame, but pulsating with an undeniable power. The whisper came once more.

"The key was never lost... only hidden."

The flame swirled, then expanded into the shape of a robed figure—a translucent being with no discernible face, its body composed of pure golden light. Aleister recognized the energy. This was no demon. No ghost. It was a memory. A remnant of Doctor Crowe himself.

The glowing figure turned toward them, though it had no eyes to see.

"If you have found this place, then you are closer than I ever was," the voice said, echoing through the ruins. "I am Father Crowe. Or rather, what remains of me. If you seek the Staff of Infinite Light, know this: power alone is not enough."

Aleister stepped forward. "The key. We need it to unlock the staff's full strength."

"Yes. The key is not an object, but a bond—a union of forces. The Staff of Infinite Light can only reach its true power in the hands of one who is bound to both the Divine... and the Mortal."

Blaze crossed his arms. "Well, that's vague and unhelpful."

"Divine and Mortal? What does that even mean?" Victoria asked.

Aleister's mind raced. The staff was in his possession, but he had always assumed it was merely a tool to be wielded. Now, it seemed to be something more—something that required a deeper connection.

Father Crowe's form flickered, the remnants of his memory weakening.

"Time is short. The answer you seek lies where the war began. Where Heaven's first warriors stood against the darkness. Find it... before Asmodeus does."

With that, the light collapsed in on itself, leaving only darkness and silence.

The group stood in silence, absorbing what had just happened.

Damian ran a hand over his face. "I swear, I am so tired of riddles."

"The place where the war began? That could mean a hundred different things." Blaze said.

Victoria, however, looked deep in thought.

"Not necessarily." She turned to Aleister. "The war between Heaven and Hell has many battlefields, but only one true beginning."

Aleister met her gaze. "Eden."

Blaze let out a low whistle. "Oh, you've got to be kidding me."

"If the key is tied to the Staff of Infinite Light, then it has to be connected to the Tree of Life." Aleister said.

"And let me guess. No one knows where that is, either." Damian said.

"Actually... I might." Victoria said.

"Wait, what?" Blaze said slightly confused.

She gestured for them to follow.

"Come on. If we're going to find Eden, we have a long journey ahead of us."

The weight of their new objective settled over the group as they left the ruins behind, stepping into the unknown once more. The whispering presence of Father Crowe was gone, leaving only his cryptic message lingering in Aleister's mind.

"The answer you seek lies where the war began... Find it before Asmodeus does."

Victoria led the way, her posture tense with thought. Blaze, as usual, was the first to break the silence.

"So, Eden. Just to be clear, we're talking about *the* Eden, right? The Garden of Life, the place where all the bad blood between Heaven and Hell started?"

Aleister nodded. "That's what it sounds like."

"No offense, but it doesn't exactly show up on a map. Where are we supposed to start?" Damian asked.

"Eden isn't a place anymore." Victoria said. "Not in the way most people think. It existed once, but when Adam and Eve were cast out, the gates were sealed. The garden itself was... removed."

"Removed?" Blaze said. "You mean it just vanished?"

"No," Victoria said. "It was hidden. Guarded. The Tree of Life still exists, but only those deemed worthy can find it."

"And you know how to get there?" Aleister asked.

Victoria hesitated for only a moment before nodding.

"I know *who* to ask."

The journey took them northward, deeper into uncharted territory. The air grew colder, the landscape shifting from dense, mist-covered forests to barren hills of jagged stone. The very land seemed untouched by time.

They traveled for hours before Victoria finally stopped at the base of a towering cliffside. A winding path led upward, vanishing into the thick fog.

"This is where we find our answers," she said.

Aleister studied the rock face. "What's up there?"

"An old acquaintance." Victoria said. "A being older than time itself."

"Fantastic." Damian said with a huff. "Another ancient mystery person. Let me guess—he'll demand some impossible test before helping us?"

"Oh, I *hope* so." Blaze said with a grin. "Wouldn't be a proper adventure without one."

Victoria ignored them and started up the path. The group followed in silence, their footsteps echoing off the rock walls. As they climbed higher, a strange hum filled the air, an energy that made the hair on the back of Aleister's neck stand up. Then, at the summit, they found themselves standing before a massive archway carved into the mountain. Beyond it, an immense stone chamber stretched into darkness. At its center stood a lone figure, draped in tattered robes of deep crimson. The figure turned, and two piercing golden eyes locked onto them.

"Ah," the being murmured, its voice like a whisper carried on the wind. "It has been a long time since mortals sought the path to Eden."

"We need your help, Keeper." Victoria said.

Aleister exchanged a glance with Blaze. "Keeper?" he murmured.

Blaze leaned in. "I was hoping for something more ominous, but alright."

The Keeper studied them, his gaze lingering on Aleister and the Staff of Infinite Light.

"You hold a great power, but you lack the wisdom to wield it fully," he said. "You seek the key to the staff, but do you even understand what it is you truly seek?"

Aleister hesitated before answering. "Maybe not, but that's why we're here."

The Keeper tilted his head. "And what would you do with such power?"

"Defeat Asmodeus and end this war."

The Keeper chuckled, the sound like dry leaves in the wind. "Such simple words. Such mortal certainty."

"Are you gonna help us or just waste our time?" Damian said.

"You are bold, vampire. But your impatience will be your downfall."

"So, I take it there's a catch?" Blaze said.

"The path to Eden is not traveled with feet, but with will. To find it, you must face the truth that you fear most."

Aleister's stomach twisted. He had already faced his fear in the Library of Shadows, yet something told him this was different.

Victoria took a breath. "We're ready."

The Keeper extended a hand. "Then step forward, and let the past reveal the path."

The moment they did, the world around them dissolved into darkness.

Aleister blinked, his heart pounding. He was no longer in the mountain chamber.

He was... *home.*

His study, the fire crackling beside him, the scent of old books filling the air. But something was *wrong.* Across the room, a figure sat in the chair opposite him.

Himself.

Aleister's mirror image stared at him, eyes filled with a cold, knowing sorrow.

"You think revenge will save her," his doppelgänger said, voice eerily calm. "You think it will bring peace?"

His twin leaned forward. "And when you kill him? When Asmodeus falls? Will that bring Mary back? Will it undo what was done?"

Aleister hesitated.

The mirror image smiled sadly. "You already know the answer."

"No. No, I can't stop now."

"You let her go once," his twin continued. "Not because of Asmodeus. Not because of demons. But because you chose this war over her. And now? Now you tell yourself you're fighting for her."

"I am," Aleister growled.

The image shook his head. "No. You're fighting because you don't know who you are without this war."

The words cut deep. Aleister wanted to refute them, to deny them. But deep inside, he knew. Mary had begged him to stop. She had pleaded for him to leave this life behind. And he hadn't listened. The revenge had become *everything.*

The mirror image stood, stepping closer. "You will never defeat Asmodeus with hatred alone. The *key* you seek... is love."

Aleister gasped as a rush of light overwhelmed his senses.

And then—

He was back.

The chamber reformed around them, and Aleister staggered back, his breath coming in sharp, uneven gasps.

The Keeper watched him closely. "You have seen the truth."

Aleister swallowed hard. His hands were shaking. "The key... isn't a thing."

The Keeper nodded. "It is a bond. The staff requires both light and humanity to reach its full strength. If you wish to defeat Asmodeus, you must embrace what you have spent your life running from."

"Well, that's poetic." Blaze said.

"So, we've been looking for an object when the answer was inside Aleister all along?" Damian asked.

Victoria gave Aleister a long look. "Not just inside him. The staff will only respond when wielded with *love*. It's not just about power—it's about purpose."

All this time, he had thought strength came from vengeance. But now? Now he realized... *it was love that gave him strength all along.*

The Keeper turned his gaze to the rest of the group.

"The path to Eden is not a road of conquest. It is a trial of the soul. If you continue forward, you must understand this—power is not given freely. It is a burden, and if wielded with darkness in your heart, it will destroy you."

Silence hung in the air.

Aleister closed his eyes. He didn't want to hear it, but deep down, he knew the Keeper spoke the truth.

Blaze, arms crossed, finally broke the tension. "So... are you letting us through or what?"

The Keeper regarded him for a long moment before extending his hand.

A doorway of golden light appeared at the far end of the chamber.

"The path is open," The Keeper said. "Go forth and may the Light guide you."

The group stepped through the portal, emerging into a vast and desolate expanse. The skies above were no longer blue, but an eerie silver-gray. The land stretched before them, barren and unforgiving, with towering mountains in the distance.

Victoria looked around. "Is this... Eden?"

"No," Aleister said. "Not yet."

Blaze exhaled. "Great. More walking."

Damian studied the surroundings with sharp eyes. "We're not alone." Aleister followed his gaze.

In the distance, along the ridge of the mountains, dark figures stood watching.

"Well, that's unsettling." Blaze said.

"Who are they?" Victoria asked.

Aleister felt the weight of the Keeper's words still pressing on him. Then he realized—these were not demons. These were something else.

A voice carried over the wind.

"Turn back."

Chapter 18

THE PATH TO EDEN

The wind howled through the desolate landscape, carrying with it an eerie stillness that set Aleister's nerves on edge. The figures on the ridge stood unmoving, their dark silhouettes blending with the jagged peaks behind them. There was no demonic presence, no corrupting energy in the air—these were not creatures of Hell. They were men. And yet, Aleister felt something just as dangerous radiating from them—a conviction that was absolute, unwavering.

"Turn back."

The voice was deep, commanding, and filled with warning.

Aleister stepped forward, gripping the staff.

"Who are you?" he called out.

The figures did not move.

Then, one of them descended from the ridge, his dark cloak billowing as he approached with measured, deliberate steps. As he came into view, Aleister took in his features—weathered yet strong, his piercing gray eyes carrying the weight of a thousand battles. He wore dark leather armor

195

reinforced with steel plating, and an insignia was emblazoned on his chest: a silver veil crossed by a sword.

"My name is Solomon," the man announced. "Guardian of the Veil."

Aleister had heard the name before—spoken in whispers among occult scholars and buried within forbidden texts. The Guardians of the Veil were a secretive order, their origins shrouded in mystery. Some believed them to be ancient warriors tasked with keeping divine artifacts hidden from mortal hands. Others claimed they were zealots, willing to kill to prevent any man from wielding power beyond his station.

Solomon's gaze swept over them, landing on the staff in Aleister's hands. His lips tightened.

"You have gone too far," he said. "The staff does not belong to you."

"What?! Blaze said angerly. "We just went through a hell storm of banshees, demons, and crypt-dwelling witches for this thing, and now you're telling us we're not allowed to use it?"

Solomon's face did not waver. "Power corrupts," he said. "Always."

"We don't seek to abuse the staff," Victoria said firmly. "We're trying to stop Asmodeus. If we don't, he'll bring Hell to this world."

"That war is not yours to fight." The warrior said.

"It *became* my fight the moment Asmodeus took my wife." Aleister said. "The moment demons tore my father apart in front of me."

Solomon regarded him in silence, then exhaled.

"I have seen many men like you, Aleister Kane. Men who believed they could wield holy power, that they alone could turn the tide of war."

He took a slow step forward, lowering his voice. "And every one of them fell to the same fate. Corruption. Despair. Madness."

"You think I'll become like them?" Aleister asked.

"I know you will," Solomon answered. "Because the staff is not meant for human hands."

A silence stretched between them.

"I'm not turning back." Aleister said.

Solomon sighed. "Then we have no choice."

At his signal, more figures emerged from the ridges—dozens of them, warriors clad in dark armor, each bearing weapons forged in celestial fire. They moved with precision, surrounding Aleister and his companions with practiced ease.

Damian cursed under his breath. "Oh, this just keeps getting better."

Blaze rolled his shoulders. "Alright, so how are we playing this?" He cracked his knuckles. "Are we fighting or running?"

Aleister's pulse pounded in his ears. His first instinct was to fight—he wasn't about to let anyone take the staff from him. But these weren't demons. They were men who *believed* they were doing the right thing. Was he truly prepared to kill them? Before he could decide, Solomon raised his blade.

"Seize them!"

The Guardians moved swiftly, their attacks precise and calculated. Victoria met the first warrior head-on, her blade clashing against his in a fierce exchange of strikes. Damian danced through the chaos, his twin daggers flashing as he deflected incoming blows. Blaze, ever the unconventional fighter, ducked and weaved through the battlefield, using defensive spells to keep the warriors at bay. Aleister found himself surrounded. Two Guardians lunged toward him, their blades aiming for his hands—to disarm him, not kill. He reacted instinctively, swinging the Staff of Infinite Light. A wave of radiant energy pulsed outward, sending the warriors tumbling back. But they did not stay down. Aleister hesitated. He didn't want to kill them. He wasn't here to fight humans. Then he saw Solomon striding toward him, eyes locked on the staff. Aleister braced himself.

Solomon attacked.

Their weapons met in a clash of power—Solomon's blade, forged from divine steel, struck the staff with force that sent shockwaves through the battlefield. Aleister staggered back, his arms vibrating from the impact.

"You are unworthy!" Solomon snarled, pressing forward.

Aleister gritted his teeth. "Then come and take it!"

He thrust the staff forward, releasing a burst of divine light—but Solomon anticipated it, twisting his blade in a defensive arc, absorbing the energy with his own celestial aura. This wasn't just any warrior. Solomon knew how to counter the staff.

Aleister's mind raced. They couldn't keep this up forever. They had to find a way to escape. Then—an idea struck him.

"Blaze!" Aleister shouted over the clash of battle. "Create a decoy!"

Blaze grinned, ducking under a Guardian's sword. "You got it!"

He slammed his palms against the ground, chanting an incantation. A pulse of green energy spread outward, and suddenly—three identical copies of Aleister, Victoria, and Damian appeared, running in different directions.

The Guardians hesitated.

Solomon's eyes flickered with uncertainty.

"After them!" he ordered.

The warriors took the bait, chasing after the illusions. Aleister didn't waste a second.

"Go!" he barked.

The real group darted toward a gap in the ridges, moving fast before the Guardians realized the deception.

They ran, the wind howling around them.

And then—they were free.

By nightfall, they had put enough distance between themselves and the Guardians to finally stop. The group gathered around a small fire, the tension from the battle still thick in the air. Aleister stared into the flames, his mind racing.

Victoria sat beside him. "You did the right thing," she said. "We didn't need to kill them."

Aleister exhaled. "I know."

But something about Solomon's words lingered in his mind. *Power corrupts. Always.*

Blaze, stretching his sore arms, let out a tired chuckle. "Nothing like being hunted by both demons *and* humans."

"Still, I'm curious... why do they fear the staff so much?" Damian asked.

Victoria answered first. "Because they know the truth. The staff isn't just a weapon. It's a responsibility."

"And if I fail... they might be right to fear it." Aleister said.

The fire crackled, casting flickering shadows across the camp. Aleister sat with the Staff resting across his lap, his fingers absently running over the smooth surface. But his attention wasn't on the staff. It was on Blaze. More specifically, on the tattoo that seemed to pulse faintly in the firelight—a strange, shifting symbol on Blaze's forearm, one that Aleister could have sworn had not been there before.

The ink shimmered like silver under the glow of the flames, its shape twisting in ways that defied logic. It was alive, or at least, something more than mere ink.

Aleister narrowed his eyes. "Blaze?"

Blaze, who had been lazily sipping from a flask, tilted his head.

"Hmm?"

Aleister gestured toward the strange marking. "That symbol on your arm. It's... moving."

Blaze tensed. His fingers instinctively curled into a fist, obscuring part of the tattoo as if to shield it from view.

Victoria and Damian turned their heads toward him, drawn in by Aleister's words. Aleister wasn't letting this go.

"It's more than ink, isn't it?"

Blaze locked eyes with him. For a long moment, it looked as if he might deflect, brush it off with one of his usual quips. But something in Aleister's gaze stopped him. A flicker of resignation passed over Blaze's face. He took another swig from his flask before speaking, his voice quieter than usual.

"You ever hear about the Rites of the Forsaken?" he asked.

The name was familiar whispered in old, forbidden texts. A ritual, known only to those desperate enough to face the horrors of Hell itself.

Victoria's expression darkened. "You mean the ritual that binds a human to the knowledge of demons?"

Blaze let out a humorless chuckle. "That'd be the one."

"Are you saying... you went through it?" Damain asked.

Blaze rolled up his sleeve, exposing more of the tattoos—intricate sigils, ancient symbols of both protection and power. He flexed his fingers, and for a moment, the ink shimmered, as if responding to something unseen.

Aleister could feel it. Magic. Old magic.

"I didn't just go through it," Blaze said. "I survived it."

Blaze's voice dropped lower as he stared into the fire.

"I was a kid when I saw my first demon," he said. "And I wasn't ready for it." He exhaled sharply, shaking his head. "My family was slaughtered in front of me. I was the only one left. And I should have died too, but something—someone—saved me."

Aleister leaned forward. "Who?"

"His name was Ezra Blackthorne. He was a demon slayer. The best I'd ever seen." Blaze said.

"I've heard of him. He vanished years ago." Victoria said.

Blaze nodded. "Yeah. He found me, barely alive, half-buried under the rubble of my burning home. And instead of walking away, he took me in. Trained me."

Aleister felt a strange pull at those words. The way Blaze spoke—it wasn't just gratitude. There was something deeper there.

"He told me something I've never forgotten: 'If you want to fight monsters, you must understand them first. So," Blaze continued, "he told me about the Rites of the Forsaken. A forbidden ritual that could carve the knowledge of demons into human flesh, binding their secrets to your very soul."

Victoria's eyes widened. "And you... chose to undergo it?"

Blaze nodded slowly. "It wasn't a choice I made lightly. But after what happened to my family, I *needed* an edge. So, Ezra led me to an old temple, deep in the ruins of an ancient city, where the ritual could be performed."

Aleister could barely believe what he was hearing. The Rites were dangerous—only a handful had ever attempted them, and even fewer survived.

"And these markings... they aren't just knowledge, are they?" Aleister asked.

"No. They're a map." Blaze said.

Aleister felt a chill run down his spine. "A map to what?"

Blaze looked at him, his expression unreadable.

"To the Well of Light."

The fire crackled.

"You mean... the very place where the Staff of Infinite Light must return?"

Blaze nodded. "Yes. The Well isn't just a power source—it's a seal. A prison, of sorts. And my markings? They don't just lead to it. They explain its purpose."

Aleister processed this information. The staff only held power for a limited time before it needed to return to the Well to recharge. But if Blaze's markings explained the Well's true purpose...It meant that the staff was never meant to be used as a permanent weapon.

"And you're just now telling us this?" Aleister said.

"Look, it's not like I was hiding it. I just never thought it mattered until now."

Victoria crossed her arms. "It matters."

Blaze ran a hand through his hair. "Yeah, well. That's why I don't talk about it much."

Aleister studied Blaze's markings. They weren't just symbols of power. They were warnings. Instructions. And if they contained the true purpose of the Well of Light, then that meant they still didn't understand everything about what they were dealing with.

Aleister finally leaned back, staring into the fire.

"So, what do we do now?"

"Simple. We keep going."

Chapter 19

DEMON WHISPERS

The night was quiet. Too quiet. Aleister lay on the cold earth, his body exhausted but his mind restless. The fire had died down, leaving only glowing embers, and the others had already drifted into uneasy sleep. His thoughts swirled like a storm—Blaze's revelation about his tattoos, the relentless pursuit of the Shadow Knights, and the warnings from the Guardians of the Veil. The Staff rested beside him, its presence a constant weight in his mind.

Then, without warning, the world around him dissolved. The embers, the cold wind, the murmured breaths of his companions—all of it vanished into a suffocating blackness.

Aleister was no longer in camp.

He stood in a ruined cathedral, its once-grand walls now fractured and overtaken by creeping vines. Pale moonlight filtered through shattered stained glass, casting eerie patterns across the cracked stone floor. The air was thick with dust and decay, and in the distance, the sound of whispering voices echoed. He had been here before. Or at least, it felt that way. Footsteps echoed ahead. Aleister turned his gaze toward the grand altar at the cathedral's center. A figure knelt before it—a man cloaked in dark robes. His shoulders heavy with exhaustion.

Doctor Crowe.

Aleister had never seen the famed demon hunter in life, but every description he had read, every whispered legend, pointed to the man before him. Crowe's hands rested on something. A staff. Not just any staff.

The Staff of Infinite Light.

It pulsed with a divine glow, faint but unmistakable, its carved wooden form exuding a radiance that seemed at odds with the ruined darkness surrounding it.

"Doctor Crowe?" Aleister asked.

The man did not react. Instead, a new voice filled the space. Deep. Cold. Mocking.

"Do you wish to see how it all began, Aleister Kane?"

Aleister stiffened. He knew that voice. Asmodeus. The shadows at the edges of the cathedral writhed, pulling away from the walls like living things, forming into dark, watching figures. Their red eyes burned like embers, flickering with something cruel and ancient.

Crowe, unaware of Aleister's presence, slowly lifted his head. The doors to the cathedral burst open with a thunderous crash. A horde of demons poured in—twisted, monstrous things with blackened flesh and skeletal wings. Their snarls filled the cathedral, their hunger radiating from them in waves.

Crowe rose to his feet.

But then—a new presence entered. A towering figure stepped through the ruined doorway; his form wreathed in darkness. His eyes burned like two molten suns, and his long, clawed fingers dripped with black ichor. Asmodeus himself.

Aleister's jaw dropped as he saw his greatest enemy in full form. Crowe did not cower. Instead, he planted his feet, raising the Staff of Infinite Light before him. Its glow brightened, pulsing with raw, celestial power.

Asmodeus chuckled. "You think you can wield it?"

"I already have."

Without another word, he thrust the staff forward. A blast of divine energy erupted from its tip, engulfing the room in a blinding flash. The demons screamed as the holy light ripped through them, reducing them to little more than ash. The cathedral's broken walls shook, the very foundations groaning under the sheer force of it. But Asmodeus did not burn. He laughed. And then—he stepped through the light as if it were nothing but mist. Crowe barely had time to react before Asmodeus was upon him. The demon grabbed the staff, forcing it down with monstrous strength. Crowe gritted his teeth, struggling to hold his ground. But Asmodeus was too strong. In one brutal motion, he struck Crowe across the chest, sending him hurtling across the cathedral. He slammed into the stone floor, the staff rolling away from his grasp.

Aleister could feel the pain. As if some part of this dream was forcing him to experience it firsthand. Doctor Crowe gasped for breath, clutching his ribs. Asmodeus loomed over him, dark wings unfurling.

"You cannot kill me, mortal."

Doctor Crowe's gaze burned with defiance.

"I don't need to."

With his last bit of strength, Crowe clawed at the ground—tracing something in the dirt with his own blood. Asmodeus hesitated.

The symbols glowed. A massive seal erupted beneath them—golden chains of holy energy springing forth, binding Asmodeus where he stood. The demon snarled, his form flickering like smoke caught in a storm.

Crowe coughed, blood dripping from his lips.

"You won't have it."

With a final whisper of a prayer, he lifted the staff one last time and vanished—the weapon disappearing from the cathedral in a flash of light.

The last thing Aleister saw before the vision snapped—before he was yanked back into his body—was Asmodeus's furious, burning gaze.

"You think you are stronger than him, Aleister Kane?"

Aleister gasped, his eyes snapping open. The fire had burned to embers. The wind howled through the night. He sat up, his heart hammering in his chest. It had been a dream. But the scent of sulfur still clung to the air. And in his mind, Asmodeus's words lingered.

"You will fail, just as he did."

He wouldn't fail. No matter what it took. Aleister stood and stepped away from the camp, needing space to think. He walked a short distance, his boots crunching over dry leaves and stones, until he reached the edge of a cliff overlooking the valley below. The sky was still dark. The stars stretched across the heavens like distant watchers. Somewhere, in the vast unknown, Heaven and Hell continued their war.

"You will fail, just as he did."

Asmodeus's words echoed in his mind, seeping into his thoughts like poison. For the first time in a long time, he wasn't sure if he could win.

"You look like you've seen a ghost," a voice said behind him.

Aleister turned, his muscles tensing. It was Victoria. She stood just beyond the tree line, arms crossed over her chest, her golden hair catching the moonlight. She wore a knowing expression—the kind that told him she had been watching him longer than he realized.

Aleister sighed, turning back toward the valley.

"Not a ghost," he muttered. "A demon."

Victoria stepped up beside him, her presence calm, unwavering.

"A dream?"

Aleister nodded. "More like a vision."

She didn't ask questions right away. Instead, she let the silence settle between them, waiting for him to speak on his own terms. Aleister appreciated that about her.

"I saw Doctor Crowe," he admitted. "I saw him in the moment he first took possession of the staff."

Victoria glanced at him, intrigued. "And?"

Aleister hesitated. "And I saw him fail."

A flicker of something crossed Victoria's face, but she remained composed.

"Tell me what you saw."

Aleister recounted the vision—the ruined cathedral, the demons pouring in, Crowe's desperate attempt to fight back. He told her about Asmodeus, about how he walked through the divine light of the staff unscathed, as if it meant nothing to him.

"And that's why you're out here," she surmised. "Because you're afraid the staff won't be enough."

Aleister didn't answer right away. Then, quietly, he admitted, "I don't think it is."

Victoria studied him for a moment. "And yet, you haven't turned back."

Aleister let out a dry chuckle.

"Because if I do, my wife dies. The world dies. And I can't let that happen."

"Aleister," she said gently, "every warrior has doubts. Even the greatest of us."

"And how do you fight them?"

"By remembering what I fight for."

"Right now, all I have is a demon whispering in my ear, telling me I'll fail."

"Then make sure he's wrong."

Aleister held her gaze, the fire in her words rekindling something inside him.

By sunrise, the group was on the move again. Blaze led them through the winding trails, his knowledge of the land proving invaluable as they navigated treacherous terrain. Damian scouted ahead, his keen vampire senses picking up on dangers before they could become real threats. Victoria stayed close to Aleister. He knew it wasn't just coincidence. She was watching him. Making sure doubt hadn't consumed him. As they moved deeper into the wilderness, Blaze eventually halted at the mouth of a massive ravine.

"Well," he muttered, hands on his hips. "This is new."

The ravine stretched for miles, a gaping wound in the earth. There was no bridge, no clear path across—only the endless drop into fog and shadow below.

"How the hell do we get across?" Damian muttered.

"Guess it's time for some old magic." Blaze said.

"Meaning?" Aleister asked.

"Meaning we're about to wake something ancient."

Before anyone could question him, Blaze stepped forward, pressing his hands to the ground. His tattoos flared gold, pulsing with energy. He muttered something in an archaic language—words Aleister didn't recognize. And then—the earth trembled. A low groan rumbled through the air, and suddenly—stone began to rise. Piece by piece, an ancient bridge formed, stretching across the ravine as if it had always been there, hidden beneath time itself.

Aleister stared. "You could have done that this whole time?"

Blaze wiped sweat from his brow. "Nope. This only works when we're exactly where we need to be."

"And what if it hadn't worked?" Damian asked.

Blaze grinned. "Then we'd have a very long climb ahead of us."

"Let's move before it collapses." Victoria said.

One by one, they stepped onto the bridge, moving swiftly. But as they reached the halfway point—The fog below began to shift. Something moved beneath them. Something ancient. The air grew thick as Aleister stepped forward, his boots pressing against the ancient stone bridge Blaze had summoned.

The fog below swirled, moving in unnatural patterns, as if something was shifting beneath its dense veil. Aleister noticed something. The others noticed it too—a presence, vast and unseen, watching them from the depths below.

Victoria walked beside him, hand resting lightly on the hilt of her sword, her gaze sharp and alert. Damian moved silently; his unnatural senses tuned to whatever unseen horror lurked beneath them.

"I don't like this," Blaze muttered. "Not one damn bit."

"You sure this bridge is stable?" Aleister asked.

"Physically? Yeah, should hold. Spiritually? That's another story." Blaze said.

As if responding to his words, the bridge trembled beneath their feet. A deep, echoing groan sounded from below, resonating through the chasm like a beast stirring from slumber. And then... the whispering began. Low, ancient voices, rising from the fog in a language Aleister had only ever heard in his darkest studies. A tongue older than time.

"That's not the wind." Damain said.

Blaze's tattoos flared gold, reacting to the unseen force rising beneath them. Then came the first scream. It didn't belong to any of them. It came from the fog itself—a high-pitched, wailing shriek, followed by the sudden, violent emergence of shadowy figures clawing their way upward. Wraiths. Countless faceless, writhing spirits—creatures of suffering, bound to the abyss below. Their glowing white eyes locked onto the group as they ascended, their translucent, clawed hands reaching for any living soul to drag back into the depths.

Aleister's heart pounded. He'd seen these kinds of spirits before—souls that had been damned to an eternal prison. Blaze was the first to react. He slammed his hands together, chanting an incantation as his tattoos pulsed, forming a barrier of golden energy between them and the incoming wraiths.

The spirits howled as they slammed into the barrier, their forms sizzling against the light. But it wouldn't hold for long.

"We have to move!" Victoria shouted.

"We can't outrun them. We must fight." Aleister said.

With that, he raised the staff, its light blazing to life in his hands. The moment the divine energy pulsed outward, the wraiths recoiled, their shrieks becoming agonized screeches.

Damian unsheathed twin daggers, their silver edges glinting under the flickering light. "Let's make this quick."

The wraiths surged forward. Victoria was the first to strike, her blade singing as it sliced through the air, cutting through the ghostly bodies with divine-infused steel. The spirits wailed, dissipating into black mist.

Damian moved like a shadow, ducking and weaving between the wraiths, slashing through them with precision. Each strike sent another spirit screaming back into the void.

Aleister planted his feet, thrusting the staff forward, sending a pulse of pure radiant energy across the bridge. The blast hit the wraiths like a tidal wave, scattering them like dust in the wind. But there were too many.

"I can't hold this forever, Kane!" Blaze shouted.

"Then drop it and fight!" Aleister said.

Blaze let out an exasperated breath before releasing the barrier, allowing his tattoos to shift into combat glyphs. He slammed his hands together, and a ring of fire erupted around him, consuming any spirit that dared step too close. The battle raged, but for every wraith they destroyed, more seemed to rise.

And then...

The bridge shook violently. Something far worse was coming. The fog beneath them split apart as a colossal figure began to rise. A towering, serpentine form, its massive, hollow skull staring up at them from the abyss. It was wrapped in chains of dark iron, its jagged teeth gnashing as it emerged from the fog like a nightmare given form. Aleister could feel its power—a being older than most demons, something buried here for a reason

"That's not a wraith." Victoria said.

"Nope. That's a problem."

The creature let out a deep, rattling growl. And with a violent lunge, it slammed a clawed hand onto the bridge. The entire structure shuddered, cracks forming in the ancient stone.

"We either kill that thing, or we run." Blaze said.

"We can't kill something that big." Damian said trying to catch his breath.

"Fine. Then we run."

Victoria agreed. "Move!"

They turned and sprinted toward the other side of the bridge, the creature's roar shaking the very heavens as it pulled itself further from the abyss. The bridge groaned under its weight. It wasn't going to last much longer. The wraiths, still shrieking, swarmed behind them, their claws reaching for any exposed flesh. Aleister swung the staff backward, releasing a powerful wave of light, sending the spirits scattering once more. The creature lunged, slamming its massive claw into the bridge just behind them, shattering a large section of stone.

Blaze leaped forward, barely clearing the gap before the stone crumbled beneath his feet. Victoria wasn't far behind, gripping Damian's arm and pulling him across.

Aleister was the last one. The creature's glowing, empty eyes locked onto him. It lunged—a massive, skeletal hand reaching for him just as he leaped across the final gap. For a moment, he thought he wasn't going to make it. Then Victoria's hand caught his wrist. With a powerful yank, she dragged him onto solid ground, just as the bridge collapsed into the abyss behind them. The creature let out a furious roar, its body plunging back into the darkness, chains snapping taut as they dragged it back into its eternal prison. The wraiths, now without their master, let out a final, agonized wail before fading into mist.

And then...Silence.

The group lay there, panting, shaking, the adrenaline still coursing through them. Aleister stared up at the sky, trying to catch his breath.

Blaze let out a weak chuckle. "Next time, I'm picking the route."

"Noted." Victoria said.

Damian exhaled. "That... was close."

Aleister slowly sat up, staring at the collapsed bridge. They had survived.

But something about that creature lingered in his mind. What had it been guarding?

Chapter 20

THE ORDER OF
THE LIGHT

The group stood in silence, staring at the ruined bridge, their breathing still labored from the frantic escape. The creature had been dragged back into the void, but its presence lingered. Aleister could feel it—like an echo in his bones, a remnant of something ancient that refused to fade completely.

Damian wiped the sweat from his forehead. "That was... interesting. Never a dull moment."

Blaze let out a tired laugh, rubbing his arms.

"I don't know, I'm thinking of making a habit out of fighting gigantic nightmare creatures."

Victoria, who had been silent up to this point, stepped forward, her gaze fixed on the fog-choked abyss where the bridge had once stood.

"That thing," she murmured, "wasn't just guarding the chasm."

"What do you mean?" Aleister asked.

"It was guarding something else. Something it didn't want us to reach."

The landscape shifted as they moved deeper into the forgotten lands. What had once been jagged cliffs and dark ravines now gave way to crumbling ruins—the skeletal remains of an ancient city, long abandoned. Moss and vines twisted around fallen statues, depicting winged beings whose faces had been worn away by time. The remnants of stone roads, now fractured and uneven, stretched toward the horizon, leading them further into the unknown.

Aleister ran his fingers along a piece of broken stonework, noting the strange symbols carved into its surface.

"You recognize that writing?" Blaze asked.

Aleister shook his head. "Not exactly... but it's similar to something I've seen before."

Damian knelt beside a half-buried pillar, brushing away layers of dirt to reveal a sigil carved into the base.

"This isn't just some lost ruin. This place was built by the Order of Light."

"The Order of Light? But why would they abandon a city like this?" Victoria asked.

"Maybe they didn't abandon it. Maybe it was *taken from them*." Blaze said.

A cold wind whistled through the ruins. Aleister didn't like this. Something about this place felt wrong. Not cursed—no, this wasn't demonic corruption. But it was... empty. Like something had been wiped away, leaving behind only the hollow echoes of what once was. And then—The whispering returned. Soft at first. Just like before. But this time... it wasn't coming from the fog. It was coming from the shadows around them. Aleister turned sharply, his pulse quickening.

"Did you hear that?"

The others stopped moving, their eyes scanning the ruins.

"Oh, I definitely heard that." Blaze said.

The whispering grew louder. Multiple voices, overlapping—chanting words Aleister couldn't understand.

"Spirits?" Victoria asked.

Damian's eyes glowed faintly in the dim light. "No. This isn't the work of spirits."

"Then what is it?"

Embedded in the stone, was a golden light, pulsing like a heartbeat. Aleister stepped closer, drawn to it, his own pulse quickening as a familiar presence radiated from the glow. Then, the light took form. A shadowy figure emerged within it—a tall man, cloaked and powerful, yet worn from battle. His spectral presence flickered like a dying ember, yet the divine energy surrounding him was unmistakable.

Blaze let out a low breath. "Is that...?"

Victoria whispered, "Doctor Crowe?"

Aleister's throat tightened. The man before him was only an echo, a preserved memory of the greatest demon hunter that had ever lived. A fragment of the past left behind to guide them. Crowe's ethereal gaze settled on Aleister.

"You have come far."

Aleister nodded but remained silent. The memory of Father Crowe stepped forward, his voice a solemn whisper.

"The staff will not answer to you, not fully."

"Why?"

Crowe studied him, then lifted a hand toward Aleister's ring—the Ring of Solomon.

"Because you have not yet understood the truth of what you carry."

"The ring? It's powerful, yes, but I've had it all my life. My father gave it to me." Aleister said.

Crowe's expression remained unreadable.

"And do you know why he gave it to you?"

Aleister hesitated. His father's words from that night so long ago echoed in his mind:

"Be patient and promise to do good with it."

For years, Aleister had believed the ring was merely a protective ward, an ancient artifact passed down through generations. But Crowe's words suggested something far more important.

"The Staff of Infinite Light does not work alone," Crowe continued. "It is the instrument, but the ring is the key. Without it, the staff is nothing but a conduit of untapped potential. Together, they become the ultimate weapon against darkness."

"But why?"

"The ring's power is not just in the magic it carries... but in the bond that fuels it. The Ring of Solomon was a symbol of love, passed from father to son, its power growing not through spells, but through the strength of the connection between generations. The love between you and your father is what unlocks the true power of the staff. Without it, you will fail."

The words resonated with Aleister as a warm sensation cascaded through his entire body. The ring's power... came from his father. Lucian Kane. The man who had died before Aleister's eyes, ripped away by a demon's claws. The one person who had fought to keep him safe—even in death. All these years... all the training, all the rituals, all the artifacts he had gathered...And it had never been about power. It had always been about love.

"Then we need to find Eden. To give the staff complete power to defeat Asmodeus, it must come from God's divine light. Only the Tree of Life can provide this power." Victoria said.

Crowe's memory nodded. "Eden is not a place that can simply be found. It exists beyond this world, hidden from those unworthy."

Damian folded his arms. "Then how do we reach it?"

Crowe's gaze settled on Victoria. "Through her light."

All eyes turned to Victoria.

"Me?"

"You are of the Order of Light. The only ones who have ever walked the path to Eden. Focus on the divine light within you and allow it to guide you."

Victoria bowed her head. "I understand."

Crowe's form began to fade, the golden energy dispersing into the wind. And with that, he was gone. Aleister stared down at the Ring of Solomon, running his finger over the metal. For the first time, he didn't just see it as an artifact. He saw it as a piece of his father.

The road ahead twisted through the mist as Victoria led the way. Her newly restored celestial light dimmed, concealed beneath the veil of mortal presence. They weren't ready for Eden yet. Not until Victoria was fully prepared to cross into the sacred realm. And so, their journey led them to the ruins of the First Sanctuary—the original stronghold of the Order of the Light. A castle long abandoned, yet untouched by time. The castle stood atop a jagged cliff, its black stone towers reaching toward the heavens.

Though ancient, it was still intact, its walls etched with golden runes, glowing faintly in the approaching twilight.

"What is this place?" Blaze asked, eyeing the fortress warily.

"This was once the first home of the Order of the Light." Victoria said. "Before the Order found sanctuary in the Church of Light, before we were scattered across the world."

As the group entered the great hall, the air shifted. The torches along the walls flared to life, illuminating the grand chamber—a cathedral-like space, lined with golden banners, depicting the first warriors of the Light. And at the far end of the hall, standing before a massive altar, was a lone figure. A man, clad in white and gold armor, his long silver hair cascading down his back. His eyes—piercing and sharp—locked onto Victoria.

"You've returned," he said.

Victoria took a deep breath. "Elias."

The man stepped forward, his armor glowing with divine energy.

"Who are you?" Blazed asked.

"I am Elias. Warrior of the Light." Elias paused to observe Victoria, who remained in a state of shock. "And she...is my sister."

"I thought you were...dead? I saw you fall in battle."

Victoria moved swiftly toward Elias to get a better look at him.

"It can't be."

Elias smiled as he remembered the bond they used to have.

"You haven't changed a bit sister...it's great to..." But before Elias could utter another word, Victoria enveloped him in a long, heartfelt hug. At first, he stood rigid, surprised by the sudden affection. But then he relaxed and embraced Victoria.

"I thought I lost you." Victoria said as tears stream down her face. "Why did you never try to find me? Or let the Order know you were still alive?

"I'm sorry sister, but I'm not what you think I am."

"What do you mean?"

"I did fall in battle that day. I'm no longer part of this realm."

Victoria starts to back away from Elias, realizing what his words mean.

"You're a Guardian?"

"Yes."

"What's a Guardian? Damian asked.

"If an angel or warrior of the Order falls in battle while serving the Light, they do not perish as others do. Instead, they pass into a higher existence—a realm beyond mortality and celestial law."

Blaze tilted his head. "So, they're basically immortal protectors?"

Victoria nodded. "Yes. Each Guardian of the Light is bound to a place, an artifact, or a piece of divine wisdom. They are eternal watchers, offering guidance when needed—but they also serve as the last line of defense against those who seek to corrupt the Light."

"Come," Elias said softly, "Let us speak alone."

Victoria glanced back at Aleister and the others, then followed Elias away from the group.

Victoria stood before Elias, tears now welling up in her eyes, betraying her usual stoicism. Her voice trembled.

"I've missed you. More than you could ever know."

Elias smiled. His eyes filled with infinite kindness.

"I have missed you as well. But, sister, my absence from your sight does not mean my absence from your heart."

She wiped a tear from her cheek, her voice heavy with emotion.

"When you fell, when I lost you—I lost part of myself. Your death shaped everything I've done. Every battle, every sacrifice, every choice..."

Elias reached out, gently touching her cheek, his presence radiant yet strangely solid.

"Sister, death was never an end. Our bond through love is eternal. Our souls are forever entwined. Never forget that."

She closed her eyes, leaning into his touch, absorbing the warmth she thought she'd never feel again.

"I've tried so hard to live up to your example, to honor your sacrifice."

"You have," Elias assured softly, pride radiating from him. "You have become a warrior greater than I ever was. But now you must be prepared for what is to come."

Victoria opened her eyes, studying Elias's face, sensing the weight of his next words.

"The battle ahead," Elias said gravely, "will test your strength, your courage, and your faith beyond anything you have faced before. Asmodeus will not relent. His power surpasses the others. He seeks the end of hope itself."

"I know."

Elias's voice grew quieter, urgent.

"Aleister Kane is the key. He is chosen, yet fragile. He doubts himself deeply, but he carries something extraordinary within—a love that can wield the Staff of Infinite Light fully. You must protect him at all costs, even if it means your own life."

Victoria drew a sharp breath, eyes wide. "Elias…"

He interrupted gently, "I know what I ask is difficult. But Aleister's survival is humanity's hope. Your life, dear sister, has always been about sacrifice. The greatest sacrifice might still lie ahead. Trust in the Light, trust in your heart."

She nodded again, determination returning to her eyes. "I will protect him. You have my word."

Elias reached into the glowing folds of his celestial robe and pulled out a small object wrapped in luminous white silk.

"This is for you."

Victoria carefully unwrapped the silk to reveal a small, radiant crystal, pulsing gently with a divine inner light.

"What is this?" she whispered, awed.

"A gift from the Divine," Elias replied. "Inside this crystal is a blessing from God himself. It will give you strength when you feel weak, clarity when doubt clouds your path, and courage when fear tries to consume you."

Victoria held the crystal close to her heart, feeling warmth radiate throughout her body.

"Thank you," she said.

Elias smiled, a mixture of pride, love, and sorrow.

"Remember our bond, sister. Even when you cannot see me, I am with you. Always."

Elias took Victorias hand and turned toward the group.

"Follow me. I will show you the way so you can continue your journey."

Elias led them to the highest tower of the castle, where a path of golden light stretched beyond the horizon.

"This is the Path of the First Light," Elias said. "It will take you to the Gates of Seraphim. From there, Eden will be within your reach."

"Good. I was getting tired of walking through nightmare forests." Blaze said.

Damian smirked. "Enjoy it while it lasts. Something tells me we're walking into something worse."

Victoria turned to Elias. "Will you come with us?"

"No, sister. My duty remains here. But I'm always here when you need me." Pointing to Victoria's heart with a warm smile.

"Farewell, my beloved sister. May the Light always guide you."

Then he was gone, leaving Victoria standing alone, the crystal clutched tightly in her hand.

She closed her eyes, breathing deeply, absorbing his final words.

"Always."

Chapter 21

THE GATES OF SERAPHIM

The golden path stretched endlessly ahead, winding toward the mystical realm known only through legend and scripture—Eden. The sky shimmered with vibrant hues of amber, gold, and violet, casting surreal shadows around the weary group as they marched onward. Aleister walked with the staff, feeling its pulse radiate gently through his fingertips. Its energy seemed stronger here, vibrant and alive, as if the staff itself could sense its origin drawing near.

Blaze broke the silence, his voice lighter than usual, trying to ease the tension.

"You know, when I signed up for this quest, I never imagined actually walking toward Eden itself."

Damian gave a quiet chuckle. "Is that regret I hear, Blaze?"

Blaze smirked, eyes scanning the ethereal horizon.

"Maybe a little."

Victoria walked silently, her violet eyes focused and intense. Aleister watched her carefully, sensing a change since her talk with Elias. She seemed both strengthened and burdened. Aleister quickened his pace until he stood beside her.

"You alright?"

She looked at him briefly and offered a small smile.

"I will be."

"I know this can't be easy—your brother..."

She raised a gentle hand, stopping him. "I'll be fine, Aleister. Elias reminded me that our bonds transcend life and death. He's still with me, even if I can no longer see him."

Aleister nodded, understanding perfectly.

"He's proud of you, you know."

"I know. And he reminded me how important you are in all of this. Your survival is crucial."

Aleister exhaled heavily, nodding slowly. "I'll do my best not to disappoint."

Victoria placed a reassuring hand gently on his shoulder.

"You won't."

After walking for what felt like hours through the ever-brightening mist, the golden haze suddenly parted, revealing a sight that stole their breath away.

Before them, radiant and magnificent, stood the massive Gates of the Seraphim. Carved from pure celestial light, the gate towered impossibly high, flanked by immense pillars glowing softly. Ancient angelic runes flickered gently upon their surfaces, hinting at timeless wisdom and eternal power.

The group stopped, speechless at the beauty and the sheer majesty of what they were seeing.

"By Heaven..." Blaze murmured, awe evident in his voice.

Damian's expression softened, impressed despite himself.

"In all my centuries, I've never imagined such a sight."

Aleister moved forward slowly, feeling small beneath the gate's grandeur. His heart quickened, his pulse raced, and the weight of his responsibility pressed once more upon him.

He whispered softly to himself, "So, this is Eden."

Suddenly, from the radiant mist emerged a towering being bathed in blazing golden fire, magnificent wings unfurling gracefully. Its eyes were piercing white orbs of pure light, and its presence filled the space with an almost overwhelming sense of majesty.

"Seraphim Caelion. We come seeking passage into Eden."

Caelion's voice was deep, resonating like thunder yet gentle as a whisper.

"Victoria, warrior of the Light, your heart and your intentions are known. But entrance to Eden demands trial and truth."

Aleister, gathering his courage, stepped forward, holding aloft the Staff of Infinite Light.

"I bear the Staff. I seek the judgment of the Tree of Life."

Caelion regarded Aleister silently.

"You are Aleister Kane, the chosen but uncertain one. You come seeking answers yet carrying questions that haunt your heart."

Aleister swallowed hard but kept his gaze steady.

"I seek the power to protect humanity from the evil that threatens it. I'll do whatever is necessary."

Caelion nodded slowly, his powerful voice filled with solemnity.

"You must face the judgment of the Tree alone. No friend or ally may enter. The path ahead is for you and you alone."

Aleister glanced back at Victoria, Blaze, and Damian, who watched him in quiet understanding and encouragement. They had come so far together, faced so much. But he knew this was his task, and his alone.

Aleister took a steadying breath and turned back to Caelion.

"I understand."

Caelion spread his six radiant wings wide, the massive gates of light slowly parting, revealing the ethereal paradise beyond. His voice rang out, majestic and clear.

"Then enter Eden, Aleister Kane. Face your final trial and accept the judgment of the Tree of Life."

Victoria placed her hand on Aleister's shoulder.

"Remember, Aleister, the power you seek is already within you. Trust yourself. Trust in the love that guides you."

Blaze gave him a strong nod. "See you soon, my friend."

Damian simply smiled. "Don't let us down."

Aleister met each of their eyes in turn, feeling their faith in him deeply. With renewed determination, he faced the gateway into Eden. Taking one final breath, he stepped forward through the gates, feeling the warmth and divine power envelop him. The gates slowly closed behind him, sealing him within the sacred heart of Eden.

Chapter 22

THE TREE OF LIFE

Aleister stepped through the Gates of the Seraphim, feeling an instant shift in the atmosphere around him. The heavy burden he carried seemed momentarily lighter, replaced by a peaceful serenity that flowed gently through him. The gates closed silently behind him, and Aleister was immediately enveloped in the tranquil beauty of Eden.

His first steps took him onto lush, emerald grass, softer than any he had ever known. The air was sweet, filled with fragrances of blooming flowers and ripened fruit, untouched by corruption. The sky overhead shimmered a crystal-clear blue, adorned with wisps of golden clouds. As he walked further into Eden, Aleister heard gentle rustling in the leaves around him. He paused, glancing curiously around the serene landscape.

From the foliage emerged creatures—graceful deer, playful foxes, rabbits, and even lions—approaching without fear. Above, colorful birds descended, their wings vibrant shades of blue, gold, and scarlet. They circled softly around him, their gentle songs creating a chorus of welcome.

Aleister stood in awe as the animals drew closer, surrounding him in a circle of calm acceptance. The smallest creatures brushed softly against his legs, while larger animals lay peacefully beside him. For the first time since he began this perilous journey, Aleister felt truly at peace, accepted without judgment, without expectation. It was as though Eden itself recognized him—not for his past sins or his fears—but for the purity that still lived within his soul.

A delicate sparrow landed gently on Aleister's shoulder, chirping softly, as if whispering words of encouragement. He smiled. A rare, genuine moment of joy washing over him. Feeling strengthened by their warm acceptance, Aleister moved forward again, surrounded by Eden's creatures who accompanied him toward the heart of Eden—toward the magnificent Tree of Life. Its towering form reaching skyward, branches gracefully stretched toward the heavens. Its leaves shimmered gently, their golden edges whispering softly in the serene breeze.

As he drew near, the tree's surface rippled and shimmered with radiant energy. From within its glowing bark stepped forth a woman formed entirely of golden light and delicate foliage. Her presence radiated an ancient and powerful wisdom, yet her eyes held warmth and compassion. She spoke gently, her voice harmonizing with the whispers of Eden,

"Welcome, Aleister Kane. I am Elysia, the heart and guardian of the Tree of Life."

Aleister was awe-struck by her ethereal beauty.

"Elysia... You are the Tree?"

She nodded softly, stepping closer, the glow around her softening gently.

"Yes. I am the living spirit of Eden, the embodiment of life itself. The Tree of Life is more than mere wood and leaves.

It is the source of life and wisdom in this world. Every living thing finds its beginning here."

Aleister glanced down at the Staff of Infinite Light in his hand.

"And this staff?"

"The staff you bear was crafted from a branch of this very tree. Long ago, when Heaven first created humanity, the Archangel Gabriel took a piece of this tree to craft a divine weapon—a weapon to safeguard humanity from the darkness that would inevitably seek to corrupt it. Its power is of pure life, bound to the essence of love and creation itself."

She reached out gracefully, touching the staff. Its glow intensified at her touch.

"But the staff alone is not enough. Its power is not simply divine—it requires a heart filled with love and humility to unlock its true strength."

"I'm not sure I'm worthy."

She gazed deeply into his eyes, searching his soul.

"That, Aleister Kane, is what we must discover together."

Her golden eyes, ancient and wise, locked onto Aleister's as she spoke.

"Aleister Kane, to wield the Staff of Infinite Light, you must face judgment within your own heart. If you succumb to vengeance and anger, the staff will fail."

Aleister nodded solemnly, taking a deep breath.

"I understand."

Elysia reached forward, gently touching his forehead. "Then let the judgment begin."

Reality shifted, and Aleister once again found himself reliving the night he lost his father. He saw Lucian Kane clearly, seated in front of the fireplace, calmly assuring young Aleister that angels and demons were indeed real. He watched, helpless, as Lucian was savagely torn apart by the demon Asmodeus. Anger and sorrow surged in Aleister's heart, and a primal desire for vengeance burned brightly within him.

But Elysia's voice echoed gently in his mind.

"Let go, Aleister. Anger will not heal your pain."

His hands trembled. "I can't forgive that monster for what he did."

"Forgiveness is not for him," Elysia whispered. "It's for you."

Aleister clenched his jaw, fists shaking at his sides. He closed his eyes tightly, breathing deeply.

"I choose love, not vengeance," he whispered. "Father, forgive me—I let go of the hatred I've carried for so long."

Suddenly, warmth flooded his chest, and a gentle peace calmed his heart. The scene shifted again. He saw Mary, her eyes filled with tears, her voice trembling as she begged him to choose her over his obsession. The pain of losing her struck him anew, and guilt threatened to overwhelm him.

"Mary... I'm so sorry."

Mary's vision stepped forward, reaching out tenderly.

"You have punished yourself enough, Aleister. Let go."

"I hurt you," he whispered. "I never deserved you."

"You are more than your mistakes," she said gently. "You are worthy of love."

Tears filled his eyes. "I choose love. I choose to forgive myself for what I've done to you."

Mary smiled softly, nodding, her image fading peacefully into the gentle light. Once more, the world shifted. Aleister stood alone, facing Asmodeus himself. The King of Demons stood before him, a monstrous form of shadow and flame, laughing mockingly.

"You think you can defeat me, Aleister Kane?" Asmodeus sneered. "You are weak. Your heart betrays you."

Aleister's grip tightened around the staff. Anger surged, tempting him to strike blindly. He felt hate rise—but then Elysia's voice echoed softly.

"Remember, hatred will weaken you. Love is your true weapon."

Aleister steadied his breathing, closing his eyes briefly, pushing away the rage. He opened his eyes, calm now, his voice clear and strong:

"I will defeat you—but not through hate. I fight because I love. I fight to protect humanity from your darkness."

Asmodeus's image faltered, confusion briefly passing over the demon's face before it vanished in a puff of smoke. Aleister returned once again to Eden, facing Elysia, the golden form now smiling with deep satisfaction.

"You have passed the trials, Aleister Kane. Your heart has chosen love over hate. You are worthy of wielding the Staff of Infinite Light in its full power."

The ring on Aleister's finger, his father's legacy, radiated brilliantly, its glow merging seamlessly with the staff, illuminating the whole of Eden. Aleister felt power and peace surge within him, clarity filling his soul as the staff awakened fully to him.

Elysia's gentle voice resonated one final time:

"Go forth, Aleister. Remember always—love is the greatest weapon you possess. Do not stray from its path."

He bowed his head. "Thank you, Elysia."

The Tree of Life pulsed softly, blessing him as the gates of Eden slowly reopened. Aleister turned, stepping forward, staff raised high, ready to rejoin his friends and face their final battle.

Victoria, Blaze, and Damian stood anxiously waiting. As Aleister emerged, radiant and transformed, they gazed at him with astonishment and pride.

Victoria smiled warmly. "You did it."

Aleister nodded confidently, his voice firm. "I know what must be done. Love, not hate, is how we will win this war."

Blaze grinned. "Sounds easier said than done—but I trust you."

"We have your back, Aleister. Until the end." Damian said.

Aleister turned his gaze toward the distant horizon, toward the darkness that awaited them. Yet he felt no fear. Only certainty. Only love.

Chapter 23

THE HEART OF DARKNESS

The sky grew darker as the group moved further from Eden, the brilliance of that divine place fading slowly behind them. Silence settled among them, each of their thoughts now focused on the battle ahead—the final confrontation that would decide their fates.

Aleister walked at the head of the group, holding the Staff of Infinite Light with newfound confidence. Yet he couldn't ignore the quiet dread in Blaze's expression, which had deepened into something unsettling.

Aleister slowed his pace, falling into step beside Blaze.

"You've been quiet. What's wrong?"

Blaze hesitated, avoiding Aleister's eyes.

"We've unlocked the full power of the staff—but there's something I haven't told you."

Victoria and Damian drew nearer, sensing the seriousness in Blaze's voice.

Aleister nodded gently,

"Go on."

Blaze exhaled deeply, steeling himself.

"To truly defeat Asmodeus, we must confront him in his own domain—just outside the gates of Hell itself. It's the only way to end this permanently."

"You mean the Black Void?" Damian said.

Blaze nodded slowly.

"Exactly. To open it, I'll have to invoke ancient, forbidden powers."

Victoria's eyes widened, surprised by Blaze's words.

"The Necronomicon?" she asked.

Aleister's blood chilled at the name.

"Blaze, you can't—"

Blaze raised a hand, quieting Victoria.

"I have no choice. The Necronomicon combined with my demon-hunter tattoos is the only way to unlock the realm. Each tattoo on my body is a seal—keys etched into my flesh for precisely this purpose. The book and the tattoos together can break the seal."

Victoria stepped closer. Her expression solemn.

"But Blaze, using the Necronomicon risks corrupting your soul permanently. You could be lost to us."

"I knew the risks when I took these markings. If this is the price of saving humanity, so be it."

Aleister swallowed hard, seeing the weight of Blaze's sacrifice.

"What happens once we pass through that door?"

"Once we step through the gate into the Black Void, we cannot return—not unless Asmodeus is defeated. We either emerge victorious or remain trapped in darkness forever."

A tense silence fell over the group, the weight of Blaze's revelation settling heavily upon them.

"The Necronomicon—where exactly do we find it?"

Blaze hesitated.

"There's only one place we can safely obtain it: from my order—the Order of Shadows. They guard the book, using its forbidden knowledge to wage war against demons, even entering Hell itself when necessary."

Damian raised an eyebrow skeptically.

"Your order willingly uses the Necronomicon?"

"It's kept under strict guard. Only the strongest, most disciplined hunters are permitted to access its powers. They understand the dangers better than anyone."

"Will your order give us permission to use the book?" Victoria asked.

Blaze sighed heavily. "They'll have reservations. Opening the door to the Black Void is an act few have ever dared. But our quest has grown far beyond personal choice—humanity's survival rests on our shoulders. They will listen to me."

Aleister placed a reassuring hand on Blaze's shoulder.

"Then we'll go to them, and we'll plead our case. There's no other choice."

After hours of relentless travel, the group reached a crumbling fortress carved into a sheer mountain face. The ancient fortress known as Dreadhold Sanctum — the last bastion of the Order of the Shadows. The structure radiated strength, secrecy, and an air of solemnity that spoke of countless battles waged in shadows.

Centuries ago, during the earliest days of the war between Heaven and Hell, a group of mortals chosen by divine will were given the burden of keeping demonic forces at bay — not with miracles, but with blood, steel, and sacrifice. These were the first Demon Hunters.

The Order's founders constructed Dreadhold atop the ruins of a much older temple — a forgotten place rumored to have been scorched clean during the First Fall, when the heavens cast down rebellious angels into the pit. Beneath the surface lie catacombs and vaults said to contain fragments of angelic relics, corrupted weapons, and forbidden scriptures. Some say even a bound demon sleeps in its lowest chamber, imprisoned by ancient rites long lost to time.

Dreadhold is not just a place of warcraft — it is a sanctuary of grim wisdom. Within its obsidian halls are tomes bound in flesh, weapons etched with divine sigils, and relics too dangerous to see the light. Only the most disciplined may walk its corridors unscathed. The air is heavy with incense and blood, and the walls whisper prayers — or curses — depending on who listens.

The Order of the Shadows has always operated in secrecy, feared even by those they protect. They believe the only way to fight true darkness is to walk the edge of it — to wield its own weapons while never surrendering to its temptation. Their motto is carved above the great hall:

"We become the shadow, so the Light may endure."

At the fortress gates stood two imposing sentries, their bodies covered in intricate, glowing tattoos similar to Blaze's own.

Blaze stepped forward, revealing the markings that lined his arms and face.

"I am Blaze Barton, Demon Hunter of the Order of Shadows. I seek an audience with Master Corbin."

The sentries exchanged wary glances before finally bowing deeply and stepping aside.

"Enter, Brother Blaze."

Inside the fortress, the group was escorted through winding passages into a large, torch-lit hall. At its far end, an elderly yet powerful figure waited: Master Corbin, head of the Order of Shadows. His body bore markings even more intricate than Blaze's—symbols of countless battles and sacrifices. Master Corbin regarded them calmly, his voice resonating powerfully.

"Blaze Barton, why have you come?"

Blaze stepped forward respectfully, bowing his head.

"Master, we need the Necronomicon. The time has come to confront the demon king Asmodeus in his own domain."

Corbin's sharp gaze narrowed, studying Blaze deeply.

"You realize what you ask? Opening the door to the Black Void is forbidden for a reason. You risk eternal damnation."

Blaze nodded solemnly.

"I understand the risk—but we have no choice. Aleister Kane wields the Staff of Infinite Light. He has passed Eden's judgment. He is our only hope to defeat Asmodeus."

Corbin's eyes shifted to Aleister, who met the elder's gaze steadily, standing firm.

"Master Corbin, we face darkness itself. We must risk everything to protect humanity." Aleister said.

Corbin studied Aleister carefully. Finally, he nodded slowly.

"I sense truth in your words. You possess courage. But know this: The Necronomicon demands a terrible price from all who use it."

"I accept the cost." Blaze said. "It's mine alone."

"The Necronomicon is not merely a book—it is an artifact of pure evil, an embodiment of corruption itself. Its pages were penned by the darkest beings to ever exist, crafted from human suffering, despair, and torment. To touch it unprotected, even for an instant, would corrupt your soul irreversibly."

"Master Corbin, I thought my tattoos—"

Corbin raised his hand firmly, silencing Blaze.

"Your tattoos grant protection from demons, Blaze, but the Necronomicon's evil surpasses mere demonic threats. No human—not even a warrior as strong as yourself—can handle it directly without being consumed by its malevolence. Only I, after decades of training and sacrifice, possess the strength to safely wield its dark power."

"Then what must we do?" Victoria asked.

"I alone must perform the ritual to open the portal to the Black Void. I alone will bear this burden. If any of you attempt to interfere, or even approach the book, your souls will be lost."

Aleister nodded solemnly, understanding the immense sacrifice Corbin was making.

"We will heed your warning, Master. What comes next?"

"Follow me," Corbin instructed firmly.

Corbin led the group down a hidden stairwell into the fortress's deepest level. The air grew colder, charged with tension and ancient magic. They stopped before a massive iron door engraved with countless protective runes, crosses, and powerful holy symbols.

Corbin pressed his hand against the heavy door, murmuring softly. A surge of holy energy flowed through the runes, unlocking the ancient barrier. The door slowly creaked open, revealing a room that radiated pure, intense holiness. The chamber was lit by hundreds of candles and encircled by countless holy crosses. Elite warriors of the Order stood silently along the walls, their faces hidden beneath dark hoods, weapons ready. At the room's center floated the Necronomicon, suspended within a glowing orb of shimmering golden magic. It pulsed gently, exuding darkness despite the layers of protective enchantments.

Corbin's voice was barely a whisper.

"Do not cross the circle. The protective spells are all that keep the book's evil at bay."

He stepped into the circle of crosses alone. The book reacted instantly, its pages fluttering aggressively as Corbin drew near. Raising his arms, he spoke powerful incantations, the symbols on his own body glowing fiercely, resisting the malevolent energy that poured from the book.

"By the powers of Light and Darkness, by the will of the Order," Corbin commanded, "I break this seal!"

With a blinding flash, the protective orb shattered, and the book fell gently into Corbin's outstretched hand. Even as strong as he was, his face twisted momentarily with pain, fighting against the flood of evil that threatened to consume him. He regained his composure swiftly, holding the book carefully away from his body.

"Quickly," he instructed. "Follow me. The ritual must begin now."

They moved swiftly down another passageway into a chamber etched with ancient, complex symbols. Corbin carefully placed the Necronomicon on a stone pedestal at the center.

"Remain at the edge of the circle," Corbin warned firmly, stepping back into the middle, "and do not move, no matter what you see or hear."

Blaze's eyes were shadowed with concern.

"Master, are you certain?"

"Trust me, Blaze. This is my burden, my responsibility. Your destiny lies beyond the Black Void—not within this circle."

Aleister nodded respectfully.

"We're ready."

Corbin opened the Necronomicon, his voice unwavering despite the immense evil pouring from its pages. He spoke words of a forbidden tongue, his tattoos glowing brilliantly, resisting corruption as the power of the dark book surged outward, cracking the air with malevolence. The chamber shook violently. Reality itself seemed to warp and twist around them. A swirling portal, black as night, began to manifest before Corbin. The terrifying vortex grew, howling with dark winds and shadowy flames. With the ritual completed, Corbin slammed the book shut, immediately stepping back from it, his breathing heavy with strain. He gestured sharply toward the portal.

"Now! Go swiftly!"

One by one, they stepped into the swirling black portal, disappearing into the abyss—leaving the fortress behind, entering the Black Void, toward their ultimate confrontation with the King of Demons.

Chapter 24

THE RIVER STYX

The darkness was absolute, a void so consuming it swallowed all sensation of time and space. Suddenly, a flash of crimson fire erupted, and Aleister, Victoria, Blaze, and Damian found themselves standing upon bleak, barren ground. Behind them, the black portal closed silently, leaving them stranded in a land that radiated death and despair.

Blaze immediately scanned their surroundings, tension etched deeply on his tattooed face.

"We're at the threshold of the underworld," he warned. "This is the domain between worlds—the place mortals were never meant to tread."

Victoria glanced around, her hand hovering near the hilt of her sword.

"Where do we go from here?"

Blaze pointed toward a dark horizon.

"The River Styx lies that way. If we want to reach Asmodeus, we have no choice but to cross it."

"Never thought I would go across the River Styx willingly. Damian said. "The ferry man really creeps me out."

"I thought vampires were fearless." Blaze said with a slight chuckle.

You'll see, everything here will scare you too."

They traveled swiftly through the oppressive gloom until a faint sound reached their ears—the slow, mournful whispers of countless lost souls. Soon after, they reached a dark, desolate shore. Stretching out before them was the legendary River Styx, its waters dark and murky, swirling with spectral currents. Lost souls writhed beneath its surface, moaning softly, desperate for release that would never come. At the edge of the shore stood a hooded figure upon a worn, ancient ferry. The figure slowly turned its head, eyes glowing faintly from beneath the dark hood. The ferryman had sensed their arrival. Charon, the keeper of the River Styx, stretched forth a skeletal hand, speaking in a hollow, chilling voice that echoed across the still waters.

"Travelers, you seek passage across the Styx. But no one crosses without payment."

Blaze stepped forward calmly, nodding respectfully.

"We know your price, Charon. We carry the obols for passage."

Charon's empty gaze studied them silently for a moment. "Then approach, mortals, and pay the toll."

Blaze reached into a hidden pouch, carefully retrieving four ancient silver obols, coins etched with sacred symbols worn smooth by time. He handed one to each companion.

"Remember, offer your coin silently, and do not speak until Charon accepts it. Any refusal, and we're doomed to wander this shore forever."

Aleister stepped forward first, heart pounding. Silently, he extended the coin. Charon's cold fingers brushed against his palm, taking the obol slowly. After a tense pause, the Ferryman nodded, motioning him onto the ferry. Victoria followed. Her fierce violet eyes unwavering as she offered her coin. Charon examined her briefly, then accepted her payment and motioned her aboard. Damian stepped forward, eyes glinting faintly with unease. His coin rested in Charon's hand longer than the others—but finally, the Ferryman accepted it, granting passage.

"I'm not mortal." Damian said under his breath. Shying away from the ferry man's haunting appearance.

Lastly, Blaze stepped forward, offering his obol. Charon took the coin carefully, pausing briefly as if sensing the deep burden Blaze carried. Finally, with a silent nod, the Ferryman gestured for him to board.

As the ferry pushed away from the shore, silence enveloped the group, punctuated only by the haunting wails and whispers of lost souls swirling endlessly beneath the dark waters of the River Styx. Aleister moved slowly to the edge of the ferry. He gazed deeply into the black, swirling currents, feeling a cold shiver race through him. Faces rose and fell beneath the surface—ghostly visages frozen in eternal torment, eyes wide with grief and pain, staring up at him as though begging for salvation that would never come. In their suffering, Aleister saw himself, a reflection of his own inner torment and regrets. He thought of his father, Lucian Kane, whose violent death had set him on this dark and dangerous path. Aleister's heart tightened painfully. He wondered if Lucian's soul had known peace—or if, somewhere in this vast realm of torment, his father suffered still, forever trapped. His thoughts turned to Mary, the woman he had loved more deeply than he'd ever allowed himself to show. He imagined her gentle eyes, her warm touch, the sadness he'd caused her by choosing vengeance over their love.

His chest ached sharply, realizing fully now how much he had sacrificed, how much he had lost chasing shadows and vengeance.

"Mary," he whispered softly, barely audible against the river's lament.

"I'm so sorry for everything. Wherever you are, please hold on—just a little longer."

The souls below reached upward, spectral fingers brushing against the ferry's side, their empty gazes pleading desperately for relief, for redemption. Aleister stared down at them, struck deeply by the path his life had taken. How had he, a collector and scholar of occult relics, found himself standing here, sailing across the River Styx itself? It felt surreal, a dream turned nightmare, a fate he'd never imagined possible. Yet this was his reality. His choices had brought him here, to the brink of Hell, to a place few mortals had ever ventured and fewer still had returned from. A gentle touch on his shoulder startled him from his thoughts. He turned to find Victoria standing quietly beside him, her eyes full of understanding and compassion. She too gazed into the river, watching the restless souls.

"I know," she said softly, barely above the whispering currents. "The weight of this war—it's too much for any heart to bear alone."

Aleister met her eyes, sensing the sincerity behind her words. "I never thought I'd find myself here," he admitted quietly.

"We've both lost those we loved deeply. But it's our love for them, not our pain, that will carry us through."

Aleister nodded slowly, the truth in her words settling within him. He glanced back toward the dark river, the souls beneath still reaching upward.

"I can't fail them, Victoria," he whispered.

"We won't fail. We'll face this darkness together."

Aleister felt a warm resolve settle deep in his heart, bolstered by her words and presence. The Staff glowed brighter in his grip, responding to the purity of his newfound determination.

"Together," he echoed firmly, turning from the river of souls to face the bleak shore ahead, prepared now to confront the ultimate evil awaiting them.

Charon navigated the dark currents expertly, steering them deeper into the underworld. Eventually, a dark shore became visible ahead—an abyssal landscape cloaked in shadow and despair. The Ferryman's hollow voice broke the silence, chilling them to their bones.

"We have arrived. Remember, few who cross into this realm ever return. Your fates lie before you now."

The ferry bumped gently against the shore. The group stepped onto the bleak, rocky ground. Charon watching silently from the ferry. As they moved forward, Charon's voice whispered one final warning through the gloom.

"Take heed, mortals. Beyond this shore lies only death."

Blaze took a deep breath.

"This is it my friends, I hope you're ready for what awaits us. Not sure I am."

Aleister stood tall, holding the staff before him like a beacon against the darkness.

"We're ready."

Aleister, Blaze, Victoria, and Damian stood at the threshold of a bleak and lifeless realm, a landscape etched from shadows and despair. Behind them, the dark waters of the River Styx whispered their eternal lament. Blaze surveyed the barren horizon.

"We must now travel toward Tartarus—the deepest pit of torment in all of Hell. That's where we'll find Asmodeus. But first, we must reach the banks of the River Phlegethon."

Damian eyed the distant darkness skeptically.

"The river of fire itself. How reassuring."

Aleister squared his shoulders, gripping the Staff firmly.

"Then lead us, Blaze. We've come too far to turn back now."

Blaze nodded solemnly and took point, guiding them through a twisted landscape of jagged rock and lifeless earth. The air grew heavier, thickened by an oppressive heat that built slowly with every step they took. After what felt like an eternity of traversing barren wasteland, the distant glow of fire illuminated the horizon. Soon, the travelers arrived at the banks of the River Phlegethon—a blazing torrent of molten flame cascading furiously through a blackened, scorched valley. Its intense heat scorched their skin, even from afar, and waves of blistering heat shimmered in the oppressive air. The roaring flames drowned out all sound, the river itself a ferocious entity, its fiery currents seething with eternal fury. Victoria gazed at the infernal river, her eyes reflecting its flames.

"How do we cross something like this?"

Blaze shielded his eyes from the searing glare.

"There's a bridge—not too far from here. It's the only way into Tartarus."

Aleister narrowed his gaze, searching the blistering landscape.

"Then let's find it quickly. It's way too hot for comfort."

Blaze and the group moved swiftly down the rocky terrain and into the unknown depths of the dark underworld.

Chapter 25

HELLFIRE

They moved carefully along the riverbank, the flames roaring deafeningly beside them. Eventually, through the smoke and fire, a narrow bride of obsidian stone came into view, arching dangerously above the molten fury of the Phlegethon. The bridge, ancient and cracked, seemed barely stable, held together by dark magic older than time. Below, flames leaped upward hungrily, eager to consume any who faltered.

Damian shook his head.

"Somehow, I imagined this differently."

Victoria eyed the perilous crossing.

"It looks ready to collapse."

Blaze stepped forward cautiously, his tattoos glowing faintly, protecting him against the searing heat.

"We have no other choice. Watch your step—one wrong move, and there's no coming back."

Aleister nodded.

"Together, carefully."

One by one, they stepped onto the narrow bridge. It trembled beneath their feet, and flames roared hungrily below, threatening to claim them. They moved slowly, deliberately, their hearts pounding with every cautious step. Finally, after what felt like eternity, they reached the far side of the bridge.

The group cautiously made their way along the blazing banks of the River Phlegethon, its flames roaring fiercely alongside them. Each step took them deeper into darkness, the oppressive heat making the journey nearly unbearable. Ahead in the distance loomed the massive iron Gates of Tartarus, etched with symbols of pain and eternal suffering. Yet, as they moved closer, the surrounding air grew tense—too quiet, unnaturally still.

Aleister suddenly stopped, raising the Staff defensively. "Something's wrong."

Blaze's tattoos flared in response.

"Stay alert!"

From the shadows around them, deep, guttural laughter echoed through the air. Emerging swiftly from the smoke and darkness came towering figures—Centaurs, fierce warriors with powerful torsos atop muscular horse bodies, their eyes burning red like molten embers. In their massive hands, each Centaur wielded great bows, already drawn back, arrows aflame and poised to fire.

Damian growled, baring his fangs.

"Looks like we have company!"

Without warning, the Centaurs released their flaming arrows. The group quickly scattered, dodging the fiery onslaught, the arrows erupting in bursts of fire as they struck the charred ground. Victoria unsheathed her sword, its blade gleaming brightly.

"We have to fight through them!"

The Centaurs charged, hooves thundering, unleashing another volley of fire arrows. Aleister swiftly summoned the staff's power, creating a protective barrier of radiant energy that absorbed the flames harmlessly. Blaze lunged forward, chanting powerful incantations, his tattoos blazing crimson, forming fiery chains that ensnared a charging Centaur, pulling it down hard onto the scorched earth. Damian moved swiftly, his vampiric speed unmatched, weaving between flaming arrows as he leapt onto the back of a startled Centaur, fangs bared. He sank his teeth deep into its neck, causing the beast to collapse, thrashing helplessly. Victoria stood defiantly in the chaos, her sword emitting brilliant light, slashing through enemy ranks with grace and deadly precision.

A fierce Centaur leader charged, bow discarded for a massive axe, bringing it down toward her with brutal force. She rolled aside, blade slicing upward, cutting deep across the Centaur's torso. It roared in pain, collapsing heavily to the ground. Aleister advanced steadily, directing pulses of radiant energy from the Staff, pushing back enemy ranks and deflecting fiery attacks. Another Centaur charged him head-on, aiming an arrow straight for his heart. Aleister swiftly raised the staff, sending a concentrated beam of pure light that exploded against the Centaur's chest, dropping it instantly. More Centaurs emerged from the smoke as their numbers became overwhelming. Blaze turned desperately to Aleister.

"We can't hold them off forever—we must get through to the Gates!"

Aleister nodded.

"Gather around me!"

The companions quickly formed a tight circle around Aleister, fending off the relentless Centaur assault. Aleister raised the Staff of Infinite Light high above his head, channeling its full power. With a surge of determination, he drove the staff into the scorched earth, unleashing a blinding wave of energy outward in every direction. The Centaurs screamed as the radiant shockwave threw them back, scattering their ranks and leaving them stunned and broken on the battlefield. Breathing heavily, Aleister raised the staff once more.

"Move! Before they recover!"

They sprinted forward, swiftly passing through the fallen ranks of their attackers, finally reaching the massive Gates of Tartarus. They paused briefly before the imposing iron gates, hearts still pounding from the battle. Blaze glanced back, confirming the Centaurs were retreating into the darkness.

Victoria placed her hand gently on Aleister's shoulder.

"You did well."

Aleister exhaled sharply, meeting her gaze.

"We all did."

Damian smiled.

"Let's get that son of a Bitch!"

Together, united once more, they pressed their hands against the ancient gates, feeling their massive weight shift beneath their collective strength. The iron doors slowly swung inward, groaning ominously as they opened, revealing the shadowy depths of Tartarus.

Aleister stepped forward, the staff's light blazing brilliantly, illuminating the darkness before them. Together, they entered the final domain of torment, ready to face the King of Demons—and end the eternal war once and for all.

Chapter 26

THE BOG OF LOST SOULS

The heavy gates of Tartarus closed behind them with a resounding, mournful groan, sealing Aleister and his companions within the bleak confines of the Underworld. An eerie stillness settled upon them, heavy with dread, as they advanced deeper into the domain of eternal torment. Blaze scanned their gloomy surroundings cautiously.

"To reach Asmodeus, we must first navigate through the Bog of Lost Souls. Move quietly—and whatever happens, do not disturb the waters."

Ahead lay a desolate swamp, its stagnant waters cloaked in a thick, ghostly mist. Gnarled trees, lifeless and twisted, reached desperately from the bog's surface, their limbs like outstretched hands pleading for release.

Victoria glanced uneasily at Blaze.

"What lurks within these waters?"

Blaze lowered his voice, a hint of fear evident. "The souls of men who committed terrible evil in life—murderers, betrayers, monsters in human form. They are trapped here forever, consumed by rage. If we disturb them, they'll drag us down, and we'll join their eternal suffering."

Damian swallowed hard, eyes narrowing suspiciously at the murky waters. "Then we tread very carefully."

Aleister nodded silently, gripping the Staff of Infinite Light tightly as the group moved forward, each step measured and cautious. Every footfall was deliberate, each breath held as they navigated the narrow paths of solid ground through the swamp. The mist grew thicker, wrapping around them like a shroud, making it difficult to see even a few feet ahead.

A faint moaning, low and filled with misery, began to rise from the dark water. Aleister's heart quickened, recognizing the anguish of countless souls tormented by guilt and despair.

Victoria stumbled slightly, and the water rippled softly around her feet. The moans intensified briefly, the surface churning with subtle movement. The group froze, their breath catching painfully, waiting for the waters to still once more. Aleister leaned toward Victoria. His voice barely audible.

"Careful."

She nodded silently, stepping more cautiously as they continued onward. They reached a narrow stone path cutting across a vast stretch of bog. Below the stone walkway, dark shapes writhed beneath the stagnant surface—ghostly visages frozen in expressions of eternal agony, distorted hands reaching toward the living, longing to pull them beneath.

Aleister felt a cold chill ripple through him. He stared downward, recognizing the desperate hunger of the souls beneath. As he stepped forward, one soul's sunken eyes opened, its face twisted with rage.

"Move!" Blaze hissed urgently.

The bog erupted suddenly in a chorus of anguished howls, the waters churning violently as souls surged upward, grasping frantically at the intruders.

Victoria drew her sword swiftly, its light driving back the wailing spirits momentarily. Blaze called forth protective wards, tattoos blazing fiercely as ghostly hands clawed at his ankles. Damian dodged swiftly, snarling as he kept his footing.

Aleister raised the Staff of Infinite Light, sending pulses of radiant energy outward, forcing the souls back beneath the waters.

"Quickly! Keep moving!"

They ran across the narrow stone path, hearts pounding, the souls reaching desperately for them, clawing inches away. As they reached the far side of the path, the howling spirits slowly sank back into the dark water, their mournful cries echoing behind them. Panting heavily, they finally emerged from the Bog of Lost Souls, its dreadful presence receding slowly behind them. Victoria leaned against a twisted tree, catching her breath, eyes haunted by the souls' eternal torment.

Blaze's voice trembled slightly. "We nearly joined them. That was too close."

Aleister's heart still raced, yet determination surged within him. "We've made it this far. There's no turning back now."

Damian stepped forward; eyes fixed on the looming cavern ahead. "Then let's finish this."

Aleister nodded, taking a deep breath.

Together, they faced the shadowed entrance to Asmodeus's cavern, resolved to face whatever darkness lay ahead.

Chapter 27

THE KING OF NINE HELLS

Aleister and the group stepped into the cavernous chamber of Tartarus, the oppressive air thick with the stench of decay and ancient evil. Darkness pulsed from the walls, tangible and suffocating.

At the far end, atop a throne carved from obsidian and bones, sat Asmodeus, the King of Demons. His monstrous, shadowy form radiated terrifying power. His body draped in layers of scorched black armor that seemed to breathe, pulsing with embers trapped beneath the surface. His wings, once divine, now twisted and skeletal, stretched wide across the cavern—tattered membranes blackened like burned parchment, glowing faintly with hellfire veins. His face was the most disturbing of all—inhumanly beautiful and utterly monstrous. A jaw too sharp. Eyes like twin black suns—pulling in the light around them. His horns coiled backward like a ram's, ridged with ancient runes carved by fire. Smoke and sulfur rolled from his mouth as he grinned. When he moved, the ground moaned. Not from weight... from fear. But Aleister's heart sank at the sight just beside the throne. His beloved Mary hung suspended by chains from the cavern ceiling. Battered and bloodied, barely alive, chains biting into her wrists. Her head hung limply, eyes closed, the faint rise and fall of her chest the only sign she still clung to life.

"Mary!" Aleister cried out, rushing forward instinctively.

Asmodeus laughed cruelly, his booming voice echoing through the cavern.

"Welcome, Aleister Kane! You've finally brought me my prize! You've played your part beautifully."

Aleister glared defiantly, clutching the staff tighter.

"Release her now, demon!"

Asmodeus laughed, unfazed.

"Poor, deluded mortal. Don't you understand yet? Everything—your journey, your suffering, even your victories—were all part of my plan. I needed someone pure of heart, guided by love, to retrieve what I could not."

Aleister shook his head, a cold dread spreading through him.

"No..."

Asmodeus rose slowly, dark power radiating from him.

"Your father's death, the capture of your precious Mary—they were simply tools to shape you into what I required. Lucian Kane's soul has languished here in Hell for decades, suffering endlessly, all his knowledge, power, and even his love for you proving utterly useless. You were always the key."

Aleister's heart shattered at the revelation, yet he knew better than to succumb to Asmodeus's deceit. Asmodeus stepped forward, towering over the group. His foul stench invaded their nostrils, but Aleister met those crimson eyes with unwavering resolve.

"What happened to you? Aleister asked. "You were once the leader of the Seraphim, God's most trusted angel alongside Lucifer himself. Why did you fall? Why did you start this eternal war?"

For a moment, Asmodeus seemed genuinely taken aback, his monstrous features softening into something disturbingly human. He spoke slowly, bitterness filling every word.

"I was God's sword, His most faithful servant. I fought His wars, destroyed His enemies, executed His judgments without question. But no matter what I did—no matter how loyal I was—it was never enough."

His voice grew louder, thick with ancient resentment.

"God used us as pawns, disposable tools. When Lucifer stood against Him, I saw clearly how meaningless our devotion had been. So, I rebelled. For my courage, my reward was eternal torment, cast from Heaven to rot in darkness forever."

Aleister felt a strange mix of disgust and pity.

"You chose your fate."

The demon king's eyes flared with renewed hatred.

"I chose freedom from servitude! From an eternity of blind obedience! If you had known betrayal as I did, you would understand why Heaven must fall. Now, give me the staff!"

Before Aleister could react, Asmodeus waved his massive, clawed hand. The Staff of Infinite Light was torn from Aleister's grip, flying across the cavern into Asmodeus's waiting hand. Aleister stumbled, shocked and vulnerable.

"No!" Aleister shouted in despair.

The demon king studied it—mock admiration lighting his eyes.

"Beautiful, isn't it?" he purred. "But useless in the hands of a god."

Without hesitation, he crushed it. The sound echoed like a scream—wood, metal, and divinity splintering into nothing. He hurled the broken pieces at Aleister's feet.

"There! Now nothing can stop me."

Suddenly, the cavern walls erupted with a cacophony of demonic laughter. Horrifying forms emerged from the shadows, monstrous demons closing in from all sides, trapping Aleister and his companions. There was no way out.

Blaze, tattoos blazing with fierce energy, prepared himself for battle. Victoria drew her sword, its blade shimmering defiantly against the darkness. Damian bared his fangs, snarling fiercely.

"Fight!" Blaze roared, as the demons attacked.

Chaos erupted within the cavern. Demons swarmed, attacking furiously from every angle. Blaze stepped forward first, tattoos pulsing with light. With a roar, he unleashed a wave of holy fire from his palm, incinerating a cluster of lesser demons in a blinding flash.

"Protect Aleister!" he shouted.

Damian transformed, his vampire nature emerging in full fury. Fangs bared, he leapt through the air, cutting down two winged fiends with the Dagger of Apollo, its golden edge igniting with every strike.

Victoria's blade sang. The Blade of Dawn blazed like a second sun, cleaving through infernal beasts with righteous fury. She fought like a woman possessed, graceful and unrelenting, wings of golden light erupting behind her as her true power surfaced.

"Aleister!" she called out. "You must fight!"

But Aleister remained still, kneeling, cradling the broken staff.

Asmodeus laughed as he watched his horde clash with the chosen warriors.

"They will fall, one by one," he said, stepping forward. "Hope dies here."

Blaze's fiery wards shielded them momentarily as Damian swiftly tore into the attackers with ruthless efficiency. Victoria fought with determination, her sword cleaving through demonic ranks. Amidst the chaos, Victoria saw her chance. She sprinted toward Asmodeus, her sword raised. Distracted momentarily by his dark triumph, he barely noticed Victoria's approach until it was nearly too late. With a roar of rage, he struck her violently, sending her sprawling painfully across the cavern floor. Victoria lay wounded, gasping for breath, her vision blurred by pain. But her resolve remained. Summoning her last ounce of strength, she lunged toward Asmodeus. Their blades clashed — hers, divine and blazing; his, made of seething black steel forged in the Dark Pit. Each blow from Asmodeus sent shockwaves through the cavern.

"You fight with light," Asmodeus growled, "but you do not understand the dark."

She sliced deep into his chest — a wound that hissed and smoked.

Snarling, he lashed out with monstrous claws, slashing across her ribs. Blood sprayed. She stumbled.

Then he struck again — hard.

She flew backward, crashing against the cavern wall. The Blade of Dawn clattered to the ground.

Aleister looked up. He saw her fall. Saw the glow fade from her body.

Victoria collapsed, her life fading, eyes meeting Aleister's one last time. "Aleister...end this. You are...the light..."

She fell silent, her body still.

Aleister froze. The words echoed through him.

"You are... the light..."

With shaking hands, he picked up a splinter of the broken staff.

And something stirred.

The pieces in his palm pulsed with warmth... then light... then power. The fragments drew together, drawn by will, by faith, by *love*.

The Staff of Infinite Light reformed in his grasp — whole and blazing like a comet.

Asmodeus stepped back. "No..." he rasped. "No, that's not possible!"

Aleister felt grief rip through him, then an overpowering sense of clarity. He grasped the staff, love and forgiveness surging through his heart, eclipsing all hatred and anger.

"You've taken everything from me!" Aleister shouted fiercely, raising the staff high, the chamber trembling with its divine power.

"But you won't take our future!"

Aleister's voice thundered, echoing through the cavern as the ground beneath their feet start to tremble.

"I banish you, Asmodeus, to a place from which you can never return!"

A surge of blinding light erupted from the staff, overwhelming Asmodeus. Behind him, a massive, swirling dark portal tore open, its inescapable force pulling him inexorably backward.

"No!"

Asmodeus roared desperately, fighting the inevitable. But the force was too great. With one final, defiant roar, Asmodeus was dragged into the vortex, vanishing into a dimension of eternal darkness and imprisonment. The portal sealed shut instantly, the cavern trembling, then falling utterly silent. The surviving demons fled into the shadows; their leader defeated.

Aleister rushed to Mary, quickly releasing her from the chains, catching her as she collapsed weakly into his arms.

She stirred slightly, opening her eyes, recognition flooding her battered face. "Aleister?"

"I'm here," he whispered tenderly, relief flooding through him.

"You're safe now."

Mary managed a faint smile, holding onto him weakly.

"I always knew you'd come."

Blaze and Damian approached slowly, their footsteps heavy, their movements weary from the brutal battle they'd just endured. Blaze's expression was etched with deep pain, a quiet sorrow reflected in his eyes as he knelt reverently beside Victoria's lifeless form. For a long moment, he hesitated, as if unable to accept the reality before him. Finally, with gentle, trembling fingers, he reached out and carefully closed her eyes, giving her the peace she deserved.

"She gave everything she had," Blaze whispered, his voice thick with grief and admiration. "She fought not just for us, but for something bigger than any one person. She gave her life so that we could succeed. She believed in you, Aleister—believed in all of us—even when we couldn't fully believe in ourselves."

Damian stood silently beside Blaze; his normally stern face softened by sorrow.

"I've lived through centuries," he said quietly, his voice unusually gentle, "but in all that time, I've rarely seen courage and sacrifice as pure as hers. We owe her a debt we can never repay."

Aleister held Mary tightly, tears streaming freely down his face as he absorbed the painful truth. The victory he'd fought for felt suddenly hollow, tempered by an ache of loss that cut deeply into his soul. He looked upon Victoria's serene face, knowing she would never again smile, never again fight bravely by their side.

"We'll never forget her," Aleister said, his voice shaking with profound emotion.

"Her courage, her heart—her sacrifice will remain alive within each of us. We'll carry her memory forward and honor everything she stood for."

He leaned down, placing a gentle hand on Victoria's shoulder, silently promising that her sacrifice would not be in vain.

Blaze knelt beside her, trembling. His knuckles white, his body aching from wounds he no longer felt.

"You were supposed to make it," he whispered. "You were the strongest of all of us."

He reached out, brushing a bloodstained strand of hair from her face. Her skin, still warm, was already fading to gray. The world fell away. He could hear nothing but the distant echo of his own breath. Just silence. Then...a faint glint of gold, barely visible beneath his coat. Slowly, Blaze reached into his inner pocket and pulled out the small silk-wrapped vial—The Tears of Eternity. For a moment, he just stared at it.

"I was going to save this for someone else," he muttered. "But maybe... this was always meant for you."

He held the vial over her heart, his hand shaking. He uncorked the vial. The air stilled. Then, with trembling fingers, he let a single drop fall onto her chest. Nothing happened at first. Blaze, still kneeling beside Victoria's still body, paused suddenly, his grief interrupted by something unexpected. From beneath the shadows that now cloaked her, he noticed a soft, almost imperceptible glow radiating gently outward. At first, he thought it was merely a trick of the dim cavern light, but as he watched closely, the faint illumination grew slightly brighter, shimmering like starlight through water.

He reached cautiously toward her, disbelief mingling with hope.

"Aleister, Damian—look! It worked!"

Aleister turned quickly; Mary still held gently in his arms.

"What is it? What worked?"

Blaze motioned urgently.

"Come closer. Look carefully."

They gathered around Victoria's lifeless form, silent and breathless. The subtle glow seemed to pulse gently, radiating warmth and purity. Blaze's eyes widened with recognition, realization washing over him.

"Her spirit—it hasn't fully departed yet," Blaze murmured in awe.

"It's gripped by a force more powerful than death itself. The Tears of Eternity have not only revived her spirit but also rekindled her soul."

Damian leaned in.

"What do you mean?"

Blaze's voice became stronger, his certainty growing with every passing moment.

"We must take her back—back to the Church of Light. They're the only ones who can help her now. Her bond with the Order and the sacred energy she wielded might be strong enough to save her."

Aleister felt hope ignite within his heart, pushing away the despair that had engulfed him moments before. He looked down at Victoria's peaceful face, feeling renewed determination surge through him.

"Then we waste no time. If there's even the slightest chance to bring her back, we'll do everything we can."

Blaze nodded solemnly; his expression determined.

"The priests at the Church will know what to do. If there's a way, they'll find it. Her sacrifice might not have to be the end."

With gentle reverence, Blaze carefully lifted Victoria's body, cradling her protectively.

"Stay with us," he whispered softly to her. "We're not letting you go—not yet."

As Aleister and his companions emerged from the darkened cavern, they stopped in stunned silence, their breath caught by the extraordinary sight unfolding before them. The oppressive darkness of the Underworld was gradually dissipating, revealing something wondrous and seemingly impossible.

From high above, radiant beams of divine light pierced through the blackened clouds, cascading down like rivers of pure, celestial gold. The glow illuminated the barren, lifeless landscape, washing away the shadows and replacing them with warmth and gentle radiance.

Blaze gazed upward in awe, his eyes wide with wonder.

"Heaven's light... it's reaching even here."

Mary, still held gently in Aleister's embrace, raised her weakened gaze, the golden glow reflecting softly in her eyes.

"It's beautiful," she whispered, her voice filled with profound peace.

Damian shielded his eyes, astonishment etched upon his normally stoic face.

"I never imagined I'd witness such a sight here. It's almost as surprising as finding garlic in my soup!"

Slowly, softly, something miraculous began to happen around them. The tortured souls, once condemned and trapped within this realm of eternal darkness, began to rise. Their twisted, pained expressions slowly relaxed into calm, their forms becoming ethereal and luminous, ascending gracefully toward the golden streams of heavenly light.

"It's redemption," Blaze breathed softly. "Their souls are finally freed."

The group stood motionless, transfixed by the wondrous ascension occurring all around them, the beauty beyond anything they had ever witnessed. It felt as though Heaven itself had opened its gates, reclaiming lost souls once condemned to eternal suffering. Then Aleister felt a gentle, familiar presence that pulled sharply at his heart. He turned his gaze to his side, and suddenly, he froze. There, bathed in radiant, celestial warmth, stood Lucian Kane, Aleister's father. His face was serene, unburdened by pain or regret, eyes gentle with the love Aleister remembered from his childhood. Lucian looked upon his son with immense pride, the lines of suffering vanished from his face.

"Father..." Aleister whispered, tears streaming freely down his face, his voice breaking with emotion.

Lucian stepped closer, his ethereal form glowing brilliantly.

"Aleister, my son... you have done it. You've ended the darkness. You've freed us all."

Aleister shook his head, overwhelmed by emotion.

"I'm so sorry, Father. I couldn't save you. You suffered for so long because of me."

Lucian smiled tenderly, reaching out to gently place a ghostly hand upon Aleister's face.

"My suffering is over, Aleister. Because of you, my spirit can finally find peace. I'm so proud of the man you've become. Your courage, your strength, your love—they're greater than you know."

Aleister trembled, his heart healing with every word his father spoke.

"I love you, Father."

Lucian smiled warmly; a final goodbye etched gently upon his serene face. "And I love you, Aleister. Always."

Slowly, gracefully, Lucian Kane's spirit began to rise into the radiant light above. Aleister watched, eyes filled with awe and gratitude, as his father's soul ascended toward the heavens, at last finding the peace that had eluded him in life. As Lucian's spirit merged fully with the brilliant celestial glow, Aleister felt a profound peace settle within him. His father was finally free, and so too was Aleister's own heart—free of guilt, vengeance, and grief.

Mary squeezed Aleister's hand gently, her touch reassuring.

"He's finally at rest, Aleister."

Aleister nodded. His voice full of gratitude.

"Yes. And now, at last, we can be too."

Blaze turned toward Aleister, a sudden realization shining in his eyes. Carefully adjusting Victoria's limp body in his arms, he approached with urgent determination.

"Aleister," Blaze began, excitement clear in his voice.

"The Staff of Infinite Light—you wield its full power now. Your heart and intentions are pure, your spirit aligned with its purpose."

Aleister stared at Blaze, confused at first.

"What do you mean?"

Blaze smiled.

"You can create a portal now, Aleister. With Asmodeus banished and your father's soul freed, the staff's true potential is finally unlocked. You have the power to open a direct passage out of this place. We don't need to journey through the darkness anymore."

Damian raised his eyebrows, astonishment evident on his face.

"A portal? You mean we can return directly to the Church of Light?"

Blaze nodded.

"Yes. It holds the power to bridge worlds, especially now that Heaven's divine light touches even here. Aleister simply needs to channel his heart and the staff's power together to take us home."

Aleister took a deep breath, feeling the weight and responsibility of Blaze's words. He glanced toward Mary, who squeezed his hand encouragingly. "You can do this," she whispered softly, her eyes filled with love and trust.

Stepping forward, Aleister lifted the Staff of Infinite Light. Its glow intensified, responding to the purity of his intention and the profound love he felt for those around him. He closed his eyes, focusing his mind, picturing the sanctuary of the Church of Light, its peaceful warmth, it's comforting presence.

"Open the way," Aleister whispered gently, pouring his heart's deepest wishes into the staff. "Take us home."

A wave of radiant energy surged from the staff, swirling gracefully in front of them. The air shimmered, folding upon itself as a bright, golden portal formed—its brilliant surface revealing the familiar grounds of the Church of Light. Together, the group stepped through the glowing portal, leaving the shadows of the Underworld behind.

Chapter 28

THE DAWN OF A NEW LIGHT

Stepping through the glowing portal, the group emerged onto the familiar, sacred grounds of the Church of Light. Warm, golden rays of sunlight streamed through the stained-glass windows, illuminating the sanctuary with hues of amber and sapphire. The air was filled with a serene stillness, carrying a gentle scent of burning incense, instantly calming their weary hearts.

Blaze gently carried Victoria's lifeless form forward; his eyes fixed ahead with solemn urgency. Aleister walked close beside Mary, supporting her carefully, while Damian stayed just behind, watchful and reverent.

The High Priest stood waiting at the far end of the sanctuary, his calm presence radiating wisdom and quiet strength. He watched them approach, immediately understanding the gravity of their mission, his eyes filled with compassionate concern as they gathered before him.

Aleister stepped forward, voice trembling with urgency. "We've defeated Asmodeus, High Priest—but the cost was great. Victoria sacrificed herself to ensure our victory. Yet her spirit...it hasn't completely left her body. Can you help her?"

The High Priest approached slowly, gazing upon Victoria with deep reverence. He reached out, placing his hand gently upon her forehead. His eyes closed in quiet meditation, sensing the faint pulse of spiritual energy within her.

After a moment, he opened his eyes, nodding slowly.

"Victoria is not like us," he explained softly. "She is a Child of the Light, a being whose spirit was born from the purest essence of divine energy. Even though her physical form has passed, her soul still clings gently to the world, awaiting its true destiny."

Blaze stared anxiously at the High Priest.

"What destiny? What must we do?

He smiled warmly, radiating gentle reassurance.

"Victoria's spiritual essence is powerful, blessed by the divine. When one like her passes from their physical body, their soul may ascend to a higher, celestial form. She may rise again—as an Angel."

Aleister felt his breath catch, stunned by the possibility.

"An Angel...truly?"

"Indeed," the High Priest affirmed, his voice calm and certain. "But she must be guided properly. A sacred ritual of transformation must be performed, one that only we, the Priests of the Order of Light, can undertake. This ritual will allow her spirit to cross the threshold into its rightful form."

Aleister nodded urgently.

"Then please—help her ascend. She deserves that peace, that honor."

The High Priest beckoned silently, and several fellow priests quietly entered the sanctuary, gathering reverently around Victoria's still form. Together, they gently placed her upon a sacred altar, surrounding her in a circle, hands clasped in solemn unity.

Slowly, the priests began to chant ancient words of divine invocation. Their voices rose in beautiful, melodic harmony, filling the church with sacred power. The air shimmered gently with a warm glow as radiant streams of celestial energy descended softly upon Victoria's still body.

Blaze, Aleister, Mary, and Damian watched in reverent awe as the ritual intensified, the entire sanctuary bathed in an ethereal light. Victoria's form began to glow softly, her earthly shell gradually becoming luminous and transparent. From her chest, a sphere of pure, radiant light emerged, floating upward gracefully, pulsing gently with her unmistakable spirit.

The chanting priests raised their arms in unison, their voices rising in harmonious climax as the sphere of light expanded and transformed. It stretched outward, taking on a new, ethereal form—a breathtaking figure of luminous beauty, wrapped in flowing garments of light. Brilliant wings of golden radiance unfolded gracefully from her back, illuminating the entire sanctuary.

Victoria, now transformed into an angelic being of breathtaking splendor, opened her eyes—now radiant and clear. She smiled lovingly down upon her friends, her voice echoing softly like the sweetest melody.

"Thank you," she whispered gently, her voice carrying infinite peace and love. "You've guided me home."

Aleister stepped forward, tears of gratitude streaming down his face.

"You saved us, Victoria. Thank you—for everything."

She smiled gently, warmth radiating from her divine form.

"Remember me always, dear friends. I shall watch over you from above."

Blaze bowed his head respectfully, overcome with awe.

"Fly high, Victoria. We will carry your courage in our hearts forever."

Slowly, gracefully, Victoria ascended through the sanctuary ceiling, passing gently into the heavens above, her presence illuminating the sky with golden brilliance. Aleister held Mary close, watching Victoria's angelic form vanish gently into the embrace of the clouds. He felt an overwhelming peace and deep gratitude. Though the journey had been long and difficult, the light had finally triumphed over darkness, love had conquered hate, and hope had risen from loss.

The sanctuary once again filled with quiet reverence. The High Priest turned toward Aleister and his companions, smiling warmly.

"Welcome home," he said gently, eyes twinkling softly with divine grace. "Your journey has ended, and Victoria's has begun anew."

Together, they stood united within the hallowed halls of the Church of Light, comforted by the knowledge that Victoria had found her divine destiny, and that their own souls, too, had been forever transformed by the power of love, sacrifice, and redemption. The golden light of the sanctuary had faded into a gentle hush, the warmth of divine energy still lingering in the air like the soft glow of fading starlight. The group had been given time to rest and reflect, but the High Priest was not yet finished. He turned toward Blaze.

"Walk with me."

Blaze exchanged a quick glance with Aleister, then nodded and followed the High Priest through the tall, arched corridors of the Church of Light. Their footsteps echoed off the ancient stone, the air around them still resonating faintly with the afterglow of Victoria's ascension.

They entered a quiet chamber off the main hall, lit only by the flicker of candlelight and a single stained-glass window depicting an angel casting down a serpent. The High Priest motioned for Blaze to stand beside him.

"I must ask you something," the Priest said, his voice low, but firm.

"Was Asmodeus truly defeated?"

Blaze hesitated. "I saw it with my own eyes," he replied. "Aleister, with the Staff of Infinite Light, opened a dark portal. It pulled Asmodeus in—screaming, fighting—but it sealed shut. He's gone. The Staff imprisoned him in a place no demon can escape."

The High Priest turned to face him fully. Though his features remained calm, there was a deep concern behind his eyes, as if he were watching storm clouds form on the horizon.

"I believe you, Blaze. But what you've described troubles me deeply."

"Why? You said yourself—the Staff holds the power of Heaven. It can banish even the most powerful of demons."

The High Priest nodded slowly. "Yes, the Staff holds divine power... but even divine power has limits when it comes to beings like Asmodeus. He is not like the others. He was once one of the Seraphim—a prince of Heaven. When he fell, he did not simply become a demon... he became a force of nature, a wound in the order of creation."

"You're saying he'll return?"

"The Underworld is healing. Light has returned, and the war has shifted. But mark my words, Blaze: Asmodeus will rise again. And when he does, he will not be bound by the laws of Heaven or Hell. He will be stronger, fueled by vengeance, and driven by knowledge of the very power that cast him down."

Blaze's jaw tightened, the old fire in his veins rekindling.

"Then we'll stop him again."

The High Priest placed a hand on Blaze's shoulder.

"You may not get a second chance unless we prepare. There is something hidden within the Lost Journals of Doctor Crowe—a secret even Aleister doesn't know. A final truth. A weapon. A key."

"Then I need to find those journals. All of them."

The Priest nodded. "Yes. And you must bring them directly to me. No one else can know what lies within until it is time."

Blaze nodded slowly, the weight of the task settling across his shoulders.

"Why me?"

"Because you still walk the space between shadow and light. You carry fire, Blaze—but you've never let it consume you. That makes you dangerous to the darkness... and valuable to the light."

But now, the Priest's tone softened. There was a gentleness to his gaze, a kindness that contrasted with the grave task he had just given.

"There's one more thing I must ask of you," the High Priest said quietly.

"I'm listening."

The Priest stepped closer, lowering his voice.

"You must do this alone. You must search for the remaining Journals of Doctor Crowe... without the others."

"Without Aleister? Without telling any of them?"

"Yes. They have carried more pain and loss than any soul should bear. Aleister has reclaimed his heart. He has saved his wife. Victoria's sacrifice gave them peace, and through your efforts, the world has been given light again."

He looked Blaze directly in the eyes. "Let them rest. Let them live. The world is safe—for now."

Blaze hesitated, his loyalty to the group warring with the wisdom he saw in the priest's eyes.

"But they'd want to help. They'd want to finish what we started."

"And perhaps one day they will," the Priest said softly. "But not now. This is a task for someone who knows the darkness intimately, someone who walks between worlds and does not flinch. This burden... must fall to you."

A long silence stretched between them. Finally, Blaze exhaled slowly, his decision settling in his bones.

"I'll do it. I'll find the Journals. All of them. And I'll bring them to you." The Priest gave a solemn nod, then reached into the folds of his robe and withdrew a small silver amulet etched with sacred runes.

"This will guide you to the places the Journals were hidden. Trust it—and trust your instincts."

Blaze took the amulet, its weight oddly comforting in his hand. He slid it into a pouch on his belt and turned toward the chamber's exit. Before he could leave, the Priest added gently,

"Thank you, Blaze. For doing what must be done, even when no one will know. That... is true sacrifice."

"Yeah. Well... I've never been one for praise anyway."

The golden halls of the Church of Light shimmered with peace and triumph. The battle was over, the wounds were healing, and for the first time in what felt like forever, a sense of calm had settled over Aleister Kane.

In the sanctuary, beneath the arched ceiling of stained glass and divine warmth, the group gathered one last time. The High Priest had given them his blessing, and now, it was Aleister's turn to send them home. With the Staff of Infinite Light in hand—no longer a weapon, but a symbol of unity and peace—Aleister called forth portals of glowing energy, each one shimmering with the essence of the home it would return them to.

Damian stepped forward first, his usual brooding demeanor softened.

"I've never fought beside anyone like you," he said, his gaze sweeping across the group. "You have my respect—and my loyalty, if ever needed."

Aleister nodded. "Thank you, Damian. May peace find you at last."

Damian gave a subtle bow and stepped through his portal, disappearing into the shadows of his own world.

Mary gave Victoria's old pendant a gentle kiss and looked up at the sky-filled dome above.

"I hope she's watching," she whispered.

Then she turned to Blaze and hugged him gently.

"Thank you... for protecting Aleister. For protecting all of us."

Next was Mary and Aleister's portal, glowing warmly with the energy of home. Before they could step through, Aleister turned to Blaze, the last still standing by his side.

"And you?" Aleister asked. "Where shall I send you?"

Blaze looked out one of the cathedral windows, watching the wind stir the golden trees beyond. His tattoos were still faintly glowing beneath his robes, their power dormant... but not gone.

"I think I'll stay here for a while," Blaze said quietly. "Catch my breath. Enjoy the peace while it lasts."

Aleister nodded, sensing something deeper behind his friend's words but not pressing further.

"You've earned that."

He and Mary stepped toward the glowing archway of their portal. Just as Aleister placed one foot through, he paused. Turning back, he walked to Blaze and offered a firm handshake, gripping his friend's hand tightly.

"Thank you, Blaze," Aleister said, his voice steady but full of emotion. "For everything. For standing with me, for saving Mary, for not giving up when everything felt lost."

Blaze's usual smirk faltered for a moment, replaced by something quieter—genuine.

"You weren't half bad yourself," he said.

Aleister's expression grew warm.

"My home is always open to you. Anytime. No matter what comes next—you're my friend. And I'm honored to call you that." Blaze looked away for just a second, blinking the emotion from his eyes.

"Likewise, Kane. Now get out of here before I start getting sentimental."

Aleister laughed softly, turned, and stepped through the portal with Mary, their silhouettes disappearing in a wash of golden light.

And Blaze... stood alone in the quiet sanctuary. But it wasn't a lonely quiet. It was a peace he hadn't known in years. He exhaled slowly, looking out into the light-soaked world beyond.

"Alright," he murmured to no one. "Time to get to work."

He reached into his pocket, feeling the cool silver weight of the amulet—the key to finding the Lost Journals. The war wasn't over. But for now, there was light. And hope.

And that... was enough.

Chapter 29

EPILOGUE

The soft crackle of firewood filled the study with its familiar rhythm, casting a gentle glow across the walls of Aleister Kane's estate. Shadows danced lazily against his shelves of ancient tomes and relics—silent sentinels of a battle long passed.

Aleister sat in his favorite chair, a glass of brandy in one hand, the other resting gently over Mary's as she leaned into him. Her head on his shoulder, her fingers intertwined with his. No monsters. No prophecies. No war. Just warmth. Just peace. He exhaled slowly, the firelight catching in his eyes as he stared into the flames. They had once symbolized the fury in his heart, the burning need for vengeance that had consumed him for so long. But now, they were calm. Gentle. Like him.

His mind drifted, as it often did in quiet moments, to the journey they had endured. Demons. Angels. A staff carved from the Tree of Life. Victoria's sacrifice. The pain. The miracles. The battles fought—not just with monsters, but within himself. He had begun that journey chasing ghosts—his father's, his wife's, his own sense of worth. But somewhere along the way, the vengeance had fallen away. And love, once locked behind walls of obsession, had broken through.

Aleister glanced down at Mary, sleeping peacefully against him. He tightened his fingers around hers.

I'll never leave you again.

He had said those words aloud to her that night they returned. And he meant them. With every fiber of his being. For the first time in his life... he was happy. And yet, as he stared into the hearth, he couldn't shake the thought lingering deep inside. A whisper he hadn't spoken aloud. This won't last. Not forever. Because the darkness always returns.

He had learned that truth well. The war between Heaven and Hell may have been paused, the world healed for a time—but evil never truly dies. It waits. In the shadows. In the cracks of the world. For the right moment to rise again. But when it did... he would be ready. And not alone.

The Staff of Infinite Light now rested above the mantle, no longer a weapon—but a promise. A reminder of who he was. Of whom he had become. Of what he would fight for, if called again. Aleister smiled softly, his eyes never leaving the fire. Let it come. Next time, I won't be the man I was. I'll be something more.

A gentle warmth filled the room. Not from the fire, but from something... divine. Aleister sat up slightly, instinct kicking in—not with fear, but awe. Two figures stood near the hearth, bathed in radiant white-gold light. They were no longer mortal. No longer bound by flesh. Victoria and Elias—wings unfurled, halos like fire, robes of celestial light that shimmered like starlight over water. Victoria smiled, her voice calm and pure.

"You've earned this peace, Aleister. It suits you."

Elias nodded beside her, his presence both commanding and kind.

"But peace, as you know... is fragile."

Aleister stood slowly, taking in their Seraphic forms.

"It's good to see you again. Both of you."

"We didn't come to bring warnings—only a promise. If your peace is ever broken, if darkness dares to rise again... we will be there. Always."

Aleister nodded, deeply moved.

"Thank you. For everything."

Elias gave a proud nod.

"The light never forgets its warriors."

With one final smile, the siblings vanished in a quiet burst of golden light, leaving only a trace of warmth and the faint scent of wild roses and rain. Aleister sat back down beside Mary, who had stirred at the presence but said nothing—she simply took his hand and held it tight.

But the peace was not to last.

A sudden shift in the air—like the drop in pressure before a storm—caused Aleister to sit up straight. The candles throughout the room dimmed, and a gust of wind stirred the flames. Then, from a pillar of radiant blue light that descended before the hearth, the Archangel Michael appeared. Regal and resolute, his armored form shimmered with divine energy. His piercing eyes met Aleister's with a gaze both proud and sorrowful.

"You've done well, Aleister Kane," Michael said, his voice echoing like a choir of distant bells. "The Staff of Infinite Light has been restored, the Underworld has been purged, and the demon king Asmodeus cast into exile. You have fulfilled a destiny few mortals could endure."

Aleister rose slowly, Mary at his side. He bowed his head slightly.

"Then it's over?"

"For now. But peace is fragile in a world balanced on the edge of Heaven and Hell."

He stepped closer, the firelight playing across the ethereal feathers of his wings.

"Asmodeus will claw his way back through the Void. And if he does... he may not return alone."

"You mean..."

Michael nodded grimly. "Lucifer. The Morning Star. He stirs in the shadows of the abyss, and if Asmodeus finds a way to reach him... the two united would bring an end not even the armies of Heaven could halt."

Silence fell. The weight of the warning pressed into Aleister's chest.

"But there's still hope," Michael continued, his gaze shifting to the worn satchel on Aleister's desk. "The Lost Journals of Doctor Crowe hold more than history. They hold prophecy. Secrets not even I fully understand. The answer may lie within them — a path not to victory, but to survival."

"Then I'll find them. All of them."

Michael placed a hand on Aleister's shoulder, and for a moment, the fire seemed to burn brighter.

"You are no longer just a man of vengeance. You are a guardian of light. And you will not face this coming storm alone."

In a burst of light and wind, the Archangel vanished, leaving only silence — and the growing realization that the true war was still to come.

Aleister turned to Mary, taking her hand. Peace was a fleeting gift. But now he was ready for what came next.

The fire whispered softly in the hearth, casting golden halos on the stone walls of the study. Aleister sat back in his favorite leather chair, the familiar scent of old books and aged wood wrapping around him like a comfort he hadn't felt in years. Across from him, Mary dozed quietly on the sofa, her hand still resting in his. She was safe. She was home.

For the first time in a long while, so was he. He gazed across the room at the relics now arranged on the mantle and shelves — the Lantern of Truth, still faintly glowing as if aware; the reforged Staff of Infinite Light, cradled in a sacred case of ash wood and gold leaf; and the Blade of Dawn, now sheathed in a case lined with runes of protection. Each piece, a memory. Each memory, a scar. He had set out seeking vengeance, driven by rage and pain. The death of his father. The loss of Mary. A hollow heart filled only with obsession. But the journey had changed him. The artifacts weren't just tools of war — they were mirrors, reflecting who he had become.

The Lantern had shown him how to see through darkness — not just in the world, but within himself. The Staff had forced him to face a truth he long denied: that strength didn't come from power, but from purpose. And the friends he had made — Blaze, Victoria, Damian — had taught him that he never had to fight alone.

And then there was Mary.

He looked at her now, her breathing slow, steady, peaceful. She had believed in him when he didn't believe in himself. Her absence had broken him. Her return had healed him. No artifact, no magic, no sacred rite could compare to the miracle of finding her again. He would never take that for granted...ever. The road to this moment had cost him more than he'd ever imagined — friends, blood, belief. But it had also given him something he never expected to find again: a reason to live beyond vengeance. He had journeyed through sacred churches and haunted forests... crossed into the depths of Hell... seen angels fall, and demons rise... and yet the greatest victory was this:

He had come back. He had saved her. And somehow, in the end, he had saved himself.

He would never lose her again. No ritual or war or demon would ever take her from him. Whatever time they had, he would treasure it. He was home and that's all that mattered.

Still... he knew peace was not forever.

Knock. Knock. Knock.

Three steady raps at the front door shattered the silence like a warning bell. Mary stirred beside him. He gently pulled himself free, pressing a kiss to her forehead. She murmured his name, half-asleep, and turned toward the fire.

Aleister crossed the room, heart calm—but cautious. His fingers brushed the edge of the Staff above the mantle as he passed, just in case. He opened the heavy wooden door. There, standing under the soft glow of moonlight and lanterns, was Blaze Barton. Cloak draped over one shoulder, tattoos glowing faintly beneath his skin. He looked almost exactly as he had the first time they met—gritty, weathered, eyes sharp as ever. But something was different this time. Something had returned with him from the shadows. Blaze met Aleister's gaze and gave the faintest hint of a grin.

"Sorry to drop by uninvited."

Aleister stared for a long beat, heart already beginning to stir with that familiar weight of destiny. Blaze's voice turned low and serious.

"I need your help."

Aleister smiled. Just a little.

"Of course you do."

A gust of wind pushed through the trees. And somewhere, far beyond the hills...something began to wake.

About the Author

Robert Massetti is an award-winning independent film-maker, author, and founder of FEAR FILM Studios, a production company dedicated to producing bold, original horror since 1999. Known for his uncompromising vision and deep passion for the genre, Massetti has written, directed, and produced numerous short and feature-length horror films that have played at festivals around the world. His work blends atmospheric tension, psychological dread, and visceral storytelling—earning him a loyal following among horror fans and creators alike.

In addition to filmmaking, Massetti is the creator and director of the *FREAK SHOW Horror Film Festival*, now celebrating over 20 years of showcasing independent horror cinema. Through this platform, he has championed emerging voices in the genre while helping to grow a thriving horror community.

Expanding his creative reach, Massetti launched **FEAR FILM Publishing**, a brand focused on dark fiction and horror comic books. His debut novel, *The Lost Journals*, marks his powerful entry into horror fantasy literature. The novel explores themes of light and darkness, vengeance and redemption, set against the backdrop of a war between Heaven and Hell.

Massetti is also the mind behind **Fredrick Fear's Tales of Terror**, a horror comic series that pays homage to the EC Comics era with modern twists, eerie artwork, and a chilling sense of fun. Whether through film, books, or comics, his mission remains the same: to terrify, thrill, and inspire.

When he's not writing or directing, Massetti engages with horror fans through his various YouTube channels, podcasts, and events. A true multi-hyphenate creator, he continues to build a dark and compelling universe that spans across media—with no signs of slowing down.

Preview

Asmodeus was only the beginning.
Lucifer has returned.
Prepare for
THE LOST JOURNALS: Book 2
coming soon

9 798999 158703